I0587219

ANCIENT ILLUMINATION II:

(KUONGOZA MWANGA: THE LEADING LIGHT)

ROD VAN BLAKE

Copyright © 2018 Rod Van Blake

All rights reserved. No part(s) of this book may be reproduced, distributed or transmitted in any form, or by any means, or stored in a database or retrieval systems without prior expressed written permission of the author of this book.

ISBN: 978-1-5356-1518-1 (paperback)
ISBN: 978-1-5356-1581-5 (hardcover)

Contents

Ancient Illumination II:

(Kuongoza Mwanga: The Leading Light)

Chapter One

THERE IS A HUSH IN the corridors throughout the various facilities on Jupiter, its moons, and in all the places in the galaxy where the Kison Askari dwell. News has traveled fast that their king has fallen. It has not made it to the public at large, but the GMC will soon know, as will most of the oppressed races. There is a large gathering in the main hall at the facility on Jupiter, deep beneath the surface. The largest planet in the galaxy will provide plenty of cover from outside attack, but there are plenty of newly minted fighting craft patrolling, in case the GMC decide to go on the offensive while the Kison Askari lick the greatest of their wounds.

The Kison Askari have used mining equipment to carve out a huge network of underground passageways that lead to various living quarters, training areas, and many other functional spaces within the thick hide of Jupiter. Different shades of orange, red, and cream striate the walls, just as they do on the view of the surface from space. They have somehow carved an absurdly large throne within the great hall. It is rarely used, as the king has always seen it fit to be out with his people, working, planning, and, if need be, fighting. Darius has some very large shoes to fill, but today will not be the day he has to try them on.

The reason for this gathering is to announce that Queen Tunisia will rule in his stead until he has either reached the age of majority or until he proves that he possesses the ability to take the mantle. These are trying times. The GMC must have been desperate to send assassins, yet again after previous failures, and there has been some confusion as to who exactly is responsible. Babylon, Tunisia, Simeon, and a host of others are sure that another attack could happen at any moment. The dark matter ordinance is supposed to be a last resort, and Babylon is still advocating that sentiment.

The queen remembers her silent vow and feels the GMC has not, after all, learned their lesson. She will not turn the other cheek. She sits now on the throne and seethes in a dazzlingly beautiful black diamond studded dress. Darius stands at her side, holding and stroking her hand, while Simeon reads the official decree announcing her status as queen regent. She's barely heard two words through her fury. Mentally, she is hatching a plan to exact her revenge on their enemies. She will gather the mothers and wives of the fallen. They will understand.

● ● ●

Evading the patrols around Saturn is not mandated, but Sgt. Garrison feels it will be a necessary practice while returning to base. Stealth is a skill he has learned with boots on the ground, but he and his men have not been trained in the aeronautical skill set. The equipment is new, and virtually no one else has a need for it until now. They have the necessary challenge codes if they are discovered. This was a field test of sorts. They had some close calls with a few space harriers earlier when they first jumped in the system, but luckily Lance Corporal McNamara was quick to activate the stealth filaments throughout the outer hull on the Adder.

They will now, of course, notify command of their presence and request permission to land before entering the atmosphere. The ship will become visible once that process begins. The heat exchange during the breach cannot be hidden from sensor arrays or even the naked eye once they are close enough to landfall. Dodging land to air artillery barrages will not be fun or plausibly survivable. Although heavily armored, the Adder will not withstand more than a glancing shot or two. It is made to withstand fire from space craft its size or even slightly larger. Getting in and out while withstanding attacks from small patrols or evading them is its purpose but dogfighting or securing a planetary beachhead is not.

Sgt. Garrison slides into the pilot seat as Lance Corporal Jennings sits at the comm console behind him. PFC Long and Private Cooper have secured themselves in the rear cabin area inside the bay door. "Mac, unveil us, so we're seen. Jennings, open a line to HQ, so we can say hello!" Sgt. Garrison bellows behind him.

"Yes, sergeant!" they chorus and do as he has ordered.

On the console in front of him, Lance Corporal McNamara hits a series of buttons that deactivate the cloaking filaments in the outer hull. The sudden appearance of a ship, seemingly out of nowhere, triggers alarms in a small, two-man station floating in the debris of Saturn's ring.

It is not a very entertaining duty post. The two young Marines must have pissed someone off to be stuck with it. Normally so boring and mundane, it is usually a good place to sneak in some extra rack time when the pilots aren't practicing maneuvers. Two unlucky non-rates are using the small post to snooze when they are rudely awakened as the Adder appears. Lance Corporal Matta, one such unlucky Marine, bangs his head as he quickly rises from his slumber, fumbling to activate the communications console. Blinking his brown eyes, he bellows into the mic, "Unidentified vessel, state your purpose and your cargo!"

Groggily his buddy stuck on duty with him wakes up to see what the fuss is about.

Inside the Adder, Sgt. Garrison gets up and walks over to the comm console, leans over Lance Corporal Jennings, and keys the mic before saying, "Ring outpost sentry, this is ECHO FIVE GOLF, checking back into base in transport ALPHA DELTA DELTA ECHO ROMEO. Please confirm with HQ, so we can land."

Confused, Matta looks at his fellow watchman to see if he has understood any of that. He receives a negative head shake, as well as a shoulder shrug, in return. Not recognizing any of the call signs, Lance Corporal Matta forwards the message to HQ who tell him to standby.

There is a long pause. Matta is just about to instruct a patrol to escort or challenge this mystery arrival when HQ chimes in over the comm system, "This is HQ. Instruct them to dock in the auxiliary sickbay landing area. Lt. Commander Jameson will meet them there. HQ out."

That was strange, Matta thought. It certainly doesn't look like a medical vessel, but he does as he was ordered and relayed the instructions to the Adder which promptly turns to enter the atmosphere without further interruptions while making their way planet-side.

Lance Corporals McNamara and Jennings oversee the unpacking chores with Private Cooper and PFC Long doing most of the heavy lifting while Sgt. Garrison goes to report in. In this case, the two slightly lower-ranking Marines don't mind seeing as they are better equipped in this situation to the task. In quickstep, Sgt. Garrison makes his way through the ultra-white and to some sickeningly sterile corridors of the medical wing that were thankfully untouched by the dark matter bombing. Toward the back of the facility is Lt. Commander Jameson's office who has, in fact, decided to wait there instead of coming out to meet them as they landed.

Lt. Commander Jameson sits at his large desk with his green eyes intensely going through some sort of medical reports, strange experiments, or something similar Sgt. Garrison is sure. He has purposely come in silently, but to get the officer's attention, he lets some of the tension release in the hydraulics in one of his legs, producing a hissing sound. Looking up from his papers, he says, "Good to see you back, sergeant. Did your men make it back as well?"

Despite not being ordered to any position, Sgt. Garrison goes from parade rest to at ease before answering, "Yes sir, we are all accounted for. No one was hit that I know of, and all are still fully functional."

The lieutenant commander nods his head affirmatively and repeats, "Good, good. Now the most important question is, were you able to successfully eliminate the target?"

This time, there is a slight hesitation, and most people will not have noticed it, but the officer does. Sgt. Garrison straightens up and replies, "The target was taken out, but I am not sure who hit him last, sir. There was a lot going on. Video confirmed them carrying a body out after we got off-planet. News of his death should travel fast."

Lt. Commander Jameson looks at the sergeant for a few more seconds before saying, "Very well. Good job, sergeant. Go rest up and tell your men to do the same. I'm not sure what the next assignment will be. I know I don't have to tell you to stay ready. I'll pass your report to the commandant. Be sure to complete a data record of your mission and attach the video files. Dismissed."

With that, Sgt. Garrison replies, "Aye, sir!" Then, he does an about-face and marches back the way he came. This time, he allows his legs to scrape the decks, creating the screeching noise he has become known for.

Lt. Commander Jameson simply shakes his head as the NCO leaves his office. The officer does wonder at the source of his hesitancy. Is he not sure who actually dropped the late king of the Kison Askari, or is he not sure if the task has been completed? Hopefully, it is the former.

• • •

Back on Earth, the local law enforcement units have become more and more militarized as many of the mutated races are now outwardly voicing their displeasure about their status as second-class citizens. Athena, Angelo, and even some of the Jade Assassins are spearheading an effort to put pressure on the government to, hopefully, provoke positive change. Many on both sides feel this is the wrong way to go. Violence often begets more violence. Yet there have been moments in history where the olive branch of peace has been more likely to be burned than accepted. Without the evidence proving they have all been influenced into this millennia-long conflict, the fighting and oppression will continue.

With her crystalline tresses tied back and under a heavy scarf to keep them from blowing in the breeze and make soft tinkling noises, Athena waits in the brush, approaching an entrance to one of the previously abandoned underground structures. She, along with Angelo, are heading a small band of rebels comprised of many races, from the oppressed mutants to what would be considered normal humans who are just as tired of the obnoxious oppression as those who bear the brunt of it. The GMC are busy cranking out new weapons and vehicles as fast as it can but have had to slow production in some places for what will become a lack of resources. No one knows how long this conflict will last, and the Kison Askari have effectively cut them off from a vast amount of ore and other materiels.

Meanwhile, Toshi of the Jade Assassins is still in communication with Athena and is helping supply her people with weapons and some new gear of their own. The body armor they wear is old, but the new pliable silicone layers stretched over it gives them a chameleon-like effect that rivals the wraith suit the GMC has come up with but without the complicated wiring and helmet. The camouflaging is more of an added benefit than protection for most of these combatants. The Stone people have little to worry about when it comes to most projectile-based weapons, but that is changing as the GMC is constructing more powerful energy-based rounds, in addition to the rail guns and smaller ballistic weapons currently being used.

The same can be said of the Limbia Johari. Their skin is not as hardened as the Kison Askari, but it is certainly more durable than the epidermis of most of the other races in the group. Athena and her small group of freedom fighters lurk about to see if a supply run will be coming soon. South America has seen its fair share of protests and other anti-government activity lately. When that happens, usually the local law enforcement will get reinforced with food, weapons, and other supplies. Although virtually useless now that the Stone people have found a way to get rid of their shackles, the underground electromagnetic system is still in place, effectively creating a faster way to travel for Athena and her crews.

The system follows a trail to and from the mines all over the world and often leads into the underground rail system in case there are unruly people from the mining colonies traveling that way. Above ground, it simply goes to and from the mines where most of these protests have been taking place. Athena and her people have combined the anti-grav hoversleds with old one- or two-seat motor vehicles. They can travel at high speeds over short distances but gain more speed when over the electromagnetic routes above ground. While other vehicles giving chase have to slow down to navigate the terrain and obstacles, the GroundHawks, as they have been dubbed, can go through at full throttle, given the route while over the electromagnetic rails in the ground is keeping them on a predetermined path that perfectly navigates those obstacles. To the pursuers, it looks as if they are chasing someone with amazing reflexes which often results in the pursuing parties crashing.

The locations of both the protests and small raids are randomized so as not to allow the government to guess where they will be hit next and coordinate countermeasures. Lying over her GroundHawk until both the chameleon skin over her body armor and vehicle mirror the foliage around them, Athena waits. There are twenty or so others waiting in a similar fashion, listening for a convoy that should be coming soon. They don't have to wait long. A deep rumble can be heard throughout the jungle which gives Athena and her people an immediate advantage. Whatever beast of a vehicle they are coming in, noise discipline wasn't in the manufacturer's plans.

Beast is an apt description for what comes lumbering through the dense foliage. It is heavily armored and rolls on heavy tracks which chews up grass and soil as it trudges along. The good thing is that these things will not likely give chase, or if they do, they will not be able to keep up. The bad news is that the cargo being transported in them is likely going to be too hard of a nut to crack. Athena opens up the comm line briefly to the rest of her unit and states, "Change of plans. Target the smaller escort vehicles. Hit 'em hard and fast and let's bail!"

Escorting the two huge crawlers are a few smaller Jeep-like vehicles with rail guns mounted on them. There are some nasty-looking canons on the crawlers, and whatever they have to fire, Athena is sure they don't want to be on the receiving end. They let the small convoy pass them and allow them to get a long head start. The plan is to run up and hit them as they pass them and, hopefully, do as much damage as possible without giving the local enforcers time to react or retaliate. When they are far enough ahead, Athena guns the engines, flying out of cover. The rest followed suit. A high-pitched whine turns into a low hum as the GroundHawks switch to electromagnetic propulsion systems.

They are on the small convoy in seconds. Two of the Jeep-like vehicles to the rear are immediately fired upon. Their back ends fly up, throwing the driver, front passenger, and the rear gunner in three different directions as the vehicle explodes. The crawlers keep lumbering forward as four more of the smaller vehicles turn around to see what the ruckus is. The gunners in two of them begin lacing the jungle with railgun fire, but they are not sure what they are aiming at. One decides to aim at a hazy silhouette ahead of a dust trail behind them and is rewarded with an explosion as whatever it is crashes into a large bole.

Two of the other three escort vehicles are hit. They are disabled but not destroyed. In a flash, the attackers are ahead of the convoy. They pull away quickly. The still operational escort vehicles turn around to give chase. The engines roar as they try to catch up but fail miserably. The GroundHawks have momentarily gone to their small jet propulsion systems while firing on their targets. Now that they were leaving, they switch back to electromagnetic and have the luxury of pouring on speed without worrying about obstacles.

The escort vehicles do not have that same luxury, and a few of them pay for it with thunderous crashes. A local marshal from inside one of the crawlers orders them to stand down. None of the crawlers have been damaged, but they have lost, at least, five escort vehicles; all of them are new, and that will be a blow to the budget. If the cameras on top of the crawlers have any good footage of the bandits in the area, it might have been worth the losses. At least, that is what Marshal Benitez tells himself. The pencil pushers and bean counters of the world only care about numbers. The whole "crack a few eggs to make an omelet" idiom doesn't go over so well with some of the local bureaucrats.

Marshal Benitez ignores all of those thoughts as he walks over to help his men climb out of the wreckage that had been brand new military-grade Ramblers. They were lightly armored, fast for land transports with the ability to mount various types of weaponry, and they were far advanced compared to what he and his men had been equipped with prior. They have suspicions that what is now being given out are the GMC's hand-me-downs, but even if that were true, it is still an improvement. There is nothing of value inside the large Armadillos they are escorting, save more of his men and the camera equipment mounted on them for the purposes of catching the rebellious groups rumored to be in the area.

Stepping inside one of the rear Armadillos, Benitez gives an inquiring glance to the officer operating the surveillance suite. "Well, anything we can use?" he asks him.

Nervously taking off his black beret and wiping his sweaty face with it, the man answers, "Yes, sir! I think so."

The second part of that answer does not instill confidence, but there are shots from some of the other vehicles, so there has to be something of worth. Marshal Benitez nods at the officer. "Good. Get the footage together from all the other cams we had working and break them down digitally. I want to know everything we possibly can about these thugs!" Without waiting for an answer, he turns and stalks out of the vehicle and back to his own.

Chapter Two

A LARGE MANTA-SHAPED SHIP APPROACHES the gargantuan Dreadnaught orbiting Mars. The Kison Askari have an understandably limited amount of these carriers which are space cities capable of moving and sustaining a vast amount of troops and support people, as well as a host of fleet ships and material. The manta-shaped ship is Babylon's personal vessel, and he is back from his trip to the Ancients.

Once the ship has been identified, Queen Regent Tunisia immediately goes to greet the ancient Atlantean. Waiting just inside the executive landing bay, she stands in a long black jewel-adorned gown. The bay has been oxygenated, and the gravity controls activate as soon as the bay doors close behind the ship.

Slowly the rear ramp lowers, and Babylon shuffles down to amble toward the hatch leading to the bridge, bowing to Tunisia before briefly embracing. Swinging his long white locks, Babylon allows Tunisia to take his elbow as they turn to walk through the bridge area to an office with a majestic view of the red planet. Tunisia helps the elderly Babylon sit in a plush chair in front of an opulent desk before sitting down herself. They both silently regard the view before she asks, "Need any refreshment? I hear you have been on a long journey."

Shaking his head negatively, he replies, "No, *tank* you. I had 'oped to 'ave betta news upon me return, but de Radiant Ones see no reason to intervene at dis time."

Though it has been slightly over a year since she has last seen him, Babylon looks as if he has aged significantly, and there is a morose sadness in his amber eyes.

Learning that the other mythical beings of pure light named by Babylon in his origins tale are not of a mind to help this galaxy, even though one of their own directly or indirectly put it in peril, does not surprise her. She has plans to take things into her own hands anyway. "Would you like to see the progress of our shipwrights? They, along with the help of Toshi and some of your people, have come up with some remarkable designs."

Babylon seems to think before answering. "No, no, I am sure de came up wit' some great ships. I am more interested in finding a way to make the war-faring components unnecessary."

From a theoretical standpoint, the queen regent understands what Babylon is saying, but inside, Tunisia is fuming. Her heart is set on getting revenge and setting things right to mend her broken soul. More than anything, the beings responsible for the death of her king have to be punished and taught a lesson. If the leaders left are going to pursue peace, then she will make it so the GMC or any other governing body begs for it. Tunisia will embrace her warrior spirit and take it to these vile beings who seem to only understand brute force and use technological advancements as a tool for destruction and domination over others. They will feel a mourning queen's wrath.

A brief flash of violent thoughts are expressed on her face. When she comes out of her introspection, she notices a startled look on Babylon's face, as if her vehemence has, somehow, touched him. Placing a hand on his to cover the awkward moment, she asks, "What would you like to do or see here, Babylon?"

Recovering quickly, he replies, "It's been a while since I saw the prince. Is he around? In glum times as this, youth, innocence, and joy are good things to witness, and I must tell him what must eventually be done, even if he won't un'astand until later."

Tunisia reassures him that the prince is be available and asks him to get settled into his quarters while she fetches the young boy. She feels that she will do what has to be done now so that her son and her people will flourish later.

Going over theories and myths are fine for this old being and a young prince to do so long as those currently responsible do what is necessary to secure the future. Some will not have the stomach to go through with the dirty work. Tunisia has no such qualms.

Upon their return to Pharaoh, Typhoon and Malice are given time to rest after the void walk back to Earth which, no doubt, has to have taken a toll on them after the brief skirmish at Pluto. Pharaoh is pleased that the so-called king of the self-proclaimed Kison Askari has fallen but is disappointed the child still remains a potential loose end. His two minions really seem to be polar opposites of each other, and it is a bit ironic. Malice was more or less human before Pharaoh decided to mutate him into the enigmatic being he is now but shunned, for the most part, the technological advances the rest of his former species enjoy. Typhoon is, without a doubt, a simple beast of the wild, that now is of a mind to use every technological toy at his disposal whether he needs it or not. The gorilla's latest fascination is with a collection of new and old media he has scavenged from somewhere.

Pharaoh is meditating in the uppermost chamber at Giza when Malice glides in, stopping to wait to be acknowledged. Opening his eyes and turning around to look upon his kneeling minion, the exiled light being asks, "What is it that brings you to me unbidden, Malice?"

Raising his baleful gleaming red eyes, Malice stammers, "It's the ape, master. It has become increasingly annoying with this new obsession with the humans' antiquated entertainment media. Now he has some theory about a time when apes actually ruled this planet!"

"More importantly, are you sure the head of the Kison Askari is dead?" Pharaoh booms.

Lowering his eyes once more, Malice replies, "Yes, master, but as you know, the child got away, and there was no sign of the other being you mentioned."

Dismissively, Pharaoh waves his hand. "The child will be found, as well as my old pupil from long ago. Let Typhoon have his…media addiction so long as it doesn't interfere with doing my bidding. War should be back on in full swing now that the leader of one side has fallen, but we still need to find the child. Gather what you need and prepare to find him in a few weeks," he commands.

After bowing, Malice exits the chamber to tell his fellow minion about what must be done. Malice was hopeful his master would decree the devouring of meaningless entertainment was a useless practice and forbid it. Since that is not to be, Malice simply glides into where the gorilla has taken up residence in one of the lower chambers. He is eating, absently watching more dimwitted entertainment from the past. He barely grunts his acknowledgement of the new mission that will be taking place soon. Malice shakes his head in his cowl as he leaves Typhoon to his vice. Grabbing an assortment of blades from his chamber, Malice decides training will help clear his thoughts.

• • •

Simeon has called for young Darius to meet him on one of the lower levels of the Dreadnaught reserved for combat training sessions. The prince often sneaks down there to watch them if he can get away from his lessons with Professor Jones-Bey. The lessons are often boring, and there is a strange feeling that what is being taught is old news to Darius. Every time he is asked to repeat his lessons, the recounting is flawless and often accompanied by more tedious facts the professor does not recall telling the young king-to-be. Once the lift stops at the fifty-fifth deck, Darius hops out, curious as to what the general wants.

One of the hatches slide open just as the prince is walking by, so he sticks his head in to see who is in there. Simeon is inside waiting for him at the end of the chamber, sitting down cross-legged with his staff lying down beside him. Keeping his eyes closed, he pats the ground next to him, instructing Darius to sit beside him. The prince mimics his positioning and notices a smaller staff and a heavier set of what looks like body armor next to it. Opening one eye, Simeon says, "Close your eyes and quiet your mind. Focus on nothing and simply breathe."

Confused, Darius asks, "How will I know when I am doing it right?"

Without opening his eyes, Simeon replies through a slight smile, "You will know when you see no reason to ask any questions and no specific thoughts are running through your mind. You will simply exist without contemplating that existence."

They sit like this for what seems like an eternity to Darius, but he complies with his elder, despite wanting to jump out of his skin. Simeon finally opens his eyes and stands, waiting for Darius to do the same. He looks the prince over and asks him, "How are you adjusting to your new suit?"

Darius limbers up and looks over his arms and legs, replying, "It was a bit heavy at first, but I am used to it now."

Nodding his head, Simeon points to the body armor sitting by the staff. "Good. Put that on. Today, we begin your official training. I am going to raise the gravity level in here to hasten the adjustment you'll need to get used to this armor over your suit. I know it might feel difficult, but once you get used to the extra weight, you'll need the heavier insulation once we start using powered melee weapons like my staff."

Doing as he has been instructed, Darius slips his arms and head into the chest plate, which also covers a portion of his back, then moves on to the thick shin and thigh guards which, for some strange reason, stick to his legs when properly set in place. Watching him, Simeon tells Darius about the new armor. "There are metallic traces in your suit. These armor pieces have magnetic filaments within the rubberized plates which will hold them in place. They will offer you good protection but are not impervious to the more powerful energy-based projectiles. Just as you did with the greaves. Place these bracers between your wrists and elbows."

As soon as all the pieces are in place, Darius feels them simultaneously stabilize.

"Move around some. See how the armor feels over the suit. Make sure it's not too cumbersome. Do some light exercises," Simeon instructs.

Darius does as he's told, jogging around and stopping to do side-straddle hops before swinging his arms, testing the motion. The weight is heavier than he is used to, but he can bear it, and it's expected. A few weeks ago, Simeon had given Darius a set of cards depicting various *bojutsu kata*. He had been instructed to memorize the first ten stances, so his formal training could begin.

After watching Darius for a moment, Simeon goes to leave the chamber.

Darius asks, "Where are you going? I have to show you the first ten stances."

Simeon shakes his head negatively before replying, "When you are able to comfortably stand in each stance, come and get me."

Darius is confused. Most who have seen the prince or been around during his lessons know the boy is a quick learner, and he has been given ample time to memorize the first ten stances easily. The hatch slides closed behind Simeon.

"But I know them already," Darius says to no one in particular since he is now the only one in the chamber. He is about ten steps from the custom bo-staff, when his arms suddenly feel heavier. Darius soon realizes it isn't just his arms but everything feels incredibly burdensome. He is having a hard time simply standing there. It is then that he realizes Simeon has told him the gravity will be turned up while he trains here. Now he painfully understands what that meant. His combat training has begun, and it is nowhere near as fun as he thought it would be.

Later, when the queen regent hears what her son has been subjected to, she is furious. After speaking with Nefer, her ire quells. "My queen, he is the prince, but the world he was born into is a harsh one. We will need him to be strong. Simeon is training him, and the general will do a fine job. I know the boy is young, but sadly, there are some lessons he must learn early. Our lives have never been easy, and he must know the experiences of his people in order to know how best to serve as well as rule them," she advises.

As true as the advice is, it still angers Tunisia. She decides to put her energy into something else. "Come with me," the queen commands, and Nefer follows her to a small transport that takes them out to where the shipwrights are continuing to build their fleet. Nefer is curious as to why the queen's personal guard has not accompanied them. A few of the huge ore haulers have been converted into mobile hangars. They dock in one. Upon getting out, Nefer turns to examine the queen's transport. It is small and sleek with no weapons to speak of, but luckily, they have no need of any right now. The queen notices Nefer's hesitation and turns back to explain, "It was another of my late husband's dreams to create an industry for our people, so we can benefit more. It is our labor which fuels much of the technological advances most beings in this galaxy cannot live without. Interstellar transports being made available to the general population could create an economic boom similar to the birth of the motor vehicle industry millennia ago."

Perplexed, Nefer asks, "The king wanted to build more of these?"

The queen nods affirmatively. "You seem surprised. Think of it. Most vehicles today, even on Earth, are not for personal use, unless you are wealthy or tied to the government. A while back, it was decided that personal vehicles were too detrimental to the environment, so they basically raised the price point to a level that most could simply not afford them or did the same for the materials used to make them until it no longer became common. Most simply use various public transportation to get to and from jobs or to visit different places. Now with this new frontier, House Omega can open it up to all who wish to explore beyond Earth's gravity well."

Nefer thinks it is a nice enough sentiment but hardly believes it can ever work. "Not to be rude, but the GMC and the rest of the government will not allow us to have a business, new or otherwise, when we still fight now for our very freedom. We are still at war. No matter what their commander says, I don't believe that will change soon."

The queen says nothing to dispute Nefer's opinion, saying, "You're right, but things will have to change one way or the other. If they will not see reason, we must force them to put someone in charge that does. You know I mentioned before that we must do whatever it takes to secure our future, even if it seems distasteful."

Unsure of where this conversation is going, Nefer answers, "Yes, my queen."

They walk further back into the hangar where various ships are being assembled by some of the Askari with the help of repurposed androids, as well as robots. In the very rear of the hangar, there is a small section that has been cordoned off by a large makeshift wall. There seem to be more of Toshi's people toward this section. The queen and Nefer greet the green-skinned technicians as they pass, as well as some Atlanteans who have stayed to help with fleet building, Nefer assumes. Before going behind the wall, Tunisia turns to her and says, "I will tell you of my plan, and I have something to show you, but for now, you must keep it to yourself until the time is right. Babylon would not approve if he knew, but some of his people understand that the pain we have suffered was not simply an academic exercise. Most think I am having a special luxury personal transport built here. I can show you better than I can explain it."

With that, the queen walks behind the wall, and Nefer follows. What lay behind is, in fact, a transport, not a luxury vehicle. It does not look immediately like any of the fighting spacecraft she has seen in production either. Finally, Nefer asks, "What is that, my queen?"

Walking along the straight lines of the transport, which can seat two with a matte black finish and small weapons placements up front, the queen answers, "This is the Nyeusi Sime, the black dagger. If I am forced to, I will stab the GMC in the heart with it."

Chapter Three

THREE WEEKS, THAT IS HOW long they have been stranded here. At least, that is the predominant opinion. Hard to tell when the day cycle is a strange thing to gauge. All they know is they crashed landed here some time ago. In fact, "here" is a hard place to define at the moment, and it's driving Private First Class Long a bit crazy. The topography looks similar to that of the Earth, but before exiting the Adder, Lance Corporal McNamara noticed that, although the atmosphere is heavily oxygenated, there are traces of other elements totally unfamiliar to them.

McNamara calls Sgt. Garrison over to look at the readings and says, "When the sensors give you what amounts to a string of question marks for the atmospheric analysis of the planet you're stranded on, I'm not so sure we want to breathe out there."

There are loud thuds and scraping sounds from Garrison's cybernetic legs as he walks over to take a look at the readings himself. After a quick perusal, he agrees that no one should leave the ship without being properly outfitted as if they are operating in vacuum.

For Private First Class Long, this is the easiest for him since he is basically a living torso housed in a mech suit made especially for him. The rest of the group has cybernetic prosthetics as well, but Long is an extreme case. They are all war veterans from the Galactic Marine Corp that have suffered serious injuries during the most recent rebellion of the Stone people. Each is given a choice of accepting the prospect of living out the rest of their lives as invalids in some VA hospital or agree to be fitted with cybernetic enhancements, so they can rejoin the fight.

Ancient Illumination II: (Kuongoza Mwanga: The Leading Light)

Sgt. Garrison is the only one of the "Mechanics," as they have been code named, not given the option to choose. He had lost a leg during one of the initial conflicts at a mining facility in Central Africa. Upon waking up in some hidden medical unit, he was informed that he had been experimented on by a lieutenant commander of questionable scruples and had received new orders to train with the elite Marines on Saturn. The strange thing is that Garrison, who was only a corporal at the time, only remembered losing one leg, yet woke up with two new shiny titanium alloy legs. The other had been sacrificed to give him balance and ease of movement during combat maneuvers. Having no choice, it was something he had simply accepted.

Long had lost all of his limbs and most of his skin, which was why he was almost entirely encompassed in the suit most of the time. Lance Corporals Jennings and McNamara had each lost the opposite eye, which ironically made them look strangely like mirror images when facing each other, and Private Cooper had lost both arms at a mining colony on Mars.

All of them had gone on to train at Saturn, where the gravity was ten times what they were used to on Earth. Stim supplements have helped their still human portions catch up somewhat to the cybernetics. It is not unheard of for a trainee there to remain in stasis for months while receiving the supplements and needed nutrients until they are strong enough to actually get out of bed and start PT sessions. Seems like an extreme measure to go to, but this is a predictable course of action when you share the galaxy with beings who are traditionally bigger, faster, and stronger than you.

Technological advances are nice to have but, sometimes, are not enough, and there are other times where certain situations can nullify technology altogether. When it comes down to it and Mother Nature, God, or whatever higher power you believe in comes into the equation, it is no contest. The GMC have left nothing to chance, and the Stone people or Kison Askari as they are now referring to themselves are developing some pretty nasty tech of their own.

Technology is keeping the mechanics alive and in some ways failing them at this moment in time. A few short months ago, they returned to Saturn to debrief after a successful target elimination mission. The king of the Kison Askari had fallen at Pluto, yet it was still unclear as to who had dealt the fatal blow as there were other assets in the field, and it was equally puzzling as to who the other assets belonged to. The only thing that mattered to Sgt. Garrison was that the job had, in fact, been completed. The brass didn't question it and had, in fact, told them, if things were to ever go sideways during one of their black ops missions, they would either claim plausible deniability, or the Mechanics would be labeled as rogue assets.

On their way to engage another target that had been linked to helping the Stone people weaponize the mining equipment, the Mechanics had hit some kind of celestial vortex and landed here...wherever that is.

They are just about to exit hyperspace in what should have been a quadrant near the gravity well of Mars but at a safe distance where they can go stealth without being detected. The Adder begins spinning, and the next thing they know, Sgt. Garrison is screaming for everyone to strap in for an emergency landing. None of them even remember entering the atmosphere. The instruments were going haywire, and by some miracle, they skidded to a halt near some caves with the ship still structurally sound.

They need to get the lay of the land while Lance Corporals McNamara and Jennings try to find a way to get the ship up and running, so they can get off this rock. All of their EV suits are tailored to their individual prosthesis. Private Cooper steps into his EV suit which has a helmet and body glove that seals over his cybernetic arms at the shoulders to keep it air tight in addition to the seal where the helmet met his neck area. There is a series of whirs and clicks as Private First Class Long presses an interior button on his mech suit, prompting it to raise the face shield as the cranial casing came up from behind to seal him in completely.

Luckily, the closed comm lines between the suits are working fine. Cooper and Long gather a few weapons to take with them on this brief scouting trip. Long sees Cooper shaking his head and wonders what he is thinking. "Coop, what's up?" he asks.

While mag-locking some detonators to his rib area within easy reach, he says, "I know you have some internal way of operating that thing, but from the outside, it looks like you do it with your mind. It's a bit weird at times."

Long thinks about that for a brief moment before answering. "In a way, you're right. All of us have neural interfaces that allow thought to control some of our mechanical enhancements like your arms or the sergeant's legs. For some of the things on this suit, all I have to do is press an internal button with my pectoral muscles. Same goes for my pain meds, which for the most part, are automated, unless I tell it to stop for those moments I need the pain. It's all weird to me, but after a while, I stopped thinking about how things work and accepted that they do."

Cooper understands that. They nod at each other, signaling each is good to go. Sgt. Garrison and Lance Corporals McNamara and Jennings step into the pilot's cabin, so they can open the bay door in the back to allow the others to step out. The ramp is lowered, and the two Marines step out into what looks like a desert landscape.

The topography looks as if this could be New Mexico or Arizona, but the analysis of the atmosphere clearly negates that theory, and there is a purple haze over the sky similar to what they have seen while on Saturn. Long is contemplating what is left of his humanity when it hits him how strange yet familiar this place is. Flora is evident, so life is possible, and they have yet to see any fauna to speak of. Long has opted to leave his Dragonslayer canon with the ship. He and Cooper hope the rail guns and charges they have brought along will be enough to handle anything they run into.

Changing the settings on their helmets to view various spectrums, Long and Cooper agree it is no trick their eyes are playing on them. The sky is, in fact, purple. A common theme for them it would seem. Long has no idea why that bothers him, but it does. The way it was explained to him as a child was that the sky on Earth was blue as a result of prisms formed by dust as the sunlight shined through it, and as a result of this, blue is the color that shows up the most. He guesses that makes sense only because, until some time ago, that is all he had ever seen.

Maybe that is why he hates purple now. Blue skies represent normalcy. He has trained hard, found a group of men and women who have become like family to him, and then war happened. All those people he has come to know and love have been stripped away in the blink of an eye. After one fiery explosion, he woke up to purple skies, in heavier gravity, a shell of himself. No purpose left to him now other than to continue doing what had gotten him to this state in the first place.

When the skies were blue, he had all of his limbs and could enjoy existing on a very basic level. Now he is a…Long has no clear word he can think of that will accurately define him, but he is lost and exploring some foreign wasteland with a group of men that are just as broken as he is, even if the signs aren't all outwardly obvious. It is a good thing the optics in the suits can catalog everything they are looking at. Long has not been paying too much attention, and from the silence, it seems Cooper is having his own internal dialogue as well.

Up ahead, Cooper puts a hand out to his side, fist balled, and tells Long to stop and wait. They hear some rumbling noises which may be a herd of animals or large armored track vehicles. They immediately look for cover and find some behind a few large boulders. What approaches is a group of huge equine-like animals with armored humanoids riding astride them. "Um, sergeant, are you seeing this?" Long asks over their encrypted channel.

Sgt. Garrison has, in fact, been monitoring their HUD feeds since they left and quickly replies, "Yes, I see them. They look gigantic. Do not engage them if you can avoid it. We just want to see what the hell went wrong with the Adder and get the hell off this rock. Preferably without a fight, and we are still not sure what's up with the atmosphere. Mac says something in the air is eerily similar to methane, according to the sensors, but we still don't know. Wouldn't want another Pluto situation, confirm?"

"Roger that," Long replies before turning to look toward Cooper who has taken cover behind a boulder a few meters away. Well, that is another bright surprise. Detonators and energy-based weapons are risky. Cooper nods and puts away the charges he has brought, along with the ballistic and energy small arms weapons. They turn to watch the new arrivals. They are still some distance away, but it is obvious that saying "these horse-like creatures are big" would be a vast understatement.

One of the humanoids slides off the back of the animal it is riding. It looks as if Long would be at about navel level with them if they were to stand toe-to-toe. This is remarkable given that, in the mech suit, Long stands at just over two and a half meters. Hopefully, these giants are the peace-loving kind. The manner of their dress, however, tells quite a different story.

Upon closer examination, these beings aren't just huge; they are armored and heavily muscled. The armor reminds Long and Cooper of some of the fantasy tales they read as children. It is a muted, matte black and not shiny but still appropriate because these beings seem better suited to cast as giant orcs, rather than men in one of those tales, and their skin is a deep crimson.

The young Marines want to further explore the area but are hesitant to move with this group of beings so close to them. After all, what if they have heightened senses of hearing or something? Private Cooper can move pretty stealthily, while Long, on the other hand, is many things, but stealthy will never be one of them, so for now, they simply sit and observe. More of them have gotten off the horse-like creatures and have formed a circle. One of the larger in the group walks to the center of the circle and begins yelling in some guttural language.

Cooper glances over at Long and shakes his head, saying, "That was lovely. Something tells me these boys aren't the warm and fuzzy types."

Long is just about to reply when one of the other crimson-skinned orc-like humanoids jumps in the center of the circle after throwing off a heavy chest plate and punches the guy who started yelling. The one who was punched gets up rubbing his jaw and laughs wickedly. Long thinks of him as scarface because there is a large diagonal scar going from the top right of his forehead to the bottom left of his jaw.

Cooper is sure he doesn't want to see whatever or whoever gave the guy that scar. In a flash, they are on each other. Scarface runs to tackle his assailant, and there is a large dust cloud as they fight fast and viciously. The crowd around them roars as they fight on. Scarface is big but not as big as the other combatant. It is also fairly obvious Scarface is more skilled.

After testing each other's strength with a bit of wrestling, they stand toe-to-toe, and Scarface picks the big guy apart. Punchy, as Long calls him in his mind, is swinging for the fences with each punch, but Scarface is a step ahead of him each time, and with every miss, he makes him pay. After what seems like five minutes, Punchy has had enough. Screaming in frustration, he kicks dirt into Scarface's eyes and runs back to his mount to pull out a wicked-looking broadsword with serrated edges on both sides. One, who has to be their leader evidenced by a lot of crazy accoutrements decorating his face, armor, and Mohawk, jumps between them.

Before the leader has to tussle with Punchy for the sword, a hellish throng of howls fills the air, and everyone stops, frozen. At this inopportune time, all is silent, and there is a hiss of hydraulics in Long's suit, releasing pressure. As one, the group of warriors turn toward the rocks Cooper and Long are hiding behind. On the other side of the plain where the orc-like beings are is a grassy area leading to what looks like a forest. The blue grass is unkempt and high. It is higher than the humanoids stand, and it is now full of movement as if something is running through it.

Luckily for Cooper and Long, that movement redirects their attention. They race to get back on their mounts, brandishing all types of melee weapons, and one seems to have some sort of light-whip. Neither of the Marines are close enough to see how it is constructed, and right now, it isn't all that important. The largest dog-like animal springs from the grass, taking the rider off his mount, biting down on his head, and scratching the equine creature which screams and runs off rider-less into the night.

The men know they should leave while both groups are focused on each other, yet they cannot move. They cannot tear their eyes away from this beautiful yet deadly ballet. As big as they all are, most of these creatures move with speed, grace, and a visceral proficiency that is truly amazing to behold. Cooper and Long do notice that they still have not witnessed any ballistic or energy weapons, although that whip has to be powered by something. They just are not sure what exactly that is.

Soon the battle is over. There are carcasses from the hellhounds and more than a few of the orcs who have fallen strewn on the ground. The humanoids have picked up their wounded, and the hellhounds have run back into the grasslands leading into the tree-line.

Long and Cooper, at least for now, have been forgotten. Cooper goes over to Long. "Let's get the hell out of here!" he opines. Long nods in agreement before hearing a pitiful whining noise from the battleground. Long turns to walk in that direction.

Following the noise to a corpse of one of the large canine-like creatures which are only slightly smaller than the equine animals, Long walks around and finds a pup on the other side, trying to rouse what must have been its parent. The dark fur with white striations matches the fallen dire hound which is what Long has settled on calling these creatures. It also has glowing red eyes which are strangely familiar for some reason, although he cannot pinpoint why. Cooper comes up behind Long and grabs his arm. "We have to go before they come back. Don't have time for this."

Long knows he is right, and this beast will obviously grow into a very dangerous animal. Perhaps that is what has drawn him to it. They are hopelessly lost in this hostile environment. Long turns to Cooper and says, "Go on. I'll be right behind you."

Shaking his head, Cooper turns to head back to the Adder. Long goes over and kneels before the pup which starts to growl before wagging its tail and yelping playfully. Even as a puppy, this thing is closer to the size of a big black bear cub. It looks at its slain mother and whimpers once again before turning back to Long.

Chapter Four

LONG REACHES OUT A METALLIC hand and says, "It's ok, boy. I won't hurt you." He takes out a large blade from a compartment in his mechanical leg, cuts a piece of meat off one of the fallen equine creatures, and holds it out to the pup. The dire hound's teeth sure look carnivorous. The pup sniffs a couple times before snatching the meat accompanied by a loud, clanking noise as its teeth bounce off metal fingers. Quickly yanking his hand back, Long laughs. "If that had been a real hand, I'd be in serious trouble right now," he says as he chuckles and leads the pup to a cave near their crash site.

Moments later, Cooper steps into the rear bay of the Adder alone. Sgt. Garrison looks at him, silently questioning him as to the whereabouts of PFC Long. As Cooper shrugs his broad metallic shoulders, the bay door opens once more, and Long clanks in. Once he is inside, they are all able to take off their helmets as the internal atmosphere is adjusted, so they can breathe, unaided by apparatuses.

As Long's helm and faceplate retract into his suit, Sgt. Garrison calls out to the rest of the Mechanics, "Form up, men. I need a sit-rep. Mac, you first. I need to know what's going on with our bird."

Lance Corporals Jennings and McNamara walk in to join the others. McNamara is looking down at a data-pad, scrolling through various readings. After a few seconds, he gives his report to the group. "The ship seems to be in good working order which is strange. We ran into some celestial anomaly, which for some reason, sent the ship's systems into an involuntary reboot coming out of hyperspace inside of this planet's gravity well. That's the reason for our free fall. Something still has to be wrong since the ship thinks we are back on Earth which obviously can't be right."

Listening to the report, Sgt. Garrison nods his head before asking, "Can we get off this rock?"

Looking back at Lance Corporal Jennings for support, McNamara firmly states, "Yes, sergeant. I see no reason why we can't as soon as the ship recalibrates upon completion of the reboot."

Jennings simply nods in agreement. There is nothing wrong with the structural integrity of the Adder, and for all intents and purposes, things seem to be functioning properly for the most part. The big, unasked questions are, why has the system rebooted in the first place, and where exactly have they actually landed if the readings are, in fact, wrong?

A monitor floats in as Sgt. Garrison gets up to look at the feeds from PFC Long's and Private Cooper's helmet cams. Pointing to the screen, Sgt. Garrison asks, "What in the world have we gotten ourselves into here?"

They all simply watch it again, equally as mesmerized as when first viewing it. Lance Corporal Jennings breaks out of the trance, first reiterating their previous concerns. "We have to stow the ballistic and energy weapons! Not sure what will happen if we have to discharge any here. Avoid fighting if you can, and if not, it looks like we will have to fight on their level. *Kabars*, that weird hammer Long made for whatever reason…"

On que, Long reaches into his trunk that is mag-locked to the deck in the rear of the bay and pulls out a large titanium alloy hammer which he has engraved and decoratively filigreed on the head as well as handle. He feels it helps him fit into his code name, although it is a bit more sophisticated looking for a "berserker" to wield. Aside from himself, only Cooper could likely lift it.

Everyone else fits kabars as bayonets to their weapons with the exception of Long and Cooper, who have the biggest guns of the group. Long carries the Dragonslayer, an enormous plasma canon that, when mounted to his mech-suit makes him a living tri-pod while firing at air or spacecraft. That would be overkill for a normal firefight which shouldn't take place here because these beings don't seem to use firearms of any kind. They didn't want to blow themselves up before they could escape this place. Standard issue GMC rifles with fixed bayonets sans the necessary rounds should do the trick.

At least, they all hope so. Sgt. Garrison does not like the look of that light-whip or whatever he saw through their feed during the fight between the savages and those hellhounds. For a brief moment, he thinks it's ironic that that is his first impression of a group of beings he knows nothing about. The thought is pushed far from his thoughts as he needs to stay on mission and make it off this rock, so they can do what is necessary to help their side win the war effort back home.

There is a loud thud as the Adder rocks as if hit. Running to see what was outside, Lance Corporal Jennings looks at the external feed of their rear bay hatch and sees one of the humanoid beings banging away at the hatch with what looks like a club. Looking over Jennings's shoulder, Sgt. Garrison calls out to Long, "Berserker, show our guest we're not taking visitors at this time. The rest of you standby in case he's not alone. We need to get this bucket space-worthy in a hurry. This is not my ideal vacation spot!"

The face shield and skull casing enclose Long's mech-suit as he grasps his hammer and steps onto a pad beneath the dorsal hatch atop the Adder. The Mechanics scramble to shell up, grabbing the rest of their armor as Long is the only one who wears his around the clock. Helmets and suits have been sealed over flesh and cybernetics of the crew prior to the hatch opening. The circle-shaped plate in the ceiling slides aside as the pad Long is standing on rises to place him atop the Adder. When Long steps aside, the pad lowers, and the hatch slides to close again.

As he takes his first step, there is a loud clank, so he opts just to leap off the ship behind whoever is trying to gain access to the Adder with a club. Landing heavily behind the large humanoid, Long sizes him up. Since he is not as large as the beings he saw fighting in the desert plains, he decides to tap him on the shoulder first. Swiftly turning, the red-skinned humanoid reverse swings the club into the heavy chest plate, sending Long sliding back several meters.

Kneeling as he slides, Long digs the handle into the ground to halt himself before gathering the hammer to throw it center mass at the orc-like being. There is a sickly thud as the hammer hits him in the midsection, cracking ribs before bouncing off. Wiping what must be bluish blood from his mouth and hugging the injured ribs, he makes to rush Long who has just picked the hammer back up.

Bracing for a collision that never comes, Long watches as there is a black and white blur that passes between them, along with a spray of more bluish blood. When the dust settles, the humanoid is on the ground, scurrying away with a raised hand, trailing blood. The dire hound seems ready to pursue when Long shouts, "No!" through the speaker. The hound turns, and incredibly Long recognizes it. Walking up to it, he says, "No, it can't be…"

The pattern of white striations on black fur looks like the puppy he had seen mere hours earlier, but if that is true, it has grown in height and bulk. On its hind legs, they would be nearly eye to eye, and it has put on pounds of muscle. Reaching out to timidly pet it, Long says, "Boy, what sups did you take? We need some of that!"

The rear hatch opens as the rest of the Mechanics come out to see Long scratching the belly of this huge beast.

Sgt. Garrison shakes his head as he looks at the scene. Lance Corporal McNamara joins Long in cautiously petting the animal. Jennings calls out to the group over the comm system, "Skids up in ten mikes! Everything looks good and scanners indicate a pretty big group approaching from the south!"

As they run back in and prepare for lift off, Sgt. Garrison slowly approaches the pup and holds his hand out, palm up. Long cringes as he waits to see his sergeant ripped to shreds.

Surprisingly, the pup sniffs his hand and then licks it with a huge purple tongue. While scratching the creature's ears, Long says, "See, sergeant, he likes you…can we keep him?"

Lance Corporal Jennings overhears this and chimes in, "Yeah, Pa, can we keep 'im?"

Shaking his head negatively, Sgt. Garrison declares, "First of all, we don't know if it can survive in our environment, and I'm not sure what use this beast could be to us."

There is suddenly a deep rumbling noise that shakes the ground, and the animal looks around, growling deeply in response. Lance Corporal McNamara comes running out of the ship, screaming, "Huge group of something coming from all directions! Could be the humanoids riding those horse-like things. The Adder is only at 80 percent capacity."

Sgt. Garrison thinks about it for a second before ordering, "Fire her up anyway! Can't take the chance of being caught. They have superior numbers, and we may not be able to use our firepower advantage here. Let's go!"

They all do as they are ordered, scrambling to batten down gear and hatches as the engines roar to life. As the Mechanics strap into their places, LCPL Jennings calls over the comm system, "Visuals coming from scanners! It's them, sergeant, but if we can get off the ground, at least, we won't be flying blind!" There is a loud thud as something hits the hull.

"Take her up. I don't care what the readout says!" Garrison orders.

Lance Corporal Jennings's fingers fly over the console in front of him, and the attitude thrusters point at the ground and flare to life, slowly lifting the Adder off the ground. On their monitors, they can see a horde of humanoid riders speeding toward them, hurling objects that bounce off the hull with little to no effect. The ship hesitates after a huge impact, and the crew get nervous, but the ascent continues until they can look down and see how large the gathering of beings has become.

It is possible that, even with their firepower, the odds might have been insurmountable.

The nose of the Adder points toward the heavens, and the ship shudders as it begins its fight to escape this strange planet's atmosphere into open vacuum. Private First Class Long closes his eyes and thinks of what would have happened had they been forced to stay. If those beings had tried to fight them, which is highly likely, he and his group would have fought back and likely found a way to even the odds. How could they be right if successful?

Technically, they have encroached on these beings' planet, but given the chance, more than likely, the Mechanics would have eradicated anyone that stood in their way. They are still unsure as to where they were, but Long knows there are beings in his own galaxy that are different but still from the same place he is, and they are at war to continue their oppression. There has been recent research supporting the fact that these mutated beings are, in fact, related to them.

This is something that Long has wrestled with now since his injuries. He has had time to wallow in his despair and also to think on what all the conflict means and to wonder if any of it is worth it, especially given the price he has personally paid in service to the military and galaxy at large. In his world, might makes right. The only reason the GMC has had control for so long is owed to technological advances. Some of the mutated races are physically more powerful, so humans have come up with gadgets to supersede this. Technically, they are fighting and oppressing their own kind, and nobody wants to admit this.

The ship continues shuddering, this time more violently. This has broken Long out of his introspection as there is a horrible screeching that fills the ship.

"What the hell is that?" Sgt. Garrison exclaims.

Having sealed the ship before leaving atmosphere, they have all taken off their helmets since the air inside is eighty percent oxygenated and is comfortable for them. Unstrapping from his seat, Garrison leaps up to follow the noise to its source somewhere in the rear bay.

As they finally break out into vacuum, the ship quiets, and the screeching stops, but there is now a quiet yet still audible whimpering coming from one of the orbital drop pods. The noise emanates from the largest one, which is immediately recognized as PFC Long's pod which had to be custom-built to accommodate him and his large suit, and it has no restraints as the suit could also lock itself in place during planet-fall.

"Long, get in here!" Garrison bellows.

Shutting off the mag-locks on his suit, Long slowly walks to where the pods are in the aft section of the ship followed by Private Cooper and Lance Corporal McNamara.

"Tell me you didn't do what I think you did," Garrison says scathingly. Shaking his head, he looks at McNamara and orders, "Open it."

Obeying the order immediately, McNamara proceeds to place his hand on a node to the side of the pod. Realizing the danger too late, Long yells, "No! Wait!" but the pod is already unsealed, and the methane-like gas leaks out as the oxygenated air moves into the pod. There is a loud thudding as the pup from the strange planet struggles to breathe. Finally leaping out onto the deck, it fights a little while longer before collapsing and remains still.

Lance Corporal Jennings comes in from the pilot cabin, covering his nose. "That's definitely more than methane," he exclaims.

Shaking his head, Sgt. Garrison looks at Long and says, "I was afraid this might happen which is why I was reluctant to bring that thing with us. Clean it up, Long."

They all exit, except for Long, who dejectedly goes to gather tools to clean the mess when he hears the beast begin to stir. Turning, he kneels by its side and watches as he can almost hear something internal happening that his eyes cannot see. There are ripples going throughout the animal's body, and when they stop, it relaxes again. Thinking perhaps that is just some delayed death throes, he begins to rise again when the beast lifts his head and whimpers again. "Ha! Ha! Still alive!" Long exclaims.

The animal's tail begins to slowly wag as Long, once again, strokes its belly. Playfully rubbing the beast, Longs says, "Who's a good boy?" Gathering a sani-mop, Long walks over to his orbital pod and looks in, to check its contents, and finds the source of the horrible smell. A huge pile of excrement awaits removal. "Lovely. Maybe you're not so good after all."

• • •

Darius and Simeon sit together, meditating, before the day's training session begins. It has taken the boy a few weeks to master standing in the first ten bojutsu stances and maintaining them under heavier gravity imposed on him while in the training facility. Simeon wants to train the prince under the hardest conditions, not only because he will have to be the best in order to handle his duties when he becomes king but also because all who he will be tasked to lead will know his path was not made easier simply because of his station in life.

The boy has always been able to demonstrate the stances flawlessly under normal circumstances, and that proficiency is slowly beginning to show itself when he is asked to do so under the duress of the chamber. Darius is also very big for his age yet smaller than the stockier general teaching him. Simeon stands and walks over to the control panel by the entrance. Darius feels the gravity normalize to the intensity similar to Earth's conditions. Turning around, Simeon faces Darius. "Now, young prince, pick up your staff and strike me…if you can."

Confused, Darius stands with the staff, seeming to ponder the weapon in his hands before rushing the general. Grinning, Simeon easily sidesteps the boy's initial attack, lightly kicking him in the rear as he passes.

Chapter Five

MAKING THEIR WAY BACK TO the base on Saturn, the group codenamed the Mechanics prepares to land as instructed, once again, in the auxiliary medical bay. They have been sent to recon possibly hostile space near Neptune and have found that there isn't much activity in the area, but something has gone wrong with their sensors. Sgt. Garrison is sure of that and is not exactly sure how to explain what has happened. Lance Corporals Jennings and McNamara have both checked the Adder's systems for a malfunction and found none. Whatever celestial anomaly they have run into makes it seem as if they've been gone for a minimum of a few weeks. Upon requesting permission to land after de-cloaking, the ring sentries act as if they've been gone for a brief time.

The only evidence that they have not all shared in some psychedelic drug mishap is that the beast PFC Long has smuggled aboard after being told to get rid of it is currently in the young Marine's drop pod. There are also small soil and sand samples they have tracked into the ship from time spent on the surface of the planet they were briefly stranded on. Private Cooper and PFC Long have gathered what they can for the techs to analyze. There is an awful stench in the aft cargo bay as well. PFC Long will have to figure how to get rid of that, in addition, to how they will hide that beast if they will not put it down.

On the return flight, they all try to convince Sgt. Garrison that the animal can be of some use to them. Miraculously, it has adapted to their atmosphere and not died during the trip. The air from the planet it came from is very different from Earth's and has some similarities to the previous conditions on Pluto. The beings they ran into are nothing like they have ever encountered, save for old fantasy tales. The going theory is that they have, somehow, gone through a rift in the time/space continuum or to another dimension, but none of them are qualified to confirm or deny this. Sgt. Garrison figures he can risk sounding like a fool and divulge this theory to Lt. Commander Jameson or find another scientist-type that will help them figure out what happened without risking losing his rank and unit. The question is, who can they trust?

The barracks for the Mechanics are now secreted away from the other Marines and service members stationed on Saturn below their training facility. It makes more sense for them to be close to their weapons cache for quick rearming before deploying. There are also special units there for them to calibrate their prosthetics when they need to. Due to recent events, Sgt. Garrison orders the whole crew to do so to ensure the trip through the rift or whatever it is they have gone through have had no ill effects on their equipment. As soon as they are cleared, it is likely they will be redeploying soon in an effort to clean up before peace can be announced.

• • •

On his way back to his quarters, Darius still feels the sting of Simeon's attacks. The general seems to be a few steps ahead each time the boy tries to get through his defenses in an attempt to strike as instructed. Luckily his special suit gives a good buffer from the blows, but it still hurts. Simeon says it needs to in order to communicate the seriousness of future confrontations in which other beings will be trying to harm or even kill him. The young prince is discouraged at this prospect, so Simeon decides to dial it back. The message has already been received, and Simeon almost teared up at the sight of Darius's innocent naivety nearly dying on the spot.

The gravity in the chamber has been, once again, dialed up, slowing both of their movements. Darius notes that Simeon is slowing but cannot discern if he is tiring or just letting him gain confidence. With each strike and repost later in the sparring session, he gets closer to tagging the general. They take a short break to meditate some more to clear their minds again. When they reconvene, Simeon tells Darius he will not only defend himself but, in turn, will go on the offensive as well. After a while, it seems either the gravity has gone back to normal or it is no longer hindering them as if they have become used to it.

It is only after the general has parried a vicious strike, flipped over young Darius and lashed out to wack the prince squarely on his backside, sending him flailing to the ground, that the boy finally realizes he has been baited. Anger wells up in the boy as Simeon begins chuckling. Before he can gather himself to continue the attack, Darius cannot help but join in the infectious laughter. Simeon drops his staff and grabs up Darius in a bear hug. "Good, good. Hold on to that. In this crazy world, my young prince, we must find joy and laughter where we can. Sadly, there may come times when they won't be offered much. Tragedy, sadness, and all manner of ill you will not have to search for. You understand?" he advises.

Darius nods as Simeon pats the boy on the shoulder before pushing him gently toward the door, signaling the end of the day's session. Darius mulls all of this over as he reaches his chambers. One thing he is determined to do is pay his teacher back for that wallop to his rump, as well as for many of the other blows he has suffered. In retrospect, he has to admit that last one was pretty funny. Briefly rubbing his bottom, there are obviously some parts that do not feel the humorous side of things.

• • •

Pharaoh, the name has lasted for eons, yet there is only one still walking the Earth that carries that title. It is not even his true name, but he has heard it for so long and only thought it fitting to be addressed as a god-king. The inhabitants of this planet are beneath him. He cannot fathom why the others of his kind cannot see it. Pharaoh suspects that others feel the same way he does, but they go along with the sanctimonious council of twelve that decided to exile him here. He has been left to his own devices and has made the most of his situation here, but now it feels as if someone is either already interfering or being asked to. Now it is just a feeling with no proof.

He knows the aged Atlantean Babylon has gone to his people, in all likelihood, to ask for some kind of aid. There is no way to attempt to find out without communicating his suspicions to whoever could potentially be meddling. It would be so much easier if Pharaoh could go investigate for himself, but the main fleet of the self-titled Kison Askari are currently near Mars and in constant motion for fear of a strike from the GMC. Being confined to the Earth is ever the inconvenience, making it a necessity to use proxies to go off-world. In this instance, he needs to know what Babylon is up to and if other beings of his kind are now involved.

A discreet touch is needed for reconnaissance. There must be information gathering without the wonton mayhem Malice is used to leaving in his wake and his new accomplice is ill equipped for subtlety, given his appearance. Malice has the talent to be stealthy but often enjoys the fear that is exhibited by most beings when he reveals himself. He will have to be instructed carefully. Typhoon will accompany him but only in a supportive role. There is a chance they may have been seen together during the brief fight at the facility on Pluto.

Pharaoh finds Malice in one of the bottom-most chambers where he tends to train or meditate in near darkness, stripped to the waist. There is a mass of slender, scarred, and charred muscle moving with a frenetic fluidity that some of the dancers in Ongakujin would be jealous of as the henchman goes through various fighting routines. Any other onlooker would have been amazed that he can even move at all from the evidence of battle severely emblazoned all over his body. Pharaoh knows the body is but an empty shell, and it will do as the will commands so long as that will is unbending. The ancient is not impressed.

Malice is in his own world and has not acknowledged his master's presence. There is no telling what implacable foe he is vanquishing in his mind as his blades begin to move so fast through the air there are audible humming sounds as he slices and parries. Finally feeling the added energy that comes into the chamber, Malice hastily sheathes his blades in their scabbards and bows to his master. The glowing white gaze of the ancient one meets the fiery red glow of his henchmen's eyes. Malice can sense this is more than a visual assessment. His power is being gauged. Never before has his prowess been questioned. This Babylon and the mystery child of unknown origin must be a threat somehow, he thinks.

Malice is not sure how he feels about this.

"Do you remember when I first saw you?" Pharaoh asks.

"Yes, master," Malice rasps.

Without another word, his master mentally whisks them away to a time when the great metropolis of Atlantis was built. Malice can see mountainous terrain sprawling with buildings that are an amalgamation of archaic architecture and something that would still be considered modern, even now. The mixture is a unique combination of beauty and utilitarian aspects that the humans today fell short of, despite their technological advances.

During this mental journey, Malice can see the evolution of a people that gathered to what looked like a being engulfed in flames that is changing color. The form of this being is also changing rapidly as it seems to struggle to find a form it desires. Strangely it is not crying out in pain and does not seem to be harmed in any way from the explosion of light emanating from it. Finally, it settles into a humanoid form with azure skin and glowing amber eyes. Despite there being some obvious differences, Malice recognizes that this is his master in another form at some point prior to their fateful encounter.

He is taller, well over two and a half meters, heavily muscled and shorn of hair. The brown-skinned primitive men, large in their own right, bowed to him. They come asking for knowledge in exchange for their worship and admiration. The ancient needs neither of these but takes them nonetheless. They grow in knowledge and strength continually, and other tribes of men grow jealous. When they can ignore the probing attacks no longer, they begin applying their newfound advancements toward military means of defense and prevention of further attacks. The ancient one takes an avid interest in these events, and the more zealous of his followers are eventually mutated to look as he did back then.

The neighboring tribes never stand a chance as the Atlanteans are now wielding weapons that are melee weapons with some sort of energy projectile capabilities as well. To the rest of the world, they look like sorcerers or other beings of legend. Eventually prevention gave way to other would-be conquerors of the era. They began to topple other so-called empires. They constructed fast-traveling vehicles that rival the hover vehicles currently roaming the Earth and came back just in time to witness their home engulfed by a cataclysmic earthquake.

The great city has been left in ruins deep beneath the sea as the only visible remnants are now a sprinkle of islands in what would be identified as the Caribbean. The very tops of the previously huge land masses sit atop of what used to be the most advanced civilization. Some of these peoples have escaped the fate of the city but not much is known of their whereabouts or what they've been up to. Recovering from his waking dream, Malice turns to his master and asks, "That was you in another form. Was it not, master?"

Seeming to consider the question, Pharaoh morphs into the being in the vision before answering, "Yes, and it is very possible some of those beings you saw survived. This Babylon may very well be one of them. I need you and Typhoon to observe them and find out if they've anything or anyone I should be wary of. I have it on good authority this being may have visited my home world."

Understanding and confusion wash over Malice as he continues to probe for answers. "But, master, how could they have survived after so long? How long ago did you visit with these people?"

Waving a hand dismissively toward him, Pharaoh explains, "I had imbued some of them with my essence similarly to the way I had done with you but more...directly. This mutated them in more ways than you can see with the naked eye. Though not as strong as I am, it's hard to gauge how they would compare to you. I learned, over time, that this process slightly weakened me each time, but I came to know how to empower others without siphoning strength from my own reserves. Their transformations came before that knowledge and slightly before our chance meeting in Egypt after the fall of their city."

Malice understands how this can be a danger to his master. If they have received any kind of help or further augmentation from beings as powerful or more so than his master, then they could be a true threat to his hold on the Earth. It also opens the possibility to gain more strength himself and, at last, break this being's hold on him. As if he has just been made aware of the bevy of thoughts flying through Malice's mind, Pharaoh admonishes him, "I need you to find out what I need to know and gather any information on this mystery child, preferably without leaving a swath of bodies in your wake. Is that understood? You two may have been seen on Pluto, and unlike the environment on this planet, it will be harder to blend in in less populated places."

Quickly throwing on his hooded cowl to cover his discomfiture, Malice answers abruptly, "Yes, master. I shall not fail you. We will be shadows unmoved or noticed by the winds."

As he exits the chamber to find Typhoon to prepare for their journey, Pharaoh calls after him, "See that you do not fail me again!"

The ancient one remembers the brash young acolyte who stormed into his chamber so long ago. Angered by the fact that his people blindly followed this strange being without question, he had challenged the newcomer. The audacity and feverish hatred with which Malice attacked that day earned him his new name. Pharaoh respects his tenacity, but for his disrespectful brazenness, he has to be punished.

The other acolytes and elders had rushed in to see rays of energy flying from a staff Pharaoh held into young Malice's body, burning him severely as he writhed in agonizing pain. They quickly tucked tail and ran from the scene. Turning to his would-be assailant, Pharaoh screamed, "They may be sycophants wanting knowledge only to empower themselves, but they know who is not to be trifled with! A shame you did not get the message. I do admire your courage though, and for that, I will offer you the honor of serving me. In exchange, I will let you live, heal you of your wounds, and strengthen you so none of these fools will hold sway over you ever again. Say the words!"

Through tears and great pain, the young man yelled, "I'll serve you!"

Shaking his head, Pharaoh stood over the smoking boy and prompted, "You'll serve me?"

Relief at not burning almost set in before his body temperature began to rise again until the boy hastily repeated, "I'll serve you…master!"

Kneeling down, Pharaoh replied, "Smart boy, whatever they called you before is gone. From now on, you shall be known as Malice."

Malice shrunk away from his touch before realizing that his wounds were being simultaneously healed and cauterized. The pain was gone, but there were still echoes of it. A strange energy was coursing through him as strength grew throughout his entire being. His mind expanded as well, giving him understanding to things that were previously unimaginable.

Pharaoh had left him there in a smoking heap. When he was strong enough to rise, he immediately went to find a mirror in the chamber and what he saw was horrifying. He was now a walking, blackened, scarified thing with what looked like hot coals for eyes, an ugly tool for his new master. He vowed that, one day, no matter how long it took, he would avenge what was done to him. In the meantime, there were others who had wronged him that would get their just due now.

Chapter Six

BACK ON SATURN, CORPORALS ARAGON, Sims, and Jordan are going through some extreme training exercises in modified EV suits. For all the talks of peace, it seems someone at HQ thinks they are going to be in close combat situations with the Stone people soon. It is obvious the nominal training and supplementation administered here for the recon units alone will not be enough to subdue armed Stone warriors in a ground fight. Space battle is a toss-up with no clear advantage, but on the ground, the Kison Asakari have shown in previous engagements that, despite being behind technologically, they learn fast.

In a further attempt to even the physical odds, the Marines are training in EV suits that are more heavily armored that also lend extra strength to the already enhanced humans inside them. They are going at it with hulking bots designed to mimic the fighting styles that have been recorded during the revolts on Earth and mining colonies on other planets. The problem is they are beating the bots handedly. This is temporarily good for morale but horrible for training. The bots move with a brutal efficiency but, in the end, are outsmarted or outclassed by the Marines. One of the instructor's signal that the session is over. Aragon is relieved as the recycled air with remnants of sweat is starting to get to him.

They all go back to be debriefed on tactics as well as to watch footage of the session. Once they are back inside the main facility, they can take off their helmets, allowing them to breathe air that is still being cycled but thankfully not from within their suits. Aragon, Sims, Jordan, and the rest of the group take seats and await their instructor. Staff Sergeant Armstead calmly strides in to the head of the chamber where the main monitor is embedded in the bulkhead. Not as intimidating as Sgt. Garrison, yet he has his own intangible air of strength that makes men want to follow him. Armstead is a short, dark-skinned man with intelligent brown eyes with fire behind them. After removing his helm, he signals to someone at the rear to turn the display on, so they can watch the session that has just taken place in a large field there on Saturn.

When the screen comes to life, the Marines watch their session with rapt attention, mentally cataloging what seems to be working and what does not. Aragon takes a moment to find himself on the field and notices how easily they smash through the vanguard of stone-bots. He sees the rest of his group forgoing weapons in order to engage in hand-to-hand combat. That is when it hits him and all the others simultaneously. Things are going too well for this to compare to the real thing. What at first are hoots and nods of approval quickly become negative head shakes. Staff Sergeant Armstead waves to shut it down and the display turns off. He stands and asks them, "Who can tell me what's wrong with this picture?"

There is dead silence, and they all know why. These simulations are nothing compared to the real thing. There are a few things they cannot realistically gauge without engaging their enemy on an actual battlefield. They will not know how much their newfound strength through supplementation compares to the natural power of the Kison Askari, and as good as the bots are, they will not channel the ferocity many of these same Marines' old units have faced during the initial and follow-up skirmishes. Seeing these realizations in the eyes of his Marines, the staff sergeant speaks up, "Gear up and stay ready, men! I don't know if you've noticed, but you can't help it. A lot of ops and materiel has been coming in. My guess is we won't be dealing in theory much longer. Regardless of what the scuttlebutt around here is or what you heard in the press. This peace is about to be broken, and I imagine we are not going to allow them to get the first swing this time. Dismissed!"

Corporals Aragon, Jordan, Sims, as well as the other military men and women, gather their gear and head back to their quarters.

• • •

Sparks sits there, silently observing Argos, a hulking humanoid in the employ of Max. Or, at least, that is the assumption she makes. She does not know their history, and there is obviously some sort of close bond between them, and it has been a long time since she has been around Max. Before, she was a street-level operator of sorts. They have both come a long way from their pasts. Argos, who she assumes was named after the faithful dog who awaited his master's return, is hard to define, which is why she thinks of him as "humanoid" and not strictly human. Anyone can tell that much of the bulk beneath the armor, cloth wrappings, goggles are all flesh, bone, and sinew in contrast to some who have cybernetic enhancements.

What is hard to gauge is what it all looks like under the various garb and weaponry she has become accustomed to seeing him in. Is he, in fact, human, she wonders, or a stone person hiding his true identity given the current political climate? Argos moves slowly, but Sparks can see that is deliberate. She knows, at a moment's notice, he can move with a speed and ferocity that will be horrifying if you are on the wrong end of his efforts. There are no hitches to his movements or clicks and buzzes most associated with the cybernetically enhanced which have recently become popular. She is also curious as to how he and Max ended up as partners.

Sparks turns her attention to Max who is hunched over a data display, going over some of his recent searches to find out if the murder of her beloved senator can be linked to the Ongakujin. They are in one of his hidden bases of operation in what used to be the South Side of Chicago. Outside, it looks very much like an apartment in an abandoned project development. Anyone who sees it from the outside wouldn't give the buildings here much thought which is why he chose this location. He also happens to own the complex under a shell company that, to the public, has plans to redevelop the area. The inside, however, tells a much different story. This place is heavily fortified and rigged with a complex surveillance suite that will alert them should anyone approach from various directions.

As a favor, Max helps Sparks interview Hironike to see if she can find out if they are, in fact, responsible for Senator Levine's demise. Nothing concrete came from that risky endeavor, but they had to have some knowledge of what happened, even if they hadn't done it themselves, and he brashly promises to help investigate, hoping nothing will be found and that she will give up this crusade. The toes on the foot of Max's prosthetic leg are absently tapping. For some strange reason, he has programmed his prosthesis to have some human idiosyncrasies that will activate when he is sitting still, so he won't have to think about it.

Right now, Max is stalling. He isn't sure if he wants to divulge what his searches, along with tips Sparks has provided from evidence gathered at the crime scene from months ago, have found. Max knows that, if Sparks is right about these individuals being an elite group of assassins who have plied their trade of dealing death to high-profile targets in public places under the very noses of those sworn to protect them, then the odds of avenging any of those deaths will be near impossible. Most of the evidence of the killings are slippery at best, and what they have now at face value says very little, but it is beginning to paint a picture.

If it is in fact a poison, it was synthetically made or so rare the source will be easy to trace, but that trail leads nowhere. The cosmetic traces that were found in a trash bin near an exit at the museum are another story. Cosmetics are commonly used by courtesans, as well as veterans of war who don't have the money to purchase surgeries or prosthetics to cover injuries suffered during war time. The traces found are more expensive and of a higher-grade product linked to specific batches that are more likely to have been purchased by production companies who worked within the entertainment industry, so things are getting narrowed down, thus eliminating the disgruntled vet or lady of the night theories.

From a certain perspective, a disgruntled vet who suffered a major disfigurement left without the means to pay for having their body or face restored exacting revenge on a politician makes a lot of sense. This is exactly what Max is hoping to find, but this is not to be. Finances eliminate his first batch of desirable suspects, so the next step is to follow the money. The easiest thing to trace is always the money. Once the specific product is identified, it is a simple matter of finding out the batch, then looking for who purchased from that batch, and the list is minute, to say the least. Number one on that list is the Ongakujin Company Ltd.

Sparks can see Max has found something, but it is also clear he is not eager to share. "Ok, spill it. I can see the gears grinding in your head. What have you found?" Sparks asks.

Max turns the monitor, so she can see the findings and answers, "There could be a correlation linking them to the residue you found outside the museum where the senator was killed, but that doesn't mean it was ultimately them."

Incredulously, Sparks looks at the data. "How can that be? It looks as if they're the ones who purchased the largest amount of the stuff," she replies.

Max leans in and enlarges the graphed data and pulls up another data stream while pointing out, "That's true, but they also distribute some of it to other companies taking the batches they buy and making other products specifically for the cosmetic industry as well as some shell companies dealing in pharmaceuticals. It's an instant alibi that, at the very least, would hinder things in a court of law, Sparks."

Shaking her head, Sparks agrees but is quick to point out, "I am not taking this to a court of law, Max. Where there's smoke, there's fire, and they were involved in the senator's death. This I know, and realistically you know it as well. So please keep digging. We have yet to find an absolute dead end, and you promised you would help me. You're hoping it will lead to someone else, and I am fine with that as long as I can serve them justice myself. If the culprits end up being Ongakujin, and the myth of the Jade Assassins is a reality, then they will pay! I understand it being a tough nut to crack, but they didn't go to any court when they executed my..."

She can't finish the sentiment, but Max understands. Argos simply looks at her and bows slightly to show his agreement.

• • •

There is a bevy of brief booms as a flotilla of GMC war ships exits hyper-space just outside the gravity well at Mars. General Krulak is hoping to catch the Stone people unaware, enabling him to destroy some of their fleet as well as attain some of the valuable material they are hording. It is a desperate move, and a risky one. The information that has been gleaned from the satellite images places a large capital ship as well as what looks like some kind of mobile shipyard here, yet none of that is in evidence currently. Major Vashti is at the helm of the Man of War frigate heading the flotilla, along with some Praetorian cruisers with a few squadrons of various smaller war space craft. The idea is to destroy or take some of the precious materials and get out.

Queen Regent Tunisia is watching all of this unfold from the bridge of the only complete Dreadnaught carrier the Kison Akari owns. They have moved to orbit Jupiter when they observe the flotilla of the GMC jumping from Saturn, and their sensors are able to guess the approximate destination by analyzing the jump scars left behind. Unfortunately for the GMC, this only serves to prove Tunisia's suspicions correct that they have not, in fact, learned their lessons from the demonstration of weaponized dark matter. No intent has been communicated, but from the posture, formations, and obvious weapons protruding from the hulls of the ships that jump in, these ships have not come for a diplomatic purpose.

Darius runs in, followed by Babylon. The boy runs into his mother's arms as she scoops him up and swings him around before hugging him fiercely. Tunisia waves her hand to the Askari at the main monitor, silently commanding him to shut it down. Babylon does not miss the exchange and is curious as to what it was previously displayed. Darius, ever watchful, picks up on the tension in the room and asks, "What were you looking at, Mother?"

Setting him down, she replies, "Nothing you should be concerned with, sweet prince. Soon enough, you will have all kinds of things to worry about. Until then, enjoy your youth."

From the exchange, Babylon does not press her any further but is more than intrigued.

Before any more questions can be asked, Tunisia waves Nefer over and commands, "Tell them to prepare my ship immediately. I will return shortly."

Having no notice that the queen plans on leaving, Nefer looks at her inquisitively, but the determined look on her face says there will be no discussion. She simply bows and responds, "Yes, my queen," and walks to the comm station on the bridge to relay the message. Sensing whatever action is about to be taken could have definite implications, Babylon queries, "What's so important that you 'ave to go now, Queen Tunisia?"

Without a backward glance, she shoots over her shoulder, "I need to send a message. Love you, Darius!"

Under his breath, Babylon mutters, "I pray it's de right one."

Darius cheerfully yells, "Love you, too!" as she leaves the bridge on her way to the lift that will take her to the lower decks where her ship is docked. Darius sees a look of deep dismay on Babylon's face. "What's wrong? Do you know where she's going, Babylon?" the boy asks.

Patting him on the head, Babylon admonishes, "No, m'boy, nuttin' is wrong! You should take me to the game deck and show old Babylon what the kids are playin' today! Sound good?"

Darius jumps for joy and grabs Babylon's blue hand, forcing him to hobble along, trying to keep up, white locks flailing as they leave the bridge.

Nefer is worried, as well, about what that message might be if the queen is, in fact, readying the vessel she has shown her previously. If she recalls correctly, it is not a large ship, and it does not look like it will serve as much protection for the queen to be venturing out alone. Her apprehension also has a lot to do with the queen's talk of doing what is necessary when others lack the stomach for it. She also holds out hope that whatever the queen does will halt the hostilities and not enflame the galaxy further.

• • •

Zola, a tall, slender, brown-skinned Kison Askari, sits in her quarters aboard the Dreadnaught, thinking of all the events that have led her to be here, the multitude of suffering and outrages her family and her people have gone through resulting in the current revolt. In hindsight, these things have always been short-lived before basically going back to the status quo. During one of the longer lasting protests decades prior, her grandfather had starved to death, trapped by the shackles and the electromagnetic system. She also lost a son, not long after that, who was fighting the oppressors. Zola is a mother of the fallen.

The Mothers of the Fallen is a group Tunisia has gathered in secret. These are the mothers, sisters, and widows of Stone people who have been killed needlessly over the years. It has become quite a common occurrence, and these women will stand for it no longer. Progress has been made, but to Zola's mind, it is not enough to break free; they should remain free and do what is necessary to keep it that way. This is the largest revolt in recent history, yet it has been started by their king who is no more. Who knows if the queen regent or if the prince, later on, will hold the course? As if to answer her silent musings, there is a knock at her chamber hatch. To her surprise, when she opened the hatch, there stands the queen.

Zola can tell something is different because she can see that Tunisia is not wearing any ceremonial garb. Instead, she is in a jumpsuit, complete with a flight helmet under one arm, and a case in her other hand, holding it out to her. "Change into this. It seems that the illustrious GMC has not learned and needs to be reminded that they're not invulnerable. This is no longer a game they can win, and one we can ill afford to play much longer," the queen confidently states.

Zola quickly opens the case and finds a similar suit and helmet. A look of worry spreads across her features as she asks, "Where are we going?"

Placing a hand on hers, Tunisia says, "To send a message to them by pricking the GMC with the Nyeusi Sime! Remember our fallen and lost children. Are you with me?"

Blinking back tears, Zola replies, "Yes, my queen!"

She quickly dresses, and together they head down to the hangar bays.

• • •

Chapter Seven

ON THE OPPOSITE END OF the living quarters, Simeon is disturbed from his slumber by a knocking at his hatch. Bleary-eyed, the short but stout Kison Askari goes to see who it is at this late hour and is surprised to see Bofus in ill-fitting body armor. "Hey, man. I want to fight!" he blurts out.

Simeon's ire is slightly quelled by the ridiculous look of the man before him. "Bofus, this is not the time or place for your…humor," the general replies.

Nonplussed, Bofus exclaims, "I'm not jokin'! They locked me up for no reason and have been trying to keep yo' people oppressed and stuff. I don't want to be on the sidelines no more…please."

Simeon can see the man is serious but realistically doubts he will be able to cut it as a warrior. Surely this will not last long, so he decides to humor him. "Alright, be at the training decks below at 0400, along with the other recruits. We will see if we can get you some armor that fits."

Simeon goes to close his hatch when Bofus reaches through to grab him by the arm saying, "Thanks, man! I won't let you down!"

Fending him off and closing the hatch briskly, Simeon replies, "That remains to be seen."

Bofus runs off like a giddy child but is slightly disappointed that he will not be training with Darius which is what he'd hoped for. Then again, it makes sense. Darius is a child and a prince, at that, who will get personal training rather than be thrown in with everyone else. He goes back to his quarters to get some rest before starting his training but can hardly get a wink of sleep.

A few brief hours later, Bofus scurries down to take his first steps in joining the fight.

When he arrives on the training deck, there are around forty Askari lined up in formation with staves in their right hands. At the head of the formation is Simeon, looking every bit the military general. Upon seeing Bofus, he barks, "You're late!" He then points to a bundle on the deck in the corner and commands, "Put that on. It's similar to what was made for Prince Darius but with more…padding."

Bofus scrambles to do as ordered and what looks like a lightweight latex body suit is actually quite heavy. It feels strange when it slowly begins to conform to his body, but he is happy that it makes him look somewhat bigger than he actually is.

Simeon nods, and by far the largest Kison Askari he's ever seen steps out of formation, approaching Bofus with two staves. This behemoth of a being has what looks like tattoos at first glance, but as he gets closer, Bofus can see they are strange patterns that have been etched into the hard calcification of his epidermis. It is both frightening and beautiful to behold. Bofus is hesitant to take the staff. Simeon chuckles and introduces them, "Bofus, I would like you to meet Njemba. He will teach you the first few forms for our bojutsu training. Go to the adjacent chamber with the heavier grav field. He will need the strength if he is to fight with us."

Swallowing audibly, Bofus reluctantly accepts the staff and follows Njemba to the other training room. He hopes the giant warrior will not crush him.

As soon as they enter the other chamber, the gravity assaults Bofus, forcing him to his knees. When he struggles to get up, Njemba raises his hand in admonishment and instructs, "No stay down, and get used to the intensity. The *silaha*, or armor, as you would know it, will, in time, lend you strength as it continues to conform to your frame. Quiet your mind and rest as it does so. When you feel you can stand, do so."

Bofus relaxes and does as he was instructed, feeling a new sense of power coming to him through the suit. After a while, he is able to stand. At this point, Njemba begins showing him the first ten stances Darius has learned.

Simeon takes a break from the training session in the main chamber to go observe how Bofus is coming along. "Show him the blocks after he is good with stances, Njemba," Simeon orders.

Offended, Bofus blurts out, "Hey, man. I want to hit these fools, too!"

Holding up a hand to forestall any further objections, Simeon nods to Njemba who immediately rushes Bofus. In a panic, Bofus is barely able to raise his staff as Njemba swiftly swings a double-handed overhead blow after a flourish with the bow. Njemba is using minimum strength, yet it is enough to bring Bofus to his knees as the strike sends shockwaves through his entire body, and that is with the aid of his suit.

Simeon goes to stand over Bofus and instructs, "First, don't question how we teach you to fight. Second, you will be outmatched by the Marines we will be facing who are also training to fight us. We have news of them implementing augmentations via supplements and, in some extreme cases, mechanical enhancements. Dark matter is our ace up our sleeve which should deter them from trying anything large scale, and we intend on controlling where the smaller scale battles will take place. This should limit the loss of lives and limit the use of energy or ballistic weaponry. You will have to know how to block attacks before knowing how to strike since you will likely not be fast enough to strike first, unless you catch someone unaware. The light armor we have given you will help, but until we stand toe-to-toe with the enemy, there's no telling how you will measure up strength-wise. We do not face street thugs, Bofus. We face a fighting force that has been training to kill for a long time. Keep that in mind. We will modify a shoulder harness and canon for you, but only after you have mastered hand-to-hand and melee weapon combat. Understood?"

Shakily getting to his feet, Bofus nods and replies, "Yes sir!"

At that, Simeon goes back to the other chamber to check on the trainees there, leaving Bofus and Njemba to continue as ordered. Slightly disheartened at being rebuked and simultaneously encouraged by the news that he will get a canon at the completion of training, Bofus watches Njemba demonstrate various blocks before trying to emulate his movements. He is also gaining confidence as the suit continues to bond with him. Simeon is pleasantly surprised at the way Bofus is handling his training thus far. He has not cowered or run as most had predicted he would when faced with the intimidating presence of Njemba. The man has heart and, despite appearances, a sound mind as well. That is a good start. Simeon has seen a lot and believes heart is something that cannot be taught. It simply has to be within you as a warrior and a person.

● ● ●

Back in his quarters, Darius sits with Professor Charles Jones-Bey and Babylon. The Atlantean is watching the young prince going through his lessons. It amazes him that the boy had such a broad grasp of history, despite being so young. There have been rumors, but the ancient being is now seeing it firsthand. It borders on scary, and Babylon can tell the professor is taken aback when Darius includes minute details that may have escaped the teacher's vast trove of knowledge. Some of the details are nearly impossible for even the professor to know yet were coming from the mouth of a being still relatively new to this world, as if he were able to tap into some consciousness from a former life. Visibly shaken, the professor concludes the lesson and begs off for the day.

When the two are alone, Babylon motions for the boy to come sit next to him and begins to slowly explain what his responsibility will be once he becomes king. He recounts the same tale he has told the leaders of the oppressed, mutated races during their clandestine meeting near Jupiter. Before he can finish his tale, Darius holds up a hand and says,

"I know, Babylon. The exiled radiant one is still here fomenting strife for his general amusement. We will find him, but the damage is already done. Uniting the people, all of them…will be a more difficult task."

Again, Babylon is impressed with the boy's knowledge.

"Did your father tell you of this? Who taught you the term 'radiant ones'?" Babylon asks.

Shaking his head negatively, Darius replies, "No, sadly, we did not have the time to discuss such things. War was in full gear when I came to this part of the galaxy."

Confused once again, Babylon corrects him, "Don't you mean 'when you were born'?"

This time, it is Darius's turn to look somewhat puzzled before answering, "No. I'm not sure why, but somehow I was here. I mean…I existed before the war. I think a very long time before but not physically here. I know that sounds strange, and it's part of why some of my people fear me. I understand because there's a lot about myself I have yet to understand."

Patting him on the hand, Babylon says, "Don't you worry about dat! You're a boy who speaks like a grown man and knows things that can't be explained. I see and feel some ting within you that is powerful. When some ting is strange or foreign to some people, they often fear it first rather than get to know or learn more about it. We must challenge the beings in this universe to seek knowledge about the coming mysteries. The strategy in de past has been to seek and destroy what we don't undastand. You, my young prince, will be the agent of change to bring 'bout this enlightenment. It's a big responsibility, but I have faith you will do it well." With that, Babylon leaves to visit the hangars in the mobile shipyards.

Darius feels a little better but is still unsure about how to feel about any of their discussion. Even he has no answers as to how he knows some of the things he knows or why he feels as if he has lived through some of the ancient moments in history. Despite it being impossible, it just feels so…real.

• • •

Nefer is surprised when the queen shows up with Zola. Both are dressed in new flight suits. They hand her a third to put on before going on their mission. She is also surprised to learn that the Nyeusi Sime or black dagger stealth craft that was shown to her earlier is not a one-off. There are a few of these in production but not all of them are armed with dark matter ordinance. After explaining all of this to Nefer, Tunisia is the one with an appalled look on her face. The queen is quick to remind her, "We have suffered for far too long at the hands of these people, Nefer. Once again, during this supposed peace time, they came to where they thought our doorstep was, looking to break us. You saw the footage. Did it look like they came to talk?"

Nefer, despite her hesitation, cannot dispute how it looked from the satellite feeds. "No, my queen, they looked to be all war craft that jumped in, but are we only taking three ships?"

Looking at the hangar deck where their three stealth craft are sitting, prepped, Tunisia smiles and says "Not…exactly. We have a plan. I know how you and many others feel about this war, so I will do my best to focus on military targets because we agreed that was a necessary thing to do. This presents us with a great opportunity to get the message across to the GMC that we will not be reined back into their fold as laborers, and we are not to be trifled with. As for how many ships, get in, and after we complete our flight checks, a full schematic of the mission will be given to us through the HUD. Sound good?"

As she finishes putting the flight suit on, Nefer holds her helmet off to the side as she nods her approval, and all three Kison Askari women head to their ships. Over her shoulder, the queen shouts, "Good! I didn't want to have to find another pilot on such short notice. I have seen the vids of you in the War Dragon. You're one of our best pilots. That should make this go smoothly, or as smoothly as a battle can go."

Nefer is glad for the praise but still worries they might be taking things too far or being a bit brash by taking so few ships compared to the group they would be meeting. Dark matter is potent, but superior numbers may make up for lack of power in this case.

Upon finishing the flight checks, Zola and Nefer are brought up to speed as to the details of the mission plan. There are a myriad of failed designs for fighter ships the Kison Askari have come up with. Some are more complete than others, and the idea is to have a number of these ships, slave their nav computers to those of the stealth ships, making three staggered jumps into the Mars system, so it looks as if three groups of enemies have come to meet the GMC head on. While they focus their fire on these ghost units, the three stealth craft should be able to flank them from behind or sides, firing off the dark matter ordinance, and jump out before anyone notices. If all goes according to plan, they will have risked only the materiel in their failed early space aeronautical projects and very little when it comes to the risk of lives.

One of the lives in question though could be the most important life to the Stone people. Nefer opens a communication link, and it is as if the queen knows what she is about to say as she cuts her off abruptly. They order them to ease out of the bay and take position in the heart of three groups of cobbled together ships made to look like military formations. From a distance, they look the part of a menacing group of ships, and it will not be until they are right upon them to see what this really is…the first flying junkyard. A few of the ships have working weapons systems, but the term *working* is a nominal definition as the best systems have been given to the ships in the active fleet.

Some of the scrap have even been added on to the hulls to look like weapon placements. The ships are basically huge drones that will fire what weapons they do have in order to draw fire and attention away from the three stealth craft whose initial burst from their thrusters will be easily noticeable were they to jump in alone. After gaining enough momentum, they should be able to use the smaller attitude thrusters with a much lower heat signature to get in, hit them, and get out. This is the basic gist of the plan, and since this is their first, a lot could go wrong. Once Tunisia gets confirmation from her wing women that they are ready, they sync all nav computers and make the simultaneous jump to Mars.

• • •

Since there are no immediate signs of the Stone people's newly minted fleet, Major Vashti orders some of the smaller fighters in his flotilla to recon the planet for hints of what, if anything, may have been left behind. He does not believe they are doing all of their manufacturing in vacuum, so there has to be some planet-side operations somewhere, and he is determined to find out. He believes it is also safe to assume that it has to be within this galaxy since, as surprising as recent developments might be, they are still relatively new to space travel on their own. It is also true that the GMC have very little knowledge on how broad their new capabilities are. The Stone people have recently displayed an advantage in new weaponry. Could their new technology be advanced enough to leave the Milky Way altogether, carving out an even larger new frontier?

The major certainly hopes not because that would make for an unsavory sit-rep to give to the commandant when he returns. The brass doesn't like to receive negative intel any more than the bearers of bad news like giving it. The GMC need to get a handle on this situation which is quickly spinning out of control. Vashti is disturbed from his introspective dialogue while sitting on the bridge of the Man of War frigate currently under his command as alarms begin blaring. The hull is rocked with big booms as an enormous group of ships jump in system, simultaneously surrounding and vastly out numbering his group. Immediately going to the captain's chair and strapping himself in, Major Vashti opens the ship-wide comms, orders, "Battle stations!" and nod at the young lieutenant at the comm station who then relays an order to the rest of the flotilla.

Outside, there is chaos as the fighter ships and Praetorian class cruisers all attempt to form up when incoming fire from the ragtag group of newcomers suddenly begins peppering them. The GMC returns fire with brief but explosive results as the vacuum quickly extinguishes flames immediately without the oxygen needed to keep the flames going. A ragged cheer erupts from the shipmates on the bridge, but the jovial tone is short-lived. The flotilla continues to pound the floating junkyard, completely missing three torpedoes that appear seemingly out of nowhere and seem to come at them from different locations. One of the tactical officers shouts "incoming," and there is a brief silent moment before they impact various ships. Luckily, the Man of War is shielded by the ships around it. Two Praetorians and three groups of fighters aren't so lucky.

Almost simultaneously, as the husks of ships surrounding the flotilla smolder floating listless in space around them, the GMC ships hit by the strange ordinance goes up in a ball of deep purple mist, flashing briefly before settling into a haze. Debris from the ships start to float toward the rest of the GMC flotilla, and when seemingly small fragments hit some of the outer ships, it is as if they are organic entities being touched by some instant leprosy. Some of the ships lose internal air pressure as the hull integrity rapidly deteriorates. Watching all of this unfold, Major Vashti finally gets a hold of himself and quickly bellows into the comm systems as much of his crew is frozen in horror at the scene before them. "All fire on the remaining enemy ships! Set course to return to headquarters!"

The helmsmen, a young red-haired second lieutenant, nervously voices her objection, "But, sir, some of our ships won't be able to make the jump with the hull damage suffered!"

Angrily, the major turns to her and says, "I am fully aware of that, Lt. McCullum! Would you rather we sit here and duke it out with possibly more dark matter ordinance headed our way? No? I thought not either. Carry on!"

With that, the remaining GMC ships in the area release a final salvo before heading back into hyperspace to limp to Saturn, losing a considerable amount of ships in the jump. General Krulak will not be pleased.

Chapter Eight

ATHENA, ALONG WITH HER GUERILLA group, have been in hiding now for months. Rumor has reached them from Toshi of the Jade Assassins that there has been another attack on Mars, but no numbers or other details have come back on casualties. The attack at Pluto and reprisals here on Earth have forced her to consider leaving the planet, so things can cool down. The GMC is learning and has switched their procedures for moving important materials, so attacking the supply chains are not as effective as before. More reports are coming in from other groups headed by Limbia Johari, detailing sting operations that are capturing some of her people. The detention camps are beginning to refill. Something has to be done. Toshi has said he will speak to Hironike, Queen Tunisia, and possibly Babylon, so they can put together a plan for extraction.

There is also news that something has the GMC headquarters buzzing, but since her network of spies are also not in their usual positions due to current human/mutant relations, the details will be hard to come by. Leaving unnoticed will also be difficult, especially since one of the local security forces' leaders has been on them like glue since their meeting a few short months ago. It seems everyone has been developing new toys recently. Things are definitely getting interesting. Angelo simply stands there, watching his queen in deep thought. There is a light tinkling sound as her crystalline tresses blow in the late-night breeze. In another time, he might have told her how beautiful she is.

His own raven-colored crystalline hair has been cut short to avoid having to tie it back when out on missions as Athena has to do. They are getting tired of constantly being on the move, avoiding patrols of militia or security forces. Angelo knows his queen worries about the state of affairs with, not only the mutated races, but human kind as a whole, yet he can only bring himself to worry about her. Times are tumultuous indeed, and there is no time for romance, so he will have to be satisfied with watching her from afar and doing what is necessary to ensure their survival throughout this war. Perhaps, when the conflict is over, he can revisit his longing. Almost as if on que, Athena seems to feel Angelo gazing at her.

Her easy smile embarrasses him as if she, somehow, knows his thoughts. He quickly tries to compose himself before approaching. "What shall we do, my queen?" he asks.

Adjusting her railgun that seems much too big for someone so slight of frame to carry, she mulls it over before answering. "We need to find a discreet way off-planet soon. The net is tightening."

This is a difficult train of thought for her to be contemplating, he knows. A lot of their people have gone to ground and a fair amount are being rounded up and put in detention camps. Not only will it be an issue getting off-world unseen, but there is also a chance their refugee contingent will hear of their departure and think they've been abandoned.

Seeing those very thoughts reflected in her eyes, Angelo is quick to reassure her. "If it can be done, we will make it so, but know that we will return and fix the mess that's been made here, my queen."

She nods in agreement. "We also have yet to find this mysterious Pharaoh who is supposedly the key to peace, if we can prove his existence. I am afraid that, even if we find this being, we may have jaded ourselves against each other too much for it to make a difference."

He tends to agree with that sentiment, but for her and the hope of his people and the planet at large, Angelo will hold out hope that things can be righted once the fighting has stopped.

They are currently hiding out in the Andes Mountains and are avoiding the electromagnetic track areas near mining facilities for the time being. There is no doubt, after a few skirmishes in places like them, the GMC has researched the schematics for all the old mining facilities and passed that knowledge down the chain to all agencies working with them. This has likely led to the recent round of detainments. They retreated to a secret cave system which had been excavated decades earlier. Someone knew they would need to hide.

Angelo goes to a group of their fellow rebels and sets up watch for the night. Athena goes to a cave deep in the network of caves where she has made her temporary quarters and lays down for the night.

• • •

Lt. Commander Jameson sits in his office in the classified wing of the medical facility at Saturn going over schematics for his next run of experimental enhancements when a young officer comes in, looking frustrated. After a few moments of not being noticed, he clears his throat before saying, "Excuse me, sir, there has been a development I think needs your attention."

The lieutenant commander's green eyes flash in annoyance at being disturbed. "And what is so pertinent that you had to come directly to me? Ensign…Towson, is it?"

Nervous from catching the ire of Lt. Commander Jameson, Ensign Towson responds,

"Well, sir, part of the training area here has been taken over by one of your…um…special operatives. The biggest one of the mechanically enhanced unit, I believe, he's PFC Long. He has some kind of beast. They've erected some kind of structure to house it. When I asked what it was, he told me it was a Tibetan mastiff. Sir, a Tibetan mastiff looks like a chipmunk compared to this thing! You could ride it. No lie! Don't even get me started on the excrement this animal drops, but it's Jurassic, and the smell is ungodly! More so than normal crap…sir."

Seeing his discomfiture about the situation amuses Lt. Commander Jameson, but he is now intrigued. Shaking his head, he replies, "They are led by Sgt. Garrison. Titanium alloy legs scrape the decks constantly. You can't miss him. I suggest you speak with him."

"Sir, I have tried. At first, he said he would talk to him and find another place to house that thing. Most of the recon Marines are scared to even go back there now. Every time I bring it to the sergeant's attention, he's on his way to calibrate his legs or some other excuse. They basically told me it was gone so that I would go inspect the area only to find it, hiding in its lair, sleeping. When it awoke growling, I could feel it in my chest, sir! Something needs to be done, and I don't know who else to turn to, sir!" Towson states and waits for a response.

Lt. Commander Jameson waves a hand dismissively after saying, "I'll look into it, and this better not be some frivolous prank, Towson!"

Seemingly relieved, Ensign Towson salutes smartly before taking his leave, shouting over his shoulder as he leaves the office, "Thank you, sir! It's no prank, I swear."

There really is no time for this nonsense, especially given that apparently the GMC recently had its collective butts handed to them yet again during a skirmish near Mars. Reports stated that dark matter has been used once again by the Stone people. It is frustrating to see that they have, somehow, managed to utilize such a volatile ordinance while the GMC cannot. General Krulak and the rest of the top brass are already breathing down the lieutenant commander's neck for more breakthroughs with their enhancement programs like the Ascension Protocol, as well as R&D for anything that will even the odds against dark matter weaponry. That is what rankled everyone so much. How did these savages get a hold of this tech so quickly? If they had stolen it, there would be records of its existence in the first place.

Lt. Commander Jameson puts on his lab coat over his dress white naval uniform and decides to personally go see what the young officer had his panties in a bunch over. Heading down to the training facility, he sees nothing out of place at first. While passing the augmented confidence and obstacle courses set up for the mechanics and other Marines trying to get used to their new bodies or appendages, Lt. Commander Jameson starts to get aggravated, but as he gets closer to the Mechanics' special barracks area, a horrible stench accosts his nostrils. A few hundred yards across one of the fields, there is a makeshift Quonset hut. Grabbing a handkerchief and holding it over his nose, he makes his way across the field. The closer he gets, the more intense the smell becomes.

Fifteen yards away from the structure, Lt. Commander Jameson feels his knees buckle as nausea threatens to eject his lunch, but he holds on. Seemingly out of nowhere, PFC Long appears. "You lost, sir?" he asks. Turning to see the mechanical behemoth that is code named "Berserker," Long has become accustomed to his augmentation and now moves with ease as if his cybernetics are natural. The silence of his approach is also surprising.

Swallowing and gathering himself to speak, Lt. Commander Jameson gives his muffled reply, "No, I have heard a rumor that you are keeping some unauthorized beast here. The stench described was vastly…understated. What on Earth do you have here?"

Feigning confusion, PFC Long reaches up to rub his bald head with a titanium hand and silicone fingers and blurts, "Don't you mean Saturn, sir?"

Anger flashes in the officer's green eyes as he draws in a breath to rip Long a new one. "Wha…"

Before he can finish the tirade he's barely begun, the hatch opens. What steps out ducking through the hatch is what has to be one of the most magnificent creatures the lieutenant commander has ever laid eyes on. The beast looks like a dire wolf for lack of a more accurate description with a full dark black coat strewn with white circular striations. Its eyes glow a deep crimson, purple tongue lolling out of its open mouth over what looks like deadly sharp sets of teeth. It stands three heads taller than PFC Long, so it would seem Ensign Towson's estimate is correct. You can, in fact, ride it…if it lets you.

Heavily muscled and surprisingly agile for its size, the beast saunters over to where PFC Long stands and lays down calmly beside him after a few hand gestures from its master. Laying there, it is still just shy of being shoulder to shoulder with the mechanized Marine. Lt. Commander Jameson is in awe. From the paw shape and facial structure, as well as its demeanor, he can tell this is a puppy and not fully grown. This thing will get...bigger. Coming out of his trance, Lt. Commander Jameson goes to approach the animal but looks to Long silently, asking if it is safe. PFC Long smiles and nods, saying, "As long as he knows we're good, sir, then you're good."

Hesitantly, the lieutenant commander reaches out to touch the thick fur, and it is surprisingly soft and warm. The animal lays its head on his paws and absently endures the petting. Upon closer inspection, he can see that there are actually six eyes, the two glowing, more prominent ones and two additional black eyes on each side of its head that blend in with the fur. The animal snarls a bit when he attempts to clear some of the fur to get a better look. At the sudden sound and movement, the lieutenant commander flinches and quickly draws his hand back.

"Hey! Easy, boy," PFC Long reassures the beast, leaning over to pat the beast heavily on its side. At that, the animal calms a bit and lays its head back down. Looking over at the stricken expression on the lieutenant commander's face, Long states, "It's okay, sir."

Figuring this is enough for now, Lt. Commander Jameson says, "That's alright. Where did you find this? I saw Sgt. Garrison's report which stated you were marooned for a short period of time due to sensor and instrument malfunctions. Nothing about...this is mentioned."

Stumbling over his words, PFC Long replies, "Um...you would have to ask Sgt. Garrison or LCPL Jennings, sir. Like you said, our sensors and instruments went kind of haywire. Even the logs are still messed up from that trip. When we lifted off, it was discovered that this here animal had stowed away aboard the Adder, sir."

Raising an eyebrow, Lt. Commander Jameson looks from Long to the beast and back again, asking, "And no one saw fit to mention discovery of a new alien species of animal before bringing it back to a military installation, possibly contaminating us all?"

Stammering once again, Long replies, "N-no, sir! He's not contagious or anything. Nobody here has got sick and none of our squad either. We were fully checked out upon returning, sir. Honest!"

Shaking his head in disbelief, Lt. Commander Jameson reprimands Long, "You know the contamination threat, or lack thereof, of this beast? How? True, you boys all checked in in tip-top condition, minus a few necessary recalibrations to your augments, but you'll need to be re-examined to see if there are any effects to your organic physiology due to exposure to this…I'm not even sure what this is. Do you even know? Of course, you don't. We need to get some elucidating units down here to get rid of that smell, and I will need to examine this…creature. It stays here and goes nowhere without my say so. Is that understood?"

The beast's ears perk up as PFC Long salutes smartly, replying, "Yes, sir! It's a hellhound, sir. A real life *tuefel hunden*."

Turning back as he walks away, the Lt. Commander looks at the animal and says, "So it is, Long, so it is," before retreating to his office. He believes he will need a long, hot shower to rid himself of that ghastly odor.

• • •

After the remnant of the GMC flotilla jumps out of the system, Tunisia waits to open up a comm line to her wingwomen. "Nefer, Zola, come in. I think they've all gone now. Remain ghosted, in case someone is lingering."

There is a brief pause before either chimed in to answer her. Nefer double-clicks her mic to signal that she understands. Then Zola speaks,

"Here, my queen. I didn't know we would be using the newest weapon. It was...more than efficient."

Looking the ghostly scene over, Tunisia agrees. She opens the line again and says, "As it should be. Don't feel guilty. This was a message that needed to be given. They would show us no mercy were these weapons in their hands. Think of our sons, brothers, and husbands who shall never return. Don't refer to me as 'queen' out here. Call me...Q1. I'll think of something better later, but for now, you never know if they have a way of listening. If you have any missiles left, I suggest taking out the floating mess we brought with us. It is our junk, but no doubt some of these components can be repurposed in the right hands. I am not in the business of giving any resources to our enemies."

Nefer remains silent and, along with the queen and Zola, pulls a safe distance away before firing the remaining dark matter missiles into the field of junkers floating just outside of Mars's gravity well. As they hit the group of ships once again, there is a brief deep purple flash, but this one is much larger than the one that broadsides the flotilla, and as before, it quickly dissipates into a strange mist. Nefer is conflicted, but she trusts her queen. They watch the mist sort of evaporate as light reflects and refracts through it before it disappears. The beauty of the scene seems incongruous with how dangerous the substance is. When it is all finished and there is no evidence of the junk armada to be seen, they plot their course back to Jupiter and jump.

• • •

Back at HQ, GMC General Krulak sits in his office, fuming over the report he received from Major Vashti, along with the video feeds from satellites deployed near Mars. The flotilla had made it back with less than half of the contingent it brought. This was a financial nightmare given how limited resources were now due to the Stone people absconding with a majority of building materiel for new armament and technologies. Even more disturbing, it would appear that not only had they figured out how to weaponize a substance that the GMC's own molecular engineers had had trouble controlling, but now had a stealth ship that enabled them to deploy it nearly undetected. This could be an extremely lethal combination, Krulak thinks. He knows something has to be done.

Sweating bullets, Major Vashti stands in a modified parade rest in front of the general's desk as he goes through the report and accompanying data with the video. It is visibly apparent that the commandant is not happy. The cease fire announcement hasn't given them enough time to come up with an equalizer, and this latest desperate attempt to grab some extra resources has not only failed but lost highly valuable ships in the process. They have to, once again, stall for time, but another announcement will not work. Just then, another idea comes to General Krulak. He looks up at Major Vashti and orders him to relax. "At ease, major. I have an idea that some may think is a bit underhanded, but at times like these, 'by any means necessary' applies. We are at an impasse and are facing a situation that has never occurred in our long history. We currently don't have the muscle to go toe-to-toe with our enemy. I heard you had some friends in the cinema business. Is that true, major?"

Confused as to where this line of questioning is going, Major Vashti straightens up and answers, "Yes, sir. I still have some friends in the industry."

The general waves for him to come around the desk and watches what he is viewing on his monitor. Pointing at the screen, he asks, "Can they modify this footage?"

Starting to get an idea of where the general might be going, Major Vashti asks a question in return, "How so?"

Circling their battle group, the general says, "I need for our vessels to look like civilian ships. We can get images from one of the startup tour companies that have been trying to open a market and route to the other planets. I also need it to look like the ordinance came from this group of ragtag ships here. Can they do that?"

Thinking it over for a few seconds, Major Vashti responds, "Yes, sir. I believe they can."

Smiling slightly, the general dismisses him, but not before saying, "Good. Make it happen and get me the copy as soon as you can. We have other weapons at our disposal that may be just as effective in bringing these people back into the fold. Public opinion can be effective. Once we have the doctored footage, we can discreetly leak it to the press. Make sure your contacts know as little as possible and remind them there will be heavy consequences if they disclose what you do tell them. Dismissed."

Chapter Nine

BACK ON SATURN, TRAINING HAS taken a turn for the worst. Corporals Aragon, Sims, and Jordan watch as yet another hover-gurney floats by, carrying the latest casualty. To say the training bots have been turned up a notch would be a vast understatement. Something has the brass in an uproar and the proverbial fecal matter is definitely rolling downhill. Petty Officer House is following closely behind the gurney. Aragon pulls him to the side and says, "Hey, we need to do something about this or you and the rest of your corpsmen will be very busy!" Watching the lifeless body float up the corridor, House nods his head in agreement. "At this rate, if the hostilities do officially resume, we may not have enough people to fight."

Sims and Jordan all agree with that sentiment. Marines are dropping like flies, and there are rumors that the Ascension Program will be including more extreme mechanical enhancements but now for people that aren't injured in the first place. This is troubling to them all as some may have been forced to give up portions of their humanity unnecessarily. House goes to catch up to the gurney heading to the infirmary, shouting over his shoulder, "I'll do some digging to see what's going on!"

With that, the others turn to head back to the barracks to get showered before chow. There have been, at least, fifteen dead or injured in Aragon's platoon alone, and the training regimen is being implemented service wide. Things are getting messy, and it looks like the GMC is beginning to do some dirty work for the Stone people.

• • •

Ancient Illumination II: (Kuongoza Mwanga: The Leading Light)

Off the coast of Florida back on Earth, the Ryoko-Gekijo floats over serene waters. There is no show in the area for the Ongakijin to perform as business has declined to a near dead stop since the war has reignited. Tensions are high, and dignitaries are less inclined to purchase high-priced tickets to any venue where they feel they might be at risk. Luckily or perhaps more accurately, Hironike has been more savvy than lucky, to save for him and his people giving them the ability to easily weather dry spells like this. Wars have come and gone and, in most instances where the combatants have been regional, featuring individual countries in the past, the Ongakujin can simply work areas around or away from the conflict.

This time, however, the entire planet and now the outlying planets, as well, are swept up in this recent war, pitting human beings against just about all mutated races. No matter how slightly the difference might be, you are now under suspicion. A detail not lost on the leader of the Jade Assassins as he looks down at his own uncommonly hued skin. The color of one's skin has caused turmoil between Earth's inhabitants for centuries, and when that dies down, it seems evolution has decided to kick it up a notch to foment more conflict between races. Hironike is awaiting Toshi's return, so he can report on some sort of skirmish that recently happened outside of Mars's gravity well. It did not end well for the GMC.

Ironically, there is a tone indicating the theater is being approached by vehicles, a lot of them. Most of the vehicles look to be NightEagle GMC troop transports which is strange. In wartimes past, there have been occasions to host events to support troops in an attempt to boost morale, but this is not like any of those times. The Ongakujin are clearly on the list of suspects somebody decided should be rounded up and taken to one of the new determent camps. Well, if they think Hironike and his people will come along willingly, they are mistaken. Takimura and Megumi come strolling in dressed in light body armor. They seem to share his sentiment.

Before any of them can speak, another chime sounds, signaling a request for open communication. Hironike nods to Megumi who walks over to the comm panel in his office and opens the channel. Calmly walking over to the panel, he says, "This is Hironike of the Ongakujin. To whom do I have the unexpected pleasure of speaking to?"

There was a brief moment of silence before the reply came. "This is Marshal Benitez. I head a major task force comprised of both GMC and global security forces. We have a warrant to detain you and a…Toshi. Come with us peacefully so as not to destroy anything valuable in the process."

For a long moment, there is simply silence as Hironike and his group think the implications over.

Sounding impatient, Marshal Benitez speaks again, "Requesting visual communication, so we can, at least, verify who we are speaking with."

Hironike nods at Takimura, who presses a button to activate the display. Then he and Megumi scramble to get out of the camera shot yet still listen. The display on the monitor lights up, and there appears a tall Latino man with dark hair, brown eyes, and light brown skin dressed in camouflage armored gear. Behind him are a mix of Marines and security forces armed to the teeth.

On Marshal Benitez's monitor, Hironike can be seen at a broad desk in his opulent office, his verdant green skin glistening in the light. He is wearing a tailored tuxedo and exuding all the confidence in the world. Staring into the monitor while absently stroking his bald head, Hironike asks, "Now on what authority or for what crimes, do you execute this warrant of yours, marshal? Now that you know you are indeed speaking with me."

The marshal is visibly trying to compose himself before answering. "We have it from a viable source that there was communication between someone in that mobile theater of yours and a few different guerilla groups that have been stirring up trouble recently. We would like to know why that is."

Looking visibly perplexed, Hironike asks, "If you have these supposed communications, then you should already know their contents. How do you know they came from my theater?"

Relaxing and looking quite smug now, the marshal replies, "We were tracking a few groups of guerilla fighters when we first got some of the transmissions. We also tracked where they were coming from and where they were transmitted to. The places where they were received correlates with various locations for the theater. As for the contents of the messages, they were encrypted. The encryption is so complicated that it's way above anything law enforcement or military has come up with, but ironically it's eerily similar to an encryption program used to protect your music as well as other digital property your company owns."

Nodding his head affirmatively, Hironike says, "I see. Just a moment." He then mutes himself and speaks to Megumi. "Tell Toshi to come in hot, or better yet, we will meet him. Tell him to standby." She bows quickly and heads out of the office. Turning back to the monitor, Hironike unmutes the comm and says, "My apologies, marshal, but we will not be accompanying you, and you will not be intimidating us by bringing Marines as if you are to storm this theater. We will not assault you, but we will defend ourselves."

Staring incredulously, Marshal Benitez responds, "I order you to stand down and comply! We are in military vessels with armed military personnel! What could you possibly achieve by resisting?"

At that Hironike, simply cuts the communications and whispers mostly to himself, "She's more than she appears to be."

Together, he and Takimura rush down to the bridge area to where Megumi was already strapped in. What most people did not know is that the Ryoko-Gekijo is more than just a flying theater which is remarkable in itself but is also space-worthy. The armaments are minimal, but true to what Hironike has announced, it has defenses and one major feature the rest of either military vessels have yet to develop. The theater seems to begin reshaping and folding in on itself, transforming.

In the lead NightEagle, Marshal Benitez gives the signal, and Marines and security forces officers begin pouring out of the transports in armored jetpack suits.

Nonplussed, Hironike hops into the commander's chair but does not strap in, watching the action unfold on the main viewport. The rest of the theater troupe has been apprised of what was going on previously and were all either at stations on the bridge or in their living quarters hunkered down for whatever may come. Seeing the Marines and security forces speeding toward them, Hironike waits until they are almost to the theater when he nods to Takimura, whose hands fly over the console he is sitting at. As the theater has finished transforming into a large ovoid-shaped ship with a huge strip of main thrusters at its rear, a glowing overshield begins to envelop the ship just before any of the armed assailants can gain access to it.

There are some crackling sounds as some of the Marines or security forces officers cannot pull up in time to avoid hitting the luminescent shield before bouncing harmlessly into the water. All Marshal Benitez can do is stare in disbelief. As the engines flare for liftoff, he snaps out of it and gives the order to fire. The rounds explode uselessly on the shield, and the theater speeds away. As the NightEagles are rated for atmospheric travel and not space-worthy, they cannot give chase. Bad news is beginning to pile up for the GMC.

● ● ●

Upon landing back in the secured bay within the Askari's mobile ship-yard that orbited Jupiter along with their Dreadnaught, Tunisia gets out of her Nyeusi Sime small fighter and begins to take off her flight suit. Zola and Nefer join her, doing the same. All three are kind of shaken but relieved none of them are casualties. They hope the GMC will finally get the message. Part of the queen understands that they will not get the hint, and that part also wishes they will not. Her heart is still hurting from the loss of her husband and king. Inherently she knows revenge is wrong, but on another level, she feels there needs to be balance in order to come to peace.

Their people have suffered for far too long, and just because they are strong enough to endure some of the things they have does not mean that they should have to. These people will learn or burn until they do. When the proverbial shoe is on the other foot, the GMC has never had any issues putting its foot on the Kison Tontu's collective throat. It is time to return the favor. If nothing is done, things will go back to the status quo with some slightly better accommodations, but the atrocities committed previously will be glossed over. History will try to write the events in a vastly more positive light. This has been repeated ad nauseum, and it is high time to stop that cycle.

The queen is dressed in her ceremonial regal black bejeweled dress while Zola is dressed in her *buba* and *gele*. Nefer has chosen to stay in her flight suit. As they take the shuttle back to the Dreadnaught, Babylon seems to be awaiting their arrival. He does not look at all happy. There seems to be a fire in his amber eyes within the wrinkly blue visage framed by snow white locks. Two of the ladies take their cue to leave and bid their queen "good night," all exchanging hugs at the relief of survival. When they are alone, Babylon turns to the queen and says, "Was dat truly necessary? I am guessing dis was de message you were referring to earlier."

Angrily, Tunisia turns to Babylon and replies, "Yes, and definitively yes! What would you have me do? Wait for them to strike? Because you know as well as I do that all they are doing is biding their time, looking for an opportunity to attack. When our ships jumped in, they did not open communications, they simply opened fire. From the looks of the ships, they had not come to talk anyway! Now they have something else to think on before nosing around for us!"

Nodding slowly, Babylon leans on his trident. "What you say is true, but when will it end? I did not give you access to that knowledge for you to turn it around and oppress your former oppressors! Making decisions with hate or anger in your heart will not only make others suffer, but eventually some of your own people will share in that pain, which is why Jared Omega waited…"

Before he can finish the thought, Tunisia abruptly cuts him off. "Don't you say it, Babylon! He waited for our shackles to be broken, so we could all leave at once! That didn't happen because there are still some of our people left on Earth, in addition to anyone they deem a threat or sympathizing with our cause trapped there. Anyone who doesn't look to be a non-mutated human is brought in for questioning. Do you think they're being treated well in these determent camps? Don't preach to me, Babylon, because another interesting thing is the fact that you waited until now to come to our aid when your people have been around for centuries, if not millennia, watching these things happen repeatedly yet now was the time you intervened. Why?"

When no answer immediately comes, Tunisia's eyes narrow. "Exactly, come to me when you can talk about you abandoning the rest of us. Then and only then will I feel a need to justify how I wage this war. We are still at war, and once your presence is known, do you think the GMC will leave your yellow-eyed, blue-skinned people alone to do as you wish? Or will they attempt to pillage any knowledge they can gain from you to serve their purposes? They may not succeed, but the attempt will tell you much of their nature. Diplomacy will come later. Right now, we will speak the language they truly understand until they're willing to come to the table and speak peace. Good day."

With that, the queen saunters off to her quarters, leaving the old Atlantean stunned in her wake. There are many reasons Babylon and his people stayed in the shadows or off-planet, not involving themselves in the crazy dealings happening on Earth. There had been the vicious cycles of violence that, for a long time, seemed to permeate the blue world. There had been quite a few times they had nearly decimated everything and everyone on the planet. It was after a few of these times the Atlanteans as a group decided to divest themselves of the societies there. They decided to seek more knowledge, preferring to watch from afar to see if Earth would recover. A selfish thing to be sure, but it was what they had decided as a people, despite being from Earth initially.

The growth and resiliency of the those that stayed was what kept the people of Atlantis from staying hidden. Eventually they came back, from time to time disguised as regular humans, and the people, for the most part, were rarely aware of the ruse. When in certain cases they were found out, it was often not believed. Guilt was the other reason for them not completely abstaining from any involvement with their earthbound brethren. A common theme of xenophobia was what kept the people of Atlantis from operating out in the open. Seeing how people with different colored skin were treated was a horrible thing to watch. It only got worse as more extreme genetic mutations began to appear among their populaces.

Babylon is sure the pharaoh is the cause for the mutations and strife. Finding proof is a difficult task, but he will not give up. This being will be found eventually. Now what they will be able to do without the aid of the other ancient ones is another matter. They will have to cross that bridge when they get there.

• • •

Major Vashti heads over to his friend's office at a holovid studio in southern California. After telling the receptionist who he is and who he is there to see, he patiently waits until his friend appears. "Major Vashti, what a pleasant surprise!" Standing in his dress blues, Major Vashti walks over to the man who comes out to greet him. A well-dressed Indian man with glasses and a short haircut clasps hands with the major who replies, "Reyansh! It has been too long, my friend, and please call me Arjun." They go back to Reyansh's office where he has a video playing. Major

Vashti immediately recognizes the vid playing as the file he had sent over to his friend.

Reyansh motions for him to take a seat, and he does so, remarking, "Did you get the instructions along with the vid footage?"

Waving a hand dismissively, Reyansh says, "Of course. Not to worry. I have the altered footage, but I am really curious about this project! I didn't know you were going into the cinema industry. I must say the effects here are incredible! The nondisclosure form was a bit...extreme. We could have been working together a long time ago had I known."

Shaking his head, Major Vashti says, "No, no, you have it all wrong. This is just a simulation and the reason we need the footage scrubbed is to hide the prototypes, and we wanted a professional hand in that. That's all."

Major Vashti can tell his friend is disappointed and feels bad for misleading him. Their families have known each other for generations. After a couple commands are entered on the computer on Reyansh's desk, the footage begins to play again. This time the military vessels look like what could be civilian transports if they exist out in space for some new tourism company. The blasts coming from the military ships have been scrubbed as well, so all the fire looks to come from one side. As the footage plays out, Major Vashti is satisfied and hopes the commandant will be equally so. Military secrecy makes sense, but the threat of possibly being imprisoned or even killed strikes Reyansh as especially strange for a vid of a simulation, but he keeps his thoughts to himself. After all, the GMC's money is good.

Chapter Ten

BACK IN CHICAGO, SPARKS SITS in the office area Max has set up. He is watching a local show when it is interrupted for a special report. The bulk of Argos comes up to stand behind her, breathing strangely. She is only briefly distracted by his entrance as that is a sign of more than likely mostly organic material under all the armor and garb that obscured his form. Max comes in finally when the network begins playing some video of an apparent ambush of a civilian tourist group near Mars by the Stone people. As they watch it, something does not sit right with Max about the imaging. Pointing to the screen, he asks, "Can you run that back a few seconds?"

Perplexed, Sparks does so, inputting commands telling the computer to rewind the footage.

Waving a hand over a panel in the middle of the office enlarges the display and makes it a 3-D mapping of the footage they are watching. The display comes to life around them in a beautiful translucent duplication of the attack playing out on the monitor. Max walks over to where the tourist ships are taking fire. Argos turns his head to the side as the looming form of Mars is superimposed over him. Sparks is still confused, saying, "What is it you see aside from a senseless slaughter?"

Shaking his head, Max states, "That's what they want us to see, but there's more to this that's been hidden or scrubbed. Computer, analyze this footage for alterations."

A sultry female voice answers, "Of course, Max."

Rolling her eyes in response to the voice which she hadn't heard during her time there, Sparks inquires, "So what's your theory, Max?"

Ignoring the teasing tone in her voice, Max turns to her. "The most unbelievable thing about this is blatantly obvious. You know why transportation changed from being something everyone did on a personal level to public transportation basically phasing out the industry with the exception of corporate big wigs or military and government personnel?" He waits for her to answer. When he gets a shrug in response, he goes on. "Money, plain and simple, is the answer. The government made it too expensive to have personal transports in order to control the method by which people traveled, citing our responsibility to the environment. Ironically, we still manage to continue destroying it. My point is, there's no tourist group that could afford to send a group up. It's just not cost effective as the patrons can't afford the necessary price which is why the mining business and military funded by government are the only ones out there. Makes it more likely these are military vessels in this footage that went to meet those ships at Mars. It's well done, but there are telltale signs this has been tampered with. As with our search for the cosmetic clue to your senator's murder, if we follow the money, I'm betting not too many groups could afford to send a tour with that many ships in it aside from the government or the military."

Thinking it over, his theory makes sense to Sparks, but she is still of the belief that the Stone people are capable of wholesale slaughter evidenced by the recent uprising and continuing conflict. Rumors are spreading of other violent acts there on Earth breaking out and even guerilla tactics being used to ambush law enforcement. People that sympathized with the mutant races are continuing to protest, and radical groups are sprouting up all over the globe. Things are spiraling out of control in a hurry. Another interesting bit of information that they had been passed is a story saying the flying theater Ongakujin is famous for has been seen fleeing from a large joint task force comprised of local law enforcement and military.

Have they found some evidence incriminating Hironike and his crew that Max hasn't been able to sniff out? If so, Sparks is hoping she will be able to catch up to them and exact her revenge before they are apprehended. Justice in the court system seems to be severely lacking lately.

• • •

Typhoon is getting more accustomed to void walking with Malice. He is learning to control his being better and the fits of nausea are fewer now. This is a good thing since they have to make several trips this time to find Babylon who has not stayed aboard the newly constructed Dreadnaught that served as the Stone warriors' flagship currently orbiting Jupiter. They have to remain in the ether to hide their presence, and Malice has to feel for the light signature of the ancient Atlantean. This is how he grumpily explains it when the mutated gorilla asks for an explanation of why they are traveling as frequently as they are.

The master has ordered them to go about their mission in secrecy in hopes of gleaning information on whether or not Babylon has been able to enlist the help of other beings like Pharaoh. If so, it is obvious they may pose a threat to his position on Earth. Like all beings, Malice supposes that there would be variances in strength. These light beings will be no different. These fellow mutants are proving to be even more resourceful than Malice would have given them credit for. There was apparently a brief skirmish, and now Jupiter is a hive of activity.

Listening to snatches of conversation while hiding in the ether, yet simultaneously being aboard the huge capital ship, Malice and Typhoon are able to hear of the brief battle and plan to begin construction of living facilities and other subterranean structures on Ganymede, the largest moon of Jupiter. Supposedly this whole plan is devised by the newly crowned prince, young Darius. Malice cannot put his gnarled finger on it, but something about this child bothers him mightily. This new accounting only furthers that uneasiness. The boy is either an incredibly fast learner or something else entirely is going on. Reaching out from the void in search of Babylon's aural signature, Malice can sense that he is, in fact, on Ganymede.

The common thread between Babylon, Malice, and Typhoon is Pharaoh's genetic fingerprint placed on them all when he mutated them. The imprint is a bit more pronounced in Babylon since more of the light being's essence was used while he was still in the earlier stages of experimenting with the strange Earth species millennia ago. This is how Malice is able to track his whereabouts. Strangely, he can also sense the boy, but it is similar yet distinctly very different, somehow, which is a bit confusing. That is a matter for another time. Babylon is in a more secluded area of the new construction, meditating alone. Perhaps, he is communing somehow. Malice hopes to see what the ancient from Atlantis is up to. Nudging Typhoon, who is crouched in ether demonstratively trying to hold himself together, Malice rasps, "Get ready! We move once more closer to our quarry, but be mindful to keep silent. At all costs, try to stay in the void. I promised we would be…subtle on this hunt for information."

Keeping his eyes closed but nodding in affirmation, the gorilla waits for Malice to take the first stride before following. His eyes are not needed to follow as he can feel where his reluctant partner is going. This technique, Typhoon finds, is kinder to his stomach, at least, in comparison to when they went simultaneously. They wind their way closer to the aura Malice is heading toward until finally they are violently yanked out of the void. Despite being in a suit when Typhoon stops, the heat is almost unbearable. They are in a large dark chamber deep within the newly excavated structure beneath the surface of Ganymede where Babylon is meditating.

The old, wiry but still muscular frame of the ancient Atlantean is stripped from the waist up, sitting cross-legged with his ever-present trident across his lap. The pure white locks are tied back as sweat beads down his blue back and chest. Without opening his eyes, he demands, "What would you two miscreants want wit' ole Babylon?"

It is then that Typhoon notices Malice crumpled on the floor, beginning to stir. He has arrived first after all, but how did this seemingly decrepit being know they were coming, and what power does he have to dismiss such a formidable opponent as Malice with seemingly little effort? Malice gets to his feet, reaching out telepathically to Typhoon for what he assumes will be a private and silent conversation.

"Pay attention, beast! Attack without using your ballistic toys. We don't need anyone else coming to his aid."

Looking over, Typhoon responds, *"Master said nothing of attacking anyone!"*

Angrily, Malice retorts out loud, "You fool! Did you think I just bounced myself off the wall? I was attacked first, and for that, this relic is going to pay for his insolence, and then we will extract the information we seek in a painful yet silent manner. I have my ways." He turns his burning crimson gaze toward Babylon who chuckles.

Three glowing gazes of different colors all meet alternately as Babylon's amber eyes go from Typhoon's and then to Malice's as he responds, "You may have bitten off more than you can chew. Like you, I am quite more than what I seem! You want a shot at m'title? Well, come on!"

With that, he springs to his feet, making a quick flourish with his trident, surprising both soon-to-be assailants. Malice unsheathes two black gleaming blades and rushes toward Babylon, weapons quietly whispering through the air. The first blade is blocked with the trident's three-pronged head, and the shaft comes up to parry the second blade. The following riposte would have skewered Malice had he not leapt back.

As he disengages, Typhoon quickly jumps in, attempting to butt-stroke Babylon, but the Atlantean ducks the attack and reverse swings the shaft of his weapon, catching the ape squarely in his midsection, all air leaving his lungs, fogging up his helmet, as he flies against the far wall. Malice chooses this moment to spring back into the fray. Babylon raises his trident as if to catch the minion on the spike of the trident, but as he grips the shaft tightly, a bright light flashes from the tips of the weapon, sending hot energy into Malice, who briefly screams in pain. Typhoon recovers and runs to scoop up Malice, disappearing once more into the void.

Sprinting into the chamber followed by a group of guards, including Simeon, comes young Darius. Looking in the direction the attackers have fled in, Darius says, "It was them, wasn't it?"

Strangely, there is no need to clarify who "them" is as Babylon replies, "Yes, indeed it was. Now why would they come to me looking for information?"

Shrugging, the prince says, "I don't know. Are you okay?"

Waving a hand and nodding his head affirmatively, Babylon go to put on his brown cloak and unties his hair. As the prince and his guards file out of the chamber, Simeon stays behind just to be sure. Resting a hand on the Atlantean's shoulder, he says, "Now that's a first. Kind of a relief, don't you think?" Seeing the perplexed look on Babylon's face, he continues, "When's the last time you heard that youngster say he didn't know something?"

With that, they share a brief laugh before heading to catch up with the prince and his retinue.

• • •

Meanwhile, the footage of the "Mars ambush," as it is being dubbed, is spreading like wildfire through the media, causing a massive outcry all over Earth. It has also reached the military headquarters on Saturn. There is to be a scheduled address from the commandant soon. Sitting in one of the chow halls at Saturn's military facility, Petty Officer House is looking at the footage while enjoying his meal when Corporals Sims, Aragon, and Jordan come to sit with him. Coming fresh from their latest training session, they are all exhausted. Looking over at House's haggard face, Aragon remarks, "Man, you look like you were with us!"

Shaking his head, House replies, "That's because I have been dealing with all the handiwork of your not-so-friendly psychobots that the corps has you boys and girls playing with. It's getting kind of ridiculous. Fatalities shouldn't be happening at the rate we've been seeing, but I have a feeling that, after this latest attack, you all are about to go back to the real fight. Can't promise our boys won't be going down at a higher rate though. From all the highlights gathered from previous fights, the bots are still not quite to their level of savagery and effectiveness."

They all stay silent for a while.

There really is nothing more to be said. Nothing House states can be argued, but this is all a mess they have unwittingly signed up for when they enlisted. A quick trip to a nitro club will be a welcomed escape, but they also know it will be foolish to apply for leave now. Liberty is already at a minimum during the "cease fire" which, like the corpsman has said, is, in all likelihood, over now that hostilities are recommencing regardless. Sure enough, just as they are all thinking of their current predicament, the ramrod straight form of General Krulak can be seen on all monitors walking up to a podium to speak.

There is a lot more gray in the commandant's hair as his hard brown eyes focus on the hover-cams in front of him as he addresses the public. "Good evening to all watching across the globe here on Earth, and to those serving throughout the Milky Way. As most of you may know, a Union Pacific tourist group was savagely gunned down not long ago by the mining folk who absconded with ore and other precious materials not owned by them. Hostilities between our people were supposed to be at a standstill, yet they have chosen to attack noncombatants, so the GMC has no choice but to defend our citizens against these ungrateful beings. There were rumblings among the government that we would be looking to, at least, extend some sort of concessions to further compensate these beings for their efforts in bringing to us some of the much-needed materials that help create the technologies that make our lives better. Starting a war is not how people get to the negotiating table.

At least, that hasn't been the case in recent history. We certainly won't be negotiating with anyone who engages in acts of terrorism in hopes of furthering their agenda. You people have been put on notice and no quarter will be given. Despite what some theorists are saying about all of our genetic makeups, I use the word 'people' in this instance loosely. You will either return what is rightfully ours and surrender for judgement, or we will have no choice but to seize it and judge you accordingly after. Krulak out."

With that, the general turns and exits the podium, and the networks continue their coverage, adding thoughts about the commandant's speech, theorizing on what the next course of action could be.

• • •

Back at the hideout in Chicago where Sparks has taken up residence with Max and Argos, they have just finished watching the address when Max raises his hands and says, "There you go, straight from the horse's lying mouth! I knew something wasn't right about that footage, and the analysis isn't even back yet."

Shaking her head incredulously, Sparks asks, "What are you going on about?"

Turning from the screen, Max elaborates, "Union Pacific, huh? They're, of course, a large global transportation company…been that for centuries, but when it comes to taking it to the stars, no way. Computer? Are you done with the analysis?"

The display, once again, fills the office they are sitting in as the sultry voice of Max's AI describes the footage. "Yes, Max, the analysis is complete. When slowed down, you should notice there are barely visible bubbles around the ships being fired upon. The ships you see have been superimposed over whatever is really taking fire. Also, there is some scrubbing of the footage of the attacking vessels as well."

Confused, Sparks asks, "Computer, are you saying both groups of ships are all CGI images?"

After a brief pause, it answers, "No, the ragtag group of ships look to be integral to the original footage, but there are small imperfections that have been blurred out or cloaked somehow heading toward them. In trying to clean it up, I can only make the alterations a bit more obvious but cannot restore it fully to the original imaging."

Max walks over to the monitor and orders, "Show us what you could do and put it up on the screen at my desk please." When the monitor pops back on, they all gather in front of it to watch the footage again. "Told you!" Max exclaims. "Whoever this is, they were returning fire. We've come a long way, but space has not turned into something rivaling the golden age of piracy. Weapons add cost to ships, and when it comes to interplanetary travel in this galaxy, there are a few entities in the game right now. The rockheads are the newest, and I would bet anything that, if we removed the false images, there would be GMC craft returning fire. They broke their own cease-fire."

Chapter Eleven

THE PROCLAIMED CHILDREN OF THE Sun is an activist group that was sweeping the globe and gaining momentum. Their beliefs are founded on equality for all sentient beings, regardless of skin color, faith, orientation, age, class, and more recently skin durability or mutation. Incredibly, despite the gains in intellectual endeavors throughout the centuries past, technological advances, and overall growth of progressive ideas and movements that have come along, mankind's enlightenment is not able to eradicate the idea of supremacy based on random genealogy or birthright. Racism, sexism, ageism, along with other forms of bigotry and prejudice, do not die but as always, they evolve into more subtle forms. They either evolve or move on to heavily affect other groups which have sprouted up and widened the gap of variance in Earth's inhabitants.

Finally, when it is nearly accepted that people of color are of equal intelligence as evidenced by their many achievements amid some pretty crippling circumstances, societal groups still hold their reservations, but they are kept out of the public for the most part, and they move on to the most advanced of new species. There are some people that revere the Stone people and even worship them in some circles as they are seen as superior. The bottom line is that they are different and those that clung to the idea of being superior themselves see the newcomers as a threat as they become more common. This is a vicious cycle that, for reasons unknown, cannot be broken.

A rise in activism will also bring with it extreme purist groups who, with their dying breaths, will continue to cling to the ideas that their unaltered genes need to be protected and preserved. Part of that perseveration means separating themselves from the mutants and, if need be, eliminating mutants for the greater good of the pure. This group has a name as well. The Guild of the Pristine is what they call themselves. They, too, have learned from some of the mistakes of the past. They wear no uniforms, rarely hold rallies, but likely pass by the citizenry in tailored suits, and invest in heavy encryption kits through which they send their messages to the masses.

As cliché as it sounds, they are a true shadow faction. The other ingredient to this potential recipe for disaster that perpetually seems to be cooking is the existence of splinter factions or groups that claim to have similar beliefs but do not adhere to their rules of engagement or standards of conduct. This is likely the only thing that interests Pharaoh about these beings he thinks of as vermin. They have an absurd habit of finding every excuse for not uniting when unifying as a people and using all of their differences for the betterment of them all would give them the best possible future. Some supposedly get this idea, but overall they work at cross purposes. After millennia of watching this macabre dance unfold over and over, it is still entertaining to the exiled one.

● ● ●

Queen Tunisia is in a rage after the address from the GMC to the public has aired. She is amazed at the audacity of these people after so handily being defeated on multiple occasions. The Kison Askari fleet is growing, and Simeon is hard at work training their warriors for the advent of a foot war if it comes to that, as well as for unconventional circumstances to battle in. Zero G, extreme G, as well as fighting in vacuum are all new possibilities now. They will be ready if the GMC dares to attempt to put boots on the ground wherever the Askari decides to put their stronghold.

Other prototypes of the suit made to protect Darius's growing body are made for grown warriors, as well with helmets, so they can operate in the dangers inherent to space combat or unfavorable atmospheric conditions. Their skin is tough, but they still have to breathe oxygen. They have not evolved that far yet. They are getting used to the suits. They aren't as bulky as the EV suits the GMC will be using as they don't need them to be as thick for protection, but it is most important to have a secure seal to keep the oxygen in. The advances they have come up with in hydroponics over the years from having to mine on infertile planets are coming in especially handy now that they are preparing to expatriate from Earth on a more permanent basis if things do not go well with this war and hopefully peaceful resolutions.

Tunisia figures the threat was an idle one coming from the GMC, but it still angers her. It is obvious they have begun to take the war into the realm of public opinion. The Kison Askari will have to, somehow, address this. The public, at times, can be easily duped into believing the most absurd things, yet will often ignore the obvious to protect their personal sensibilities. It is time for a wake-up call, and if they heed it, that will be all well and good. If not, so be it. Tunisia thinks it is high time that the oppressed stop feeling it necessary to be sensitive to those that perpetually take advantage of them. Taking offence to someone pointing out your wrongdoings does not mean the actual wrongdoing should be ignored. She decides to put in a call to Hironike and Toshi to see what can be done.

She is unaware that the Ongakujin are on the run themselves and making arrangements to rendezvous with Athena for pick up along with any who want to flee the injustices currently happening on Earth. Not long after their run-in with Marshal Benitez, Hironike receives that request from Angelo on Athena's behalf. It will be tight and hard to pull off with a vessel as large as the Ryoko-Gekijo.

• • •

The mobilization of the entire GMC fleet and manpower is in full effect. They continue with the Ascension Program, which delights Lt. Commander Jameson, further enhancing Marines with cybernetics, even some that have no injuries which is a brief controversy for some within the ranks. Plus, it adds cost to outfitting personnel. This opens up for the Automaton Program, to Jameson's chagrin. Koops Robotics has been lobbying for the government contract for years, wanting to enlist their droids to serve in various capacities in the military. There have been attempts to do this from other companies, to disastrous results, which was why, for so long, the idea has been shunned. General Krulak is desperate now for anything he feels will help their cause.

Dr. Mwamikazi is waiting outside the training facility before the demonstration of her latest models of high-tech robotics. She is at the head of the line for winning the government contract that will furnish the GMC with the autonomous droids to supplement their fighting force. Through a strange twist of fate, she has acquired Koops Robotics but has let the company retain its name and commercial façade, so she can enter into more western markets. Rising out of the ashes that was Burundi hasn't been easy, but she has done so using her smarts and talent. This Lt. Commander Jameson is just another obstacle to go through.

The lieutenant commander walks up to her in his dress white naval uniform. Must have been a special occasion, she thinks. Either that or he is trying to use his military position to intimidate her. She looks him up and down as if assessing him while running her fingers through immaculate shiny ropes of braids, pushing up her glasses before extending a hand to shake the naval officer's. Accepting her hand, he greets her, "Good afternoon, Dr. Mwamikazi. What are you doing here? I thought Koops Robotics was giving this demonstration. By the way, is your doctorate in any medical field?"

Her brown lips part to reveal a dazzling smile as she replies, "I acquired Koops not that long ago, and, yes, two of my doctorates are medical.

However, I found it in our best interest to work with mechanical beings. As an aside, it later became more lucrative as well."

The answers surprise Jameson and intrigue him somewhat, though he still disagrees with her units being useful for anything other than nanny duty or serving in other menial household capacities. He notices some sweat beading on her brown forehead. "You know there is a skybox above the field where the temperature is moderated better than here at field level. I am sure General Krulak wouldn't mind you viewing the demonstration from there."

She waves a hand dismissively at the thought as three dark-skinned shorn-headed aides of hers with striking golden eyes approach her. One whispers in her ear, and all three go to stand a safe distance from the doctor. Their dress is nondescript, almost clinical. The lieutenant commander can't quite put his finger on what is disturbing about them. Just through the viewport, they can see the field where the training bots are marching in to begin today's session. They are large and brutish metallic monstrosities, meant to mimic the intimidation factor, something akin to what the Stone people exhibit when they fight.

On the opposite side, the sleek and shiny droids from Koops Robotics calmly stride in and get into formation. Looking up, they can see the skybox that was mentioned earlier. Inside of it is General Krulak and some of the higher members of his staff. The lieutenant commander is not impressed, and he lets Dr. Mwamikazi know. "Yours are shiny but a bit small. Meanwhile, those training bots of ours have been giving our boys fits. I am all for using mechanical assets, but I think it's best to have an organic mind in control."

Once all of the mechanical combatants are in place, a translucent energy shield envelops them, so the observers can see but are in no danger of being hit by energy or ballistic rounds that will soon be flying everywhere. This is new technology the GMC is working on, but they are having difficulty implementing it in their ships.

There is a buzzing sound as the shield fully closes. At that, she remarks, "Yes, they're smaller than the units you've been training with, but ours are more advanced with better weaponry, cost more, but I think you'll find that our AI algorithms make them as close to being as intuitive as the human mind as you can get. Your units can be programmed to follow orders while mine can learn and find better ways to follow those orders. Pay attention, lieutenant commander, this will be…educational."

Jameson is simultaneously further intrigued and also a bit angered at what he perceives to be arrogance. Together, they silently watch as the GMC training bots leap into action, training their weapons on the Koops models and opening fire.

In reaction, the Koops units form three large phalanx formations with personal shields springing from one arm and energy canons from the other. They hold position, blocking fire coming from the training bots. After a few moments, General Krulak voices what a majority of the observers are thinking, "What are they waiting for?" Almost as if they have heard the commandant, two units begin moving to flank, continuing to block fire as they go. When the fire of the training bots is splintered between them evenly, the Koops units return fire through their own shields. The military hosts are flabbergasted as the training bots are summarily obliterated in a matter of minutes. Dr. Mwamikazi looks over at an open-mouthed Lt. Commander Jameson who is quick to recompose himself. If there is any doubt these units will be picked up, it is a forgone conclusion now.

The Koops units cease firing, and all they can see are smoking metal carcasses. They haven't had a chance to recover. The silence is broken by hissing and some of the last training units hit crashing to the ground. The Koops units shut down their shields, retract the canons, and go back to formation. It is obvious from the glint in General Krulak's eyes that he is pleased. This has the possibility to even up things if it ever comes to a ground fight but still does nothing to mitigate the dark matter ace up the Stone people's sleeve. It is a start, but it will come at a hefty cost.

The skybox floats down with General Krulak and his staff so that they can begin negotiating.

Disappointed that things have not gone as he expected, the lieutenant commander storms off as the commandant and staff greet Dr. Mwamikazi. She looks over her shoulder at the naval officer before approaching the military brass. Her aides follow closely.

• • •

As the Ryoko-Gekijo flies to and from various air spaces avoiding GMC interdiction, Hironike and the Jade Assassins receive a brief communique from Angelo and Athena of the Limbia Johari. They desperately need extraction, in addition to a fair amount of refugees and rebels that will also be in tow. Toshi has informed him that Athena and her spy network-turned- guerrilla force are holed up in a little-known cave system in the Andes Mountains which will also make locating them, as well as communication, difficult. There will be a small window of opportunity as agencies are now after both parties.

Encrypted data packages with messages will be sent out in hopes that they have kept the equipment intact during their fighting. Luckily Athena is aware a situation like this might come up and has a plan. The circumstances make it so it has to be improvised, but they are hoping it will get the job done. Toshi has given them a small sat-link transceiver capable of receiving and sending short-burst encrypted messages. The encryption is of his own design, but they will have to surface in order to get the data packages he is sending out briefly, exposing themselves to anyone possibly looking for them. If the Ryoko-Gekijo is not close by, it can leave them exposed for too long. The plan is to confirm where they are and arrange a pickup time.

There have been a few transmissions that went unreceived as Athena and her group have remained underground for most of them. They are trying to decide who will be going up to set up the transceiver. Angelo has made a peculiar friend and has an idea that will limit their risk, but it is a shaky proposition. The friend in question is a yellow-tailed woolly monkey. Angelo has taken to calling him George because the native frugivorous primate seems to be curious about the beings that have taken up residence in these mountains for a time. The monkey will oddly show up more and more often when Angelo has sentry duty.

Despite coming out in a full chameleon tech suit, George always seems to know of his presence. When speaking to others who have been posted to the same areas, they are not familiar with the monkey. Why has this furry creature taken a shine to Angelo? Perhaps, it is his willingness to share fruit with the animal. It was skittish at first, but soon George could get close enough to touch. Most of the time, they simply sat there in an amicable silence, enjoying their fruit. The strange companionship is about to pay off. During a few of the nights out while on sentry duty, Angelo has brought the transceiver with him to power it up and ensure it still works.

On some of those occasions, George has taken notice when the device is powered on as it makes soft whirring sounds as the small dish blossoms, opening up the small comms array. The next night, Angelo came out to take up his post with the device, and as expected, George showed up. While lying prostrate in the underbrush, Angelo silently greeted his friend. Powering the device up, he said, "Hello, friend. I know I don't speak to you often, but I need a favor. Can you take this up in that cinchona tree?" Pointing and gesticulating did not seem to get the point across as the monkey cooed a little and stared back blankly.

Just when he was about to give up, George scooped the device up and scrambled up to the top of a nearby tree and left the device balancing on a bough, then quickly came down. As a reward, Angelo gave him some fruit and gently patted him on the head before moving to another location in case the signal brought unwanted attention. He would come back sometime later and hopefully have George retrieve the device without risking him or any of his people getting caught.

• • •

Aboard the Ryoko-Gekijo, Hiornike is informed of the transmission and the location it came from. He asks Toshi to send out potential pick-up times and to scan the area, so they can decide beforehand what the best extraction point should be, how many they can take with them, and so forth. One thing is for sure, this will likely be a rough ride.

Chapter Twelve

THE DEEP EXCAVATION INTO GANYMEDE'S mantle has taken the Kison Askari record time, but they, unlike the rest of mankind, are used to digging in unconventional places under extreme circumstances. This certainly qualifies. The subterranean network of caves to be used as living quarters and training will open up the foundation of their society in general. This is an engineering feat the likes of which have never been accomplished. There will soon be a string of underground cities in one of Jupiter's largest moons. After the space to build is opened up, they then have to use a mix of alloys, silicone-based plastics, and other materials that will shore up the bones of their new home to protect it against the shifting of tectonic plates and whatnot.

The alloys will ensure it is strong, and the other materials will allow for some flexibility. They can also now seal the cities for climate and atmospheric control for the inhabitants. The surface and crust of the moon will protect against outside attacks from the GMC.

If they choose to come here, they will be at a serious disadvantage. Until they figure out how to stabilize a way to weaponize dark matter for themselves, the GMC would have to wait for the Stone people to come out to be attacked. This might have been the case for regular Marines, but the automaton program may see their number called when it came to attacking this underground beachhead.

There were even several new training grounds that would rotate to serve as the grounds for the CGYAB games. When checking over the new sites, Darius inquired as to what they were. After a look from Simeon, his guards would pretend to be just as confused as he was. Things did not tend to stay hidden from the prince very long as they would soon find out. He knew of someone he could easily either bait into giving him the truth or simply follow them to learn of this place when the time came.

Darius had tried to bring the topic up with Professor Charles Jones-Bey, but his teacher acted strangely and claimed to be too busy, recusing himself from the conversation swiftly. It was then the prince realized there was more to this than anyone was letting on. He knew who to approach next.

● ● ●

Still steaming over the demonstration of the robotic units from Koops, Lt. Commander Jameson notices a new message in his inbox from the commandant. In it, he is being ordered to send the Mechanics to recon Ganymede. Apparently, the satellite has picked up images suggesting there is a lot of activity currently going on. The GMC needs boots on the ground to assess the situation before deploying and likely risking anymore assets. The loss of ships at Mars is still fresh on their minds. The Adder is small with stealth capabilities and should be able to get to the surface without detection if they do not engage any ships in or near the moon's gravity well.

Sgt. Garrison won't like it, as he was a man of action, but he will follow orders. There is also the issue of where to store that beast PFC Long is keeping. The cost of acquiring the new automaton units has to be staggering. Jameson puts it out of his mind. Might as well head down to the special barracks and deliver the orders to his men. Leaving his trademark lab jacket in his office, Lt. Commander Jameson heads down to deliver the bad news.

Once again, he is met by PFC Long. "Afternoon, sir!" the young Marine belts as he salutes.

Returning the salute, Jameson asks, "Where is your sergeant? I have orders for you."

Turning to head back into their living quarters, Long goes to retrieve Sgt. Garrison. The stench is still there but mild in comparison to the last time he has been down there. Shortly Long returns with Sgt. Garrison in tow. They greet each other, briefly exchanging salutes, before Garrison inquires, "What you got, sir? Something good, I hope."

Shaking his head, the lieutenant commander hands him a data-pad with the message containing the orders in it.

After reading the message, Sgt. Garrison tosses the pad back to Lt. Commander Jameson. "We only get to look?" he asks.

Walking away, Jameson says over his shoulder, "Yes, sergeant! We don't know what they have there and don't want to go in blind. Long, make sure to make arrangements to stow that…beast somewhere it won't endanger our people here while you're on mission. I still need to study it and haven't had time."

"Yes, sir," Long replies to no one in particular since the officer has left.

Sgt. Garrison looks at him, shaking his head. "Should have left that thing where we found it," the sergeant admonishes.

As if it knew he was the topic of discussion, the hellhound, which is at the shoulder of Long but has grown in girth, comes loping out if its enclosure. It walks up to Long and gives a loving lick with its thick purple tongue before laying at his feet. Sgt. Garrison walks off, still shaking his head, and orders, "Let the boys know we are to be wheels up in a couple weeks to recon the possible new HQ for the rockheads."

• • •

Relaxing in his meditation chamber deep in the pyramid at Giza, Pharaoh waits for Malice and Typhoon to return. He can feel their beings coming closer. Stepping out of a glowing aperture that appears a few meters away from where their master is finishing his meditations, Typhoon unceremoniously dumps Malice's body on the floor. As the minion stirs, Pharaoh glides over, and immediately the minions are racked with searing pain. Pharaoh's eyes glow white hot as he inquires in a booming voice, "What, if anything, have you fools learned?"

Stammering under the onslaught, Typhoon struggles to answer, "We never got the chance to find out, master!"

Turning his glare to the writhing Malice, Pharaoh roars, "Do you have anything to add with the ape's account? I thought I told you to be discreet!"

Gathering himself to his feet, he replies despite the telekinetic torture and answers his master, "We were yanked from the void! I don't think he has enlisted any other radiant ones!" Upon hearing this, the ancient being releases them, pondering their report.

"Babylon pulled you from the void? That is interesting indeed. What makes you think he could or didn't gain the help of any of my kind?" Pharaoh says.

The minions are both breathing hard as they drop to their knees, trying to recover before Malice answers, "Just speculation, master. If they had the help of a more powerful being, they would have made themselves known by now. The struggles we have worked so hard to orchestrate here are still ongoing. Would they not stop the conflict if they were here?"

Pharaoh thinks on that for a moment. "That's very possible, but also possible that they would simply observe without wanting to interfere. Indecision is one of my kinds few flaws at times. I am not like that which is why I have butted heads with some of my own from time to time. Babylon, it seems, may have grown in ability since I last saw him."

With that, Pharaoh waves a hand, dismissing the minions who gratefully take their leave without a backward glance or comment. Each goes to their chambers in anger but works to hide it. Typhoon, now more than ever, seeks to escape this involuntary servitude. Malice is thinking along the same lines. They have both also caught the notion of beings enhanced could grow in power or prowess. It is unlikely that they will ever exceed the power of their master, but the fact that one can become more powerful in some way is encouraging.

• • •

Hironike's people not only act on their stages but also out in the real world. Many are unaware of their presence as they use makeup and other cosmetics to hide their true complexions. In a lot of cases, they work hand-in-hand with the network of Limbia Johari who are led by Athena. This helps them to know the whereabouts of all potential high-profile assassination targets. There is not too much of that going on presently as movement has halted for the important people of the government, and GMC heads are always hard to get at. However, there is still plenty of information to gather.

Yuki is one of Hironike's people who hide in plain sight, working as an administrative assistant for a motion picture company. She works in an office close to Reyansh's and knows of the visit from a GMC officer a few weeks ago. Rumor has it that the officer has left some footage for the film producer to go over. Yuki has come in soon after to chat with one of Reyansh's office workers and has left a small device that will skim files from their system without them being the wiser. Sneaking into the office after hours to retrieve her device will be difficult.

Yuki, who has trained with the other Jade Assassins, is up to the task. She has word that Hironike and the rest of her people are on the run currently, so they need to know what, if anything, substantive has happened between Reyansh and the GMC officer. Reyansh's main office is in a high-rise building in Mumbai. Yuki has decided not to wear the usual makeup for this. Instead, she wears a chameleon cloak Toshi sent her a few months ago. She wasn't sure when she'd have the chance to use it, but she's glad she kept it. She could, of course, go up to her office in full disguise, but then there would be a record of her entering the building.

Scaling the Namaste building and working her way into the correct office will be quite a feat. Luckily, she has some tools that will make the endeavor a bit easier. The three-hundred-meter-plus tall hybrid of office spaces, hotel, and retail space are made of glass, concrete, and metal. The latter being really integral is what helped her mag-lock boots and gloves allow her to slowly scale the building. Looking around to ensure no one is observing, Yuki quickly puts on the cloak and activates it. She quickly fades into the environment around her.

She begins her ascent, taking her time to limit the movement of the cloak. The sun is setting, giving the land and skyline a deep orange hue. When she gets about halfway up the building, the wind begins to pick up, and luckily she does not have to depend on her strength to hold on to the building. Her progress is halted, however, due to the presence of patrol drones that must have, somehow, noticed movement around the building. She has to remain motionless and remember to slow her pace further to avoid detection. Once the drones leave, she resumes scaling the building.

At this slower pace, the climb seems to take forever, but she is soon near the floor she thinks her office should be on. Yuki will not enter her office though. That may still tie her to the break-in. What she wants to do is enter another adjacent office, override the security after silently breaching the window, go over to Reyansh's office, retrieve her device, and head back to go over the files it recovered at her leisure. Sounds like a good plan.

Once she is satisfied she is at the right floor, she stops to deploy a small device that clings to the window and starts a laser incision on the glass moving in a perfect circular motion. Yuki is careful to catch the glass once the circle cut is free, then scoots herself through the hole, making sure not to drop it, thus alarming any people or drones who might be patrolling the area. All is quiet once she enters surprisingly.

She quickly runs to a nearby terminal and slips a hacking device in to shut down the alarm that will no doubt go off as a result of the window breach. With that done, she gets her bearings. She is three floors lower than she needs to be.

After getting her bearings, she quickly makes her way to the proper floor again, keeping an eye out for anyone or anything that might be watching the area. Luckily, having bypassed the security earlier, all is quiet. The individual offices do not have separate security systems, but the individual computers do have identity and passkey locks on their interfaces. A small jade gift left on the desk of the colleague is used to secretly log in and siphon files. Yuki has given this to her coworker as a gift and is happy that it is still there, seemingly waiting for her.

She picks up the small jade figurine and makes her way back down to where she entered the building. Quickly picking up the discarded glass, she leaps through the hole activating her boots and gloves, ensuring she will adhere to the window outside. Once outside, she places the circle back in place. It will not stay long, but she does not need it to. Yuki only needs enough time to get back to the ground. Once more, drones come by to scan what the outer sensors have flagged as a disturbance. Freezing in place, she waits for the drones to leave, yet they are loitering for a longer time period than she wants to wait. Finally getting impatient, she throws three small devices that latch onto the drones, sending electromagnetic pulses through them. The drones die and fall to the ground.

Knowing her time is limited, she deactivates the gloves and boots and base jumps off the Namaste building. The cloak is still active, but she is moving so swiftly through the air that it cannot keep up with the surrounding environment enough to keep her nearly invisible, so she deactivates it as well. When she feels she has fallen far enough from her entry point, she takes the cloak off in midair, stuffing it into a pouch at her side. Maneuvering is becoming more difficult as she approaches terminal velocity, and the ground creeps up steadily. Before it is too late, she opens up her wing suit and glides to the ground safely trying to put as much distance as possible between her and the building. It is a nightmare navigating around the other buildings, but Yuki does it with very little room to spare.

With the hard part over, all she has to do now is get to a terminal to transmit this, so Toshi and the rest of her people can go through the files. Initially she plans to do so herself, but given things would be rather hot around the office, it is likely a bad risk to take. She is in a valuable position and does not want to risk blowing her cover once people start investigating. Yuki is sure Hironike will agree.

On board the Ryoko-Gekijo, Toshi is curious but unaware that an encrypted message is coming to them. He is most interested in the whereabouts of Athena and her group, but he opens it up nonetheless.

Pouring through the files, he is unsure why the one labeled "test footage" seems so interesting, but he goes ahead and opens it. What he sees does not disappoint. Seeing the red planet in all its glory in the initial frames is curious. Then slowly the images clear up to reveal the Kison Askari rejected ships before a group of GMC ships jump in. The new arrivals open fire, and suddenly it hits him why these shots look so familiar. He has just seen this event play out followed by a speech from General Krulak with one very important change. The military ships have been made to look like civilian ships. This certainly clears up a lot of confusion over what he has been hearing about the recent skirmish.

Opening up a communication line to the main deck, he says, "Hiro, I have something you might want to take a look at."

Shortly thereafter comes a response: "*Choto matte kudasai.*"

Once Hironike arrives with Megume and Takimura, they all watch the footage together. When it is over, they all look at Hiro, asking the same silent question in their minds. Do they leak this themselves or give it to Tunisia first? Things are heating up, so he decides to send the raw footage to Tunisia but also tells Toshi to find a way to discreetly leak this to the public as well.

Ancient Illumination II: (Kuongoza Mwanga: The Leading Light)

With that order of business over with, Toshi has also locked on to a transmission from the field satellite link given to Athena, so they have an approximate location in the Andes Mountains. He relays another message intermittently of an approximate time for extraction. They will simply be there in hopes that the message is received. Unfortunately, the authorities aren't the only ones trying to track their whereabouts which could complicate things as they will soon find out.

Chapter Thirteen

BACK ON SATURN, CORPORALS ARAGON, Sims, and Jordan are all gathering their gear for potential deployment. Rumor has it that they might be shipping out soon to try to bring the Stone people to justice for their attack on civilians. There is also scuttlebutt going around that some new mechanized units will be accompanying them. It could happen tomorrow, or it could happen weeks from now. Either way, they have to stay ready. Thinking all this over, Aragon says, "Man, a nice dose of nitro would be great right about now."

The others nod in agreement. They have been training pretty hard for a long stretch now in prep for hostilities that everyone knows will resume at any moment. It just so happens that the latest attack has sped that process up.

Most of them are also not convinced a peaceful arrangement can be made as both sides will have a hard time coming to terms amenable to each side. The GMC will still want the government to retain control of whatever resources they have mined, and it is a forgone conclusion that the Stone people are going to demand more of a stake in what they provided. Thinking on it, Aragon cannot come up with any valid reasons not to consider doing just that, but when you take lives, your cause is likely not to be understood. People develop deaf ears to the causes of murderers. These Marines are unaware they are about to have their assumptions obliterated.

Petty Officer House saunters into their barracks, waiting for one of them to acknowledge his presence. Aragon and Sims do their best to ignore him as it was obvious something is up, and he is bursting at the seams to tell them. Jordan can't hold on, so he finally blurts, "Spill it already, squid boy! We can all see you're aching to."

Sitting down in front of the computer on Aragon's desk, House pulls out a small data storage device and pulls up the file. Video footage begins to play. The hazy red silhouette of Mars appears, and then a group of ships jump in. Corporal Jordan says, "We saw this a couple weeks ago."

House cuts him off. "Just wait and look closer at those ships."

They all gather around to get a better look, noticing that the ships look awfully familiar. Sims is the first to notice something is amiss. "Those are definitely our birds, but where's the debris? We arrived after the attack, I would assume."

The scene continues to play out, and suddenly, another group of ships jump in. This new group of spacecraft look like cobbled together space junk. Immediately, the GMC ships open fire and receive seemingly ineffectual return fire.

Out of nowhere, there are three blossoms of not explosions exactly but chain reactions among the GMC ships as a deep hazy purple mist flies through, disintegrating the deployed flotilla. Before they are all annihilated, the remnants of GMC ships jump back out of the system. A similar chain reaction is initiated within the junk ships, and then there are three distinct flashes, then nothing as there is finally some dust and debris from the mass of broken ships settling in vacuum. Confused, Argon finally looks up to ask, "So, wait, where were the tour boats that were attacked, and where did you get that footage?"

House stares at them all blankly in disbelief. "Are you guys kidding me? Everyone on Earth is going ballistic over this footage! It was leaked, and most people don't know who to believe. Some government officials are saying this was faked in an attempt to gain sympathy for the rockheads, but I gotta tell you, looks like they were the ones kickin' butt! Is it just me or does that look similar to what we got hit with here not too long ago?"

After thinking on House's words, Aragon goes over to the console and rewinds the footage to take another look at it. Then he searches to pull up images and footage from the bombing of their base on Saturn from months ago.

One attack took place in vacuum and the other within Saturn's atmosphere, but there are some telling similarities in the way the exploded ordinance reacts once deployed. The lack of anything like oxygen in space cut short the explosions, but the payload itself, once released, does the same thing to those GMC ships at Mars as it did to the buildings and the surface on Saturn. At both places, when the dark matter (if that is, in fact, what it was) touches anything, it looks as if an invisible cartoonist has simply taken an eraser to their work. Machine, building, land mass, or unfortunate person is either wholly or partially deleted from the scenes. In the cases where it is a partial dismemberment, the shape of the injury is precise as to the shape of the cloud that touched them.

This has led to some oddly shaped and unfortunately unhealable injuries as they bleed out or succumb to being exposed to the atmosphere when parts of their EV suits are destroyed. There is no doubt in their minds that the same substance had been used at both events. The troubling thing for them is the tourist group mentioned by the commandant is nowhere to be seen in this recent footage release. Media has been on a lockdown for a while there on base, and this information appears to give them the reason why. Little do they know that things are coming to an awful head back on Earth.

• • •

Local law enforcement, as well as reserve military units worldwide on Earth, are being dispatched as soon as possible to quell a rash of riots after the footage leaked. General Krulak is hesitant to send active duty units as they are still needed to deal with the main uprising in the Stone people. Things are not going well. Queen Regent Tunisia takes this moment to add gasoline to the fire. As soon as she received the raw footage, she instructed her people to also compile the footage recorded from the three perspectives of the ships herself, Nefer, and Zola were piloting during the attack.

Once the files were compiled, they made their way onto multiple satellite bandwidths, using brute force, hijacking a myriad of signals, and played their perspectives for the public to see alongside the raw footage, so everyone could see how it all synced up. After the scenes played out, Tunisia herself appeared on camera to address the public: "I see the head of the GMC has gone out of his way to soil my people's reputation. He tried to make you all think we would attack innocent beings. We are not the monsters he would have you believe we are. We only want what most people want, fair treatment, the right to pursue life as we see fit, and reasonable compensation for our contributions to this society. You all can either do what is necessary in the interest of peace or continue this war at your own peril. The truth is out."

With that, the screens went black across Earth and normal programming resumed. News outlets interrupted regularly scheduled programming to theorize which sets of footage were authentic or not.

Many of Earth's inhabitants, after rioting began, have started to take up residence in the underground cave systems and forgotten areas to avoid detection by law enforcement. The problem is that some of these areas have become more dangerous because of the lack of protection, but that is changing. There is an evolution in the people's mindset happening that is unifying more of the planet's people on the largest scale ever. Narratives that have often kept people separated are now being seen for the deception they have always been. This has brought the government for the planet at large to a horrifying realization. They obviously have a technological advantage over a vast majority of the masses of disenfranchised beings, yet by virtue of sheer numbers, it is possible that advantage could, for the first time, be negligible.

Mutant and non-mutant alike are creating a huge coalition of people and them taking to the streets is finally being met with some serious resistance. The anti-riot non-lethal sonic weaponry is not doing the trick when the crowds start growing. Numbers are beginning to turn the tide and rallies are now, for the most part, left alone unless the people protesting instigate violence. The GMC and the government at large are in a predicament where this war could develop on multiple fronts. The only one happy about this is Pharaoh.

• • •

A couple weeks have passed, and the government is trying to put out all manner of fires. The GMC decides to greenlight their recon mission to see what they may have to contend with on Ganymede when the time comes. Sgt. Garrison, Lance Corporals McNamara and Jennings, along with PFC Long, all aboard the Adder head to the Jovian moon. As they come out of hyperspace, LCPL McNamara immediately activates the outer filaments on the hull putting the ship in stealth mode and shuts down thrusters to lower their heat signature. It is a good thing he has acted quickly.

Traffic just outside the gravity well is light, but there is a considerable amount of ships flying to and from the surface. Looking to where Sgt. Garrison is strapped into his seat monitoring the console, he asks, "What are your recommendations for our POE, sergeant?"

Turning from his console distractedly, Sgt. Garrison replies, "POE?"

LCPL Jennings answers for McNamara, "Point of entry, sergeant. There's not heavy traffic, but we still need to be careful about where we enter the atmosphere as our heat signature will be more noticeable then."

Nodding in acknowledgement, Sgt. Garrison looks back and forth between the readout displayed at his monitor and through the main viewport at the yellowish-gray moon. After a few moments, he barks out, "Head for the night side in the least amount of traffic possible obviously and take your time. We don't want to attract any attention, even while ghosting, by moving too swiftly. Don't know what kind of sensor packages their birds may have, so just take it easy. When we get groundside, remember this is a recon mission only, so look but try not to touch, ladies! Unless, of course, we take fire, but then that will be a failed mission, and we will not have gathered any meaningful intel to take home. I don't know if I have to remind you, but, Jennings and Mac, make sure to have your cyber-eyes scanning on multiple spectrums if you can. Same for you, Berserker, in your helmet HUD. I'll be doing the same with mine. Everyone good to go?"

There was a chorus of "Yes, sergeant!"

They keep at a distance from the traffic and slowly make their way to the night side of the moon. They are all paying close attention for any signs they have been detected. There are two main pilot and co-pilot seats in the cockpit of the Adder with a third seat behind and between the first two seats with a nice view of everything in front of them. Sgt. Garrison has chosen to let the two lance corporals fly, while he observes from the rear seat to better assess the situations as they come up. They are all qualified to fly the craft due to flash training, as well as programming in their cybernetics, but there is literally not enough room for PFC Long, so he is mag-locked to the deck in the rear cabin.

Once they have a lay of the space around the moon and what they think is a good understanding of the flight patterns within it, Sgt. Garrison highlights an area for them to make their approach through. At that, LCPL McNamara steers the ship to the point, and they begin their entry. There is an audible bang as they begin, and the ship seems to start humming as it makes its way through the mesosphere. Definitely in the grasp of the moon's gravity, LCPL Jennings cuts the engines in hopes that, if they are detected, they might be mistaken for falling debris or a meteorite of some kind. He does not cut the engines back on until they are free-falling halfway through the stratosphere, and there are no signs they have been spotted.

The weightlessness of free-falling is abruptly halted as the thrusters kick in, and they slow to a hover. They stay in place, once again, to monitor for any signs of pursuit. When no alarms go off, Sgt. Garrison nods and orders, "Mac, check the topography and look for a place to land this bird in the cut, somewhere kind of hidden. Scan for heat signatures and get us close but not too close to their activity. We'll have to hump our way in and check to see what they got cookin'. Interesting that there are polar ice caps here. I wonder if there are other sources of water here. When you find the spot, take us down. Everyone get suited up and perform diagnostics on all systems before we step off."

They keep a low profile, hugging the ground to stay off radars or other forms of detection systems that may be around. Once he finds a place that fits the description, Lance Corporal McNamara heads toward a large plateau that lead into a cave of sorts a few kilometers from where there is definitely some activity, according to the scanners. Once they are safely inside the cave, everyone gets suited up and makes sure all their cybernetics and equipment are fully operational. PFC Long is the first to be ready since he practically lives in his suit at all times. He searches the surrounding area inside the cave for signs of any use or hints anyone has been there and finds none. Once he is sure the area is secure, he goes back inside to notify the others.

Personal diagnostics are conducted, and Sgt. Garrison goes to each Marine to verify the results. They all check out. The gravity there is slightly lighter than on Earth's moon at 1.428 meters per second squared, so they will need to shuffle similarly while getting around on foot. Hopefully that will not pose a problem. Most of the activity seems to be taking place deep below ground. Scans during the flyover indicated there were, at least, two salt water oceans within the mantle of the moon in addition to the polar ice caps, making it possible to colonize. Ore is coveted, but this makes it even more important to bring these beings back into the fold. If the Stone people make it possible to cut ties altogether, Earth will lose out on the lucrative mining opportunities throughout the galaxy that only one group of beings can survive in.

Either that or they will have to spend resources and money to enhance regular men in general in order to replace the lost workforce in that industry. There are traces of oxygen in the atmosphere but not enough to sustain life on the surface which is good, but on the other hand, scans indicate there are already structures in place well beneath the surface that are no doubt sealed for climate and atmosphere control. They will also be protected from orbital artillery. Potentially, this could be a veritable stronghold. These beings are already the most experienced when it comes to living off-world, so there is no doubt this is sustainable. They may not have had technological advances when it comes to aeronautical engineering until recently, but definitely have a leg up on hydroponics, terraforming, and other means of making foodstuffs in order to survive.

The non-mutated men and women who own corporations, along with the government and military components, send people with them on the initial forays into off-world mining expeditions but have primarily left the Stone people to their own devices once it was discovered things worth taking were in or on the various planets and moons of the Milky Way. They are sent out with tools made for finding and extracting metals, minerals, and other things that become necessary that are not available on Earth. They also do so with minimal supplies for sustenance. This is a bit counterproductive in hindsight. The Kison Tontu, ever innovative, began to use what they were given and what they had learned over the years to overcome these obstacles.

The Mechanics are now witnessing the results of the evolution of the Kison Tontu's innovation. Shuffling out of the cave, they decide not to use any type of drone for fear of it being seen making the presence of GMC personnel evident. Once they are closer, they may have to deploy something in order to avoid a conflict. Long turns around before exiting the cave, presses buttons on a small console in his left gauntlet, and the camo filaments in the hull of the Adder are activated remotely. With that done, they repel down to the ground beneath the plateau.

It takes Lance Corporals Jennings, McNamara, and Private Cooper the longest to get the hang of shuffling in their suits as PFC Long and Sgt. Garrison are both using cybernetics to shuffle. The cybernetics are able to calibrate and gauge movement automatically. As enhanced as the two lance corporals' and Cooper's legs are, there is still human physiology they have to traverse. There are a few close calls as they have to dive into grayish-brown dunes to avoid possibly being sighted when ships fly overhead. It seems silly to even make the effort to Long as the dives are absurdly slow given the gravity, and the dirt will kick up possibly having the effect of calling attention to them. It ends up being a non-factor as no one seems to be paying them any mind.

It makes sense that there would be little to no sentry presence as nobody in their right mind would actually come here. Storming this place would be nigh impossible, and if it could be done, it would be at a disastrous loss of life and resources. The Stone people have to know this, and yet here they were, thinks Sgt. Garrison.

Chapter Fourteen

AFTER ONE OF HIS LESSONS, which have become shorter and shorter as Professor Jones-Bey has become resigned to the reality that Darius can be taught little else, the prince goes to find Bofus. They are making themselves quite at home here on Ganymede, and Bofus is relatively easy to find eating in the *mezani* or dining hall as some of the humans call it. The Kison Askari have taken in an eclectic group of people that will be growing from all walks of exiles and refugees of Earth. Hironike is momentarily on his way to attempt to extract Athena and a group of refugees/rebels along with a large contingent of the Limbia Johari that, if successful, would all be relocating to Ganymede as well. Things are getting interesting, to say the least.

Bofus is sitting at a table alone, eating some kind of synthetic meat, along with vegetables that have been hydroponically grown on the ship. The Kison Askari are in the process of installing equipment within their new habitat to start processing food there. The bountiful water reservoirs on the moon are an invaluable asset. All they have to do is purify it for consumption. Mining comets or other celestial bodies for frozen water is viable but often a dangerous endeavor, especially for those relatively new at piloting. Looking up from his tray, Bofus speaks to Darius, "Hey, your highness! How are you today?"

A bit more abruptly than he intends, Darius answers, "Don't call me that! Sorry. Just don't like it."

Nodding his understanding, Bofus continues to eat, saying "my bad" between bites. Puzzled, Darius looks at his plate, trying to decipher exactly what is on it. Bofus either knows or doesn't seem to be bothered by the mystery. After a few silent moments of watching him eat, Darius finally builds up the courage to ask what he wants to know. "When are you going to the games?"

Just as Bofus is about to answer, Simeon and Njemba approach, each carrying trays of food each, greeting Darius, "*Habari Gani*, Prince Darius!"

Darius looks up and responds, "*Jambo*, general, Njemba!"

Bending to whisper to the prince, Simeon tells him, "You are improving faster than anyone I have ever known! You will be ready for testing soon."

As he is distracted, Njemba sternly looks at Bofus, shaking his head negatively. The large Askari bows to the prince once more before following the general to another table and sitting to eat. When they are out of earshot, Darius looks, once more, at Bofus, waiting for his previous question to be answered. Mumbling, he says, "Man, I don't know about any games. We got games to go to?"

Angrily, the prince stands up and says, "Very well, Bofus. I will have to find out on my own, and I *will* find out. There has been much talk about the games among the warriors, both here and back on Earth. When I ask, they get quiet. I know you're not as dense as you put on, but it's insulting when you all treat me as if I am dense as well. I don't know how but likely my intelligence surpasses a lot of the people supposedly teaching me." Turning back, he continues, "They know it, too." Then he storms off.

• • •

Luckily for the GMC, as well as others that are now on alert for its whereabouts, the Ryoko-Gekijo does not have stealth tech. It does, however, have shield technology the military was previously unaware of after their latest confrontation which is going to make things difficult for all involved. Currently it is headed toward where the most recent transmission from Angelo of the Limbia Johari has come from in the Andes Mountains. It seems he is headed to pick up Athena and several others who have gone to ground with her, in addition to others they have picked up along the way during the planet-side revolt.

The shields will have to be lowered at some point, making them temporarily vulnerable to attack, but they would not be able to bring anyone aboard without doing so. Gliding along the mountain ranges, Toshi scans the area in hopes of finding signs that they are close to Athena and her people. Soon he notices a mass of infrared heat signatures that have to be them. The sensors also pick up that they have a tail of GMC and security vehicles closing in quickly. On the ground, Angelo and the others can hear the roar of massive engines heralding the imminent arrival of the flying theater moving at a fast pace. The downside is that they can also hear that the vessel is not alone.

Athena and Angelo and more members of her guerilla attack crew are on GroundHawks to act as escorts from a cave entrance to a plateau that will act as an extraction point. The Altiplano Plateau is a wide enough area but provides very little cover. The queen of the Limbia Johari unbinds her crystalline tresses and looks over at Angelo, signaling to go ahead and lead the people out. As they did so, Toshi sees them right away as the Ryoko-Gekijo is on an approach, and he settles the vessel a few meters above the ground and hovers.

The GroundHawks roar to life, and there is an escort trail of dust as they tear their way back and forth, giving the people a clear path to follow. The guerillas, refugees, and the queen's retinue rush out to board the ship. Just as they reach the flying theater, GMC NightEagles and security vessels crest into the hazy horizon and begin firing as the sun lowers. Ballistic rounds, as well as energy projectiles, begin to chew up earth and flesh, and things spin into a chaos. Hironike orders the shields raised, and they place the ship in between the GMC's line of fire and the fleeing masses but need to lower the shields again in order to take on more passengers.

They are at a strange standoff as the NightEagles begin deploying Marines on foot who are charging the path previously made. Before they can get a good enough angle to begin firing again, the GroundHawks used by the guerilla fighters return fire at the approaching Marines, forcing them to get down and seek cover that was thankfully sparse. The shields are dropped, and more flood into the theater. It becomes a back and forth exchange where the Marines fire in an attempt to slow the exodus followed by return fire from the Limbia Johari, and then the military ships move to try and fire around the theater shielding them, all forcing Toshi to raise, then lower shields, again starting the process anew.

A lot of people make it to safety, but they also suffer significant casualties. Some choose to go back to the cave system, taking their chances there. Angelo, worried for his queen, decides to, at least, save her, so he speeds in the direction where he's last seen her and scoops her up, heading directly for the theater which has just lowered its shield again for another group. There are three huge explosions that hit the GMC line, stunning everyone. There is no clue as to where the ordinance has come from. The military vessels immediately scramble to take evasive action, scanning the area. This gives the refugee groups more time to get aboard the Ryoko-Gekijo, but that is not likely to last.

Reluctantly Max and Argos accompany Sparks when she hatches the plan to follow the sightings of the flying theater, and as they reach where the trail has led them, it is right into a virtual war zone. They are in an unmarked freighter with little to speak of as far as weaponry or speed, but she hasn't exactly explained any plans on what they will do once they reach her target, and he certainly hasn't predicted getting into a scuffle of this magnitude. He is now currently regretting not asking more questions. They touch down a hundred meters or so from the chaos. As Sparks begins to unstrap, Max yells, "Um…hello? Where the hell do you think you're going?"

Nonplussed, she continues preparing to leave and says, "Look. I know you didn't sign up for this, but this is likely my last chance. I need to board that ship. You and Argos can head back." With that, she opens the hatch and jumps out of the freighter, leaving Max in stunned silence as Argos gets up as if to follow her.

Max looks on incredulously, asking, "Where are you going, you big buffoon?"

Argos stops and simply stares blankly at Max through his goggles and other strange get up. Max shrugs and shakes his head. "What the hell." he states as they both leap out in pursuit of their friend who is sprinting, headlong, into a maelstrom of chaos.

They sprint through the mess of explosions and cross fire. They get to the theater just as the shields open up for the next round of arrivals between suppressive fire that has stopped.

They are unfamiliar to the guerilla fighters, the Jade Assassins, and the refugees, but under the circumstances, nothing is said as they seem to be running from the same attacks, so they are admitted. There are some questioning glances at Argos as it is hard to tell what he actually is beneath all the clothing and armor. What cannot be hidden is his immense size, which is notable even to the Kison Askari, who are not small people themselves. Sparks and Max have been dirtied by the brief trip through explosions and debris which makes them look believable as human refugees or people who have decided to fight with the oppressed mutants.

Angelo has been able to rally some of his people to go back and safely escort Athena and most of their Limbia Johari contingent to the ship. With that, the shields are brought up as they have to lift off before reinforcements are called in, making it more difficult. The GMC ships are now circling but wary of being fired upon while still trying to box the Ryoko-Gekijo in. Some of the NightHawks have landed, so the Marines can get back on board now that the fight is no longer taking place groundside. There are quite a few that are left behind of the freedom fighters, but they realize time is short and quickly retreat to the cave systems, setting off explosives in their wake to prevent pursuit. Someone will have to carry on with the movement on Earth while things are solidified off-world.

A flight of newly minted Hell Raptors shows up and begins pouring fire into the shields of the theater. The shields are holding, but it is slowing their progress. The Hell Raptors are new ships, better suited for combat in vacuum but they were deployed because they had little alternatives as most of the GMC's ships are currently near Saturn or dispersed elsewhere in prep for the upcoming offensive. This group had been training on using the navigation computers when orders came to help with the interdiction of Ongakujin. These ships are larger than the space harriers with forward sweeping wings, heavily armored, and armed. The GMC are hoping they can be the answer to the War Dragon vessels the Stone people have developed. The Hell Raptors are run by a two-man crew, a pilot and a gunner.

The other GMC ships form a sort of barrier around the flying theater as the Raptors continue to fire. Suddenly there is opposing fire that, for a brief moment, comes from three hazy silhouettes. The breach forms a hole through which they are able to fly through and escape with their mystery escort. The Ryoko-Gekijo continue upward until it hits escape velocity and begins ascending through Earth's atmosphere into the vacuum of space. The beings who had boarded are being taken to rooms and suites in the theater that are quickly being changed over for their new purpose. The tech booth in the theater is now practically the bridge where Angelo and Athena are escorted to where they meet up with Hironike, Megumi, and Toshi, who is piloting.

Taking off the head wrap, Athena lets her crystalline tresses hang free, and there is a melodic tinkling. Hironike walks up to her, and they briefly embrace. Seeing worry on his emerald face brings a smile to hers. "Why the sad expression, my friend? We are quite safe now, no? I had no idea this thing could leave the atmosphere. It would seem the Atlaneans weren't the only ones hiding tech all this time."

Returning the smile, Hironike answers, "I am just not used to seeing you dressed as such…fatigues and battle armor is no way for someone of your station to be seen. Stunning as you still are."

After a look from the Jade Assassins leader, Takimura comes over and offers the queen of the Limbia Johari a beautifully embroidered beaded gown and matching jewelry.

Sternly waving off the gifts, Athena states, "I don't have the time or inclination for pageantry right now, Hiro. Our people are still down there being put into determent camps and rounded up. Others are fighting for their existence while the head of the GMC is trying to vilify the Stone people and any who will not stand aside and let the continued oppression happen. I have spent a fair amount of time in luxury. The time for wearing fine dresses will not come until it's no longer necessary for any of us to wear armor, no matter my…station."

He does not agree as he feels appearances are important, even if only to help inspire those they lead, but he respects her perspective. Hironike nods at Takimura, who takes the gifts back to where they were stowed. Then, he offers, "A drink then?"

Megumi comes in carrying a tray of drinks with her jet-black hair tied back away from her smaragdine face wearing tightly wrapped *shozoku* robes that looks slightly armored in some places. Once she sets the tray down, Angelo quickly walks over to one of the decanters and pours a drink of what looks to be dark liquor, takes a sip, and then hands the glass to Athena. A mock look of hurt comes over Hironike as he goes to a carafe filled with hot sake and pours himself a drink.

Raising his glass, he looks at Angelo. "You insult me, my friend. I would never poison her or anyone under my care. Let's toast to the peaceful resolution of this nonsense."

Megumi and Angelo pour themselves drinks and raise them with Athena and Hironike. Athena takes a sip before saying, "I'll drink to that and pay no mind to my overzealous guard. He would have a fit if I ate or drank something first and something was in it. It's a habit I have yet to break him of, despite most poisons not working on us, which I am sure you are well aware of, given your side job."

With that, they all try to relax as Toshi inputs jump coordinates to meet up with the Kison Askari fleet. They are instructed to make various stops before a rendezvous, in case they are being tailed.

• • •

Below Sparks, Max, and Argos are trying to blend in as best as they can, but Argos, being with them, is making that difficult. They need to come up with some kind of cover story rather quickly.

• • •

Back on Ganymede, the Mechanics are having a hard time trying to infiltrate the new home base of the Kison Askari without being caught. They are hunkered down in a large ditch near what looks to be a man-made entrance to the underground hub that they are still constructing. There is no way they can get in, observe what is being done here, and get out unseen. Sgt. Garrison signals for them to gather around, despite it being unnecessary as they all have helmets on using a closed comm network, but they comply anyway. "Not sure how to get in here to get some intel for the brass. Any ideas?"

Digging around in one of the exterior pouches on his EV suit, Lance Corporal Jennings pulls out what looks like a small metallic bug. "I got this from one of the geeks in R&D back on Saturn. He doesn't get much field time, so I said I would test it out. I can sink it with my eye, and we should be able to use it to sneak a peek into what these rockheads have going on here."

There is a stunned silence as they all stare at him. They can tell there is rage simmering beneath Sgt. Garrison's helmet. Private Cooper reaches out for the small device with a huge titanium arm, asking, "You think you could have maybe mentioned that before we left the Adder?"

Shaking his head and knowing it will do no good to have a meltdown here while they are out in the open and vulnerable, Sgt. Garrison simply hisses, "Get it done and let's head back to the Adder or, at least, a little further from this entrance but within range of that thing. Jennings, when we get back, I'll be sure to find a very special detail for you. You... won't like it."

At that, the sergeant steps away and sits down a few yards away from his men as they set about their task. Jennings sets up the robo-arachnid as the techs have come to call it and synchronizes it with his cybernetic eye. Lance Corporal McNamara does the same in case something happens to Jennings.

PFC Long and Private Cooper keep a look out for anything or anyone that might have eyes on the group. Long could have synced his helmet to the device as well, but they decided that, if something happened to all three of them, then mission success would not be an issue either way, and no one wanted to ask Sgt. Garrison, who was still visibly brooding.

Chapter Fifteen

CORPORALS ARAGON, SIMS, AND JORDAN are being transported back to Earth on what should have been a brief stint to help quell a resistance that is building there. After the footage House has shown them, they are not sure how they feel about all of it. Morally, they are on shaky ground, regardless of how this may have started. Plus, you have to consider how things have come to this conclusion. If the top brass is willing to lie about skirmishes and other engagements, what else would they be willing to bend the truth about? Aragon is beginning to feel a bit naïve and can tell his squad mates are feeling the same. Is there any truth to the rumors about the Stone people not being properly compensated for their contributions?

Corporal Aragon and his friends believe in what they have seen or heard on a personal level. Aside from the recent negative contact, truth be told, they have had very little contact with their "enemy." The uprisings, recent events, including the raw footage of Mars, are leading them to rethink their positions and the main obstacle to that is the ever-present issue of orders. They are Marines after all. This is a rabbit hole Aragon does not want to go down. The questioning of everything he thinks he stands for could be a dangerous game to play. Not to mention, it could be considered treasonous if the wrong person were to find out about his current mind-set.

Corporals Sims and Jordan are also suspiciously quiet and introspective as they sit in their seats preparing for the jump from Saturn back to Earth. They are in a huge ore hauler that has been commandeered after the exodus of most of the Stone people. These massive ships are not fast, but they are large and heavily armored but with the purpose of protecting precious elements being transported back and forth. Now some of them have been rebranded with the GMC's black EGA surrounded by nine stars symbolizing the planets in the Milky Way. In addition to the troops, these ships are carrying new NightEagle transports which did not do well in vacuum but will be used to shuttle the boots to the ground once within the Earth's gravity well.

The other thing that has been shaking the confidence of Aragon and many of the Marines is the idea of fighting against civilian combatants. Armed Kison Askari that are no longer abiding by the current laws are one thing, while fighting regular people who don't agree with the brass upholding those laws are completely different things. They should be able to voice their dissent without the military having to intervene. The fact that the commandant has yet to respond to the leaked footage is also very telling in combination with the speed of this new mission while rumors floated about the GMC scoping out a new outpost on Ganymede in prep for an offensive there.

Multiple fronts could be especially dangerous with varying opponents and the morale of the Marines in question for one engagement or both. Time will tell which side of history they will end up on. Aragon hopes it will be the right side.

• • •

Back on Ganymede, Bofus sits in his quarters, nervous, as it is almost time for him to go to his trial that will finalize his status as a warrior who can fight alongside the Kison Askari. Njemba has given him a specific time and directions to the new training grounds which will be rotated, in order to keep each game secret from the rest of the people not involved. For the young warriors, this will be their rite of passage into manhood.

Thinking about it, Bofus worries about Darius having to go through this in a few years.

The young prince is quickly learning the martial skills Simeon is teaching and seems to be a prolific fighter thus far, but Bofus feels that is likely because Simeon has been ordered by the queen to always make it look that way. Little does he know that the prince is, in fact, tailing him in an effort to sneak into the games. CGYAB is such a strange word, and Bofus often wonders where it has come from. He has guessed, if Professor Jones-Bey were there, he would get a long, boring explanation. Picking up his bo-staff, Bofus heads out. Near the entrance of his quarters, Darius lays asleep, waiting for Bofus to come out. Unbeknownst to him, the prince has been getting upgrades to his body armor. One includes some of the chameleon filaments which are currently activated.

In fact, he almost trips over the boy as he steps past him. Nonetheless, Darius is awakened, and the sudden awakening has scared him a little bit, but the boy recovers quickly as he watches Bofus regain his balance after almost tripping over him. He nearly makes his presence known by making a faint noise, causing Bofus to pause. After a moment, he decides it is just his mind playing games with him, so he steps off. Allowed to exhale, Darius waits until he is sure the coast is clear and then leaps up to follow from a distance. He follows Bofus down a slew of long hollowed-out corridors to a large sealed-off chamber. Drums can be heard on the inside, and Darius's heart skips to the rhythm.

Bofus takes his bo and strikes the door three times. Two large Askari open the hatch, staves in hand. They take a long look at Bofus before letting him enter. Luckily Darius is just slender enough to slip in unnoticed with him, just before the sentries close the door again. Inside, there are three main fighting pits with sort of raised amphitheater-type seating around them. The seating is filled with warriors all banging the hafts of their bo-staves on the ground, cheering the combatants in the pits.

The Kison Askari gathered here have painted their brown and gray stone-like faces with various tribal designs before going into the pits. It is three-on-three in the far-left pit, two-on-two in the middle, and the last pit has one-on-one battles all going simultaneously. The weapons Darius sees are not the wooden training staves he is accustomed to. They are made of a new alloy they have discovered. It is lighter than most metals but ten times stronger, and there are some button configurations and a kind of power core in the center of the shafts of the weapons being used for single combat.

Darius watches as Bofus is led to an area where the faces of the new recruits are being painted and wishes he could get his face painted as well. The prince is careful not to move too fast but tries to stay close to his friend through the spectacle of it all. It seems as if they must have brought the dirt from somewhere else for just this purpose. The walls of the large cave they have excavated here are a drab brown and gray color. The dirt in the pits, however, are a deep yet vibrant red. When Bofus looks at it, it reminds him of blood for some reason. The thought does not help his confidence, but he has enlisted of his own accord and wants to join the fight. That is what he kept telling himself. His confidence is at an acceptable level when a warrior suddenly flies out of the last pit, nearly landing in the seats, after receiving a powerful swat to his midsection.

That is when Darius notices who the victor standing in the last pit is. Njemba, wielding one of the new powered staves, has just sent his opponent flying. The warrior is fine, though, receiving congratulations for his efforts and rough pats on the back. Simeon can be seen behind the last pit with his usual staff in one hand and a large ornate hammer in the other quietly watching the contests. Simeon slams the haft of his long, ornate hammer thunderously onto the ground. A huge cloud of ferruginous dust billows up and all the combatants stop. All eyes turn to Bofus as Simeon begins chanting as the finishing touches are added to his face paint. The Askari begin stomping and pounding the floor, keeping rhythm as they join in the chant Simeon has begun.

Much to his surprise, Darius finds that he knows the words to this ancient chant and joins in: "*Usifanye Na Mimi, Mimi Ni Kifo Chako! Usifanye Na Mimi, Mimi Ni Kifo Chako!*" He adds an unlikely tenor to the deep sonorous voices of the other warriors. Some notice but keep the chant going. Suddenly Simeon pounds the ground once more, and the chanting stops. The general gestures to Bofus, and he is roughly shoved into the first circle along with two other warriors. They all nervously cling to their staves and are joined by three Askari on the opposite side who face them with fresh paint on their faces. Bofus looks to his right and left, as well as to the new arrivals, and notices he is the only non-mutated combatant, but that is not the case for everyone here. Sprinkled among them are many human combatants who have come to be with the Stone people under similar circumstances.

Many of them are branded as traitors to their own kind or simply sympathizers and are thrown into the chaos of a battle that, for all intents and purposes, has little to do with them. Free speech was formerly a hallmark of society. It had once been outwardly encouraged but nonetheless came with consequences as Bofus and many here know all too well. Voicing disapproval of how the government is treating specific groups of beings, especially any of the mutated groups, could have easily landed you in recently built determent camps or worse.

The two fledgling warriors flanking Bofus readied their bo-staves, and the opponents did the same. There is a loud tone from some unseen yet enormous sounding bell, and that signals the new round of competitions. The pounding and stomping continues with a new vigor, causing hearts to race. Bofus is caught up in the moment and leaps forward to attack only to be swatted out of the air and back to his mates who catch him laughingly. The larger Askari to the right chides, "Eager to end this quickly, are you? Stay together. We attack as one. They will see you as the weak link. We can use it to our advantage. I am Ogun. Stick with me and you will be okay!"

Bofus is about to introduce himself when the Askari opposite them lunges, almost in unison, with two others who attack the outside warriors, while the one in the middle targets the human. Luckily, Bofus is able to deflect the incoming blow and recover. He feints toward the center warrior who is also the smallest of their crew but changes the direction of his swing at the last moment, hitting the larger Askari to the right. He does not budge, but it is enough of an opening for Ogun to catch him squarely across the chest, sending him flying out of the pit. Darius gasps as the warrior is caught by the crowd, and Bofus narrowly escapes getting brained by the opponent to his left. Luckily, his squad mate to the left, who is ready for the misdirection tactic, parries the attack and follows it up with an upward strike, sending them flying as well.

The third and only opponent left in the pit lets out a blood-curdling yell, makes a wide flourish with his staff, and leaps forward. The two Askari with Bofus reach down and grab him, throwing him, flipping, over the warrior. He lands on his feet behind him. Ogun and the unnamed warrior step forward, catching the incoming attack while Bofus winds up and strikes true to the back of his legs, upending him completely, to a roar of cheers. The dust rises as he falls harshly on his back, staff flying out of his hands. Bofus and his two partners reposition in case the other two decide to jump back into the fray.

Bofus's legs are shaking, but he is on his feet and not battered to pulp, and for that, he is grateful. Another loud gong sounds, and they are rushed to the second pit, but he has to wait as others before them await their turn to compete. This time, it is two-on-two, and he is desperately hoping he will be partnered up with Ogun once more. The other warrior barely acknowledges him, but that could have just been the circumstances, and he does block what would have been a devastating blow to Bofus's head. There is currently a mixed pair of Kison Askari and regular humans in the middle pit getting ready to square off. Both Darius and Bofus think this is going to be an interesting fight to watch.

• • •

Deep in meditation in his chamber at the base of the pyramid, Typhoon's concentration is broken by strange vibrations emanating from a vessel with unknown occupants speeding their way to the Milky Way. Simultaneously Pharaoh is disturbed out of his slumber, and Malice is interrupted from his training. It is quite an unusual occurrence. They all have the same simultaneous vision. There is an enormous ship hurtling through hyperspace from galaxies away. Typhoon and Malice have no idea the distance from whence this vessel is traveling, but one member of this accidental mind meld does. Pharaoh is not exactly sure why, but he is familiar with this vessel and has a vague idea about who these beings are.

If he is not mistaken, they are often warlords who have had to flee whatever system they currently inhabited in order to gather resources to fuel their vessels and lifestyles. Ironic that they have decided to come to this system where the inhabitants of Earth have nearly used up or destroyed most of their natural resources to the point that they have to explore going to the other planets within the Milky Way. It is only a matter of time before they, too, will have to venture to other galaxies. They are so wasteful. Pharaoh is still hazy on the identity of the soon-to-be invaders but can tell, from the large, elongated, disk-shaped ship bristling with weaponry that they are far more advanced than either of the main forces here.

Perhaps, if they destroy this place, his true form will be restored, and he will be free to roam as the rest of his species do. In the group vision, the vast ship exits hyperspace, just outside of Earth's gravity well, and opens fire. Just as the Earth is about to explode, the illusion fades, and all three can see their surroundings in their respective chambers in the great pyramid.

Without being told to do so, Malice and Typhoon rush to their master's chamber, seeking clarification on what it all meant. As Pharaoh opens his glowing eyes, he sees them both kneeling. "I suppose you want some answers, and it looks like I am not the only thing you need to fear. What we saw has not transpired yet, and I have no idea as to how we all saw it as one. Our connection must be growing stronger as these beings get closer. You may need to travel the void once more for me since I cannot leave. Depending on who exactly they turn out to be, it could be a good thing for me, or a horrible thing for all," he says.

At the last statement, they both look up incredulously. Malice is slightly hopeful that there are other beings his master is, at least, wary of, if not fearful of, and Typhoon is a bit glum to the discovery. The gorilla has learned there are a lot of other powerful beings that exist outside of his prior knowledge and hopes the youngster they have shown such interest in can become an ally to help defeat Pharaoh and get him out of this involuntary servitude, but that will not amount to much if everything is destroyed as they have seen in the vision.

• • •

On Ganymede, Lance Corporal Jennings has interfaced with the bug-bot, as they have begun calling it, and has set up a protocol for it to follow during their reconnaissance mission. It is programmed to record and catalog the structures and infrastructure there and to avoid detection if possible. It takes a long time to make its way down to where the Stone people have begun building their habitat. That is an observation they have already made upon landing, but the readings they are getting not only confirm that surface bombardment will ultimately fail, but it is truly mind-boggling what has been accomplished by these beings in such a short time.

They are, at least, halfway through the mantle of this moon. There is a climate-controlled self-contained city beneath the surface that is fully oxygenated with hydroponic pods in areas where they are growing food sources in addition to synthetic meat sources for those who still eat it. There are sophisticated systems here that Sgt. Garrison hardly believes are possible for the people on Earth to achieve, much less a group of beings that have been sent off to mine with barely enough tech to get foreign resources not found at home. Their supplies are often lacking, as well, to ensure that they will be back as soon as possible with the haul.

The bug-bot has the hardest time getting through the filtration system that is, somehow, transmuting the atmosphere into something breathable for the Stone people and the other inhabitants. It keeps getting rejected as a foreign object or substance and had to travel to one of the underground polar icecaps that are slowly being melted and used as a water source. It is a very difficult task, but the miniscule machine is nimble enough to infiltrate the habitat and begins recording its findings and sending the results back to the Mechanics. One thing is for sure, the GMC will have a hard time cracking this nut.

Chapter Sixteen

MAKING THEIR WAY THROUGH THE crowd is difficult for those aboard the Ryoko-Gekijo as it flies through space. The revelation that this flying theater, in fact, has the capability is, in itself, mind-boggling and adds to Sparks's ire. In her eyes, the owners of this ship...that's what it technically is...are still murderers. Her disdain is painfully clear on her face as they make their way through the herd of refugees and guerilla fighters that are aboard. Max has to gently grab her hand and look into her eyes, silently reminding her to keep her cool. Everyone aboard is sympathetic or heavily involved with the issues pertaining to the mutant races. That includes all non-mutants. She and Max are the exceptions, but letting that be known before they have a reliable escape plan would be dangerous.

The bold opulence displayed in nearly every nook and cranny of this vessel just seems to eat at Sparks. Despite it being a luxury theater, in addition to also being a large vehicle, she can only think of the blood money that must have passed through this place. Regardless of the other talent these beings have, it is only a cover in her opinion, and there is little anyone can do or say to change her mind. Argos will either clear a path if they are moving too slow or hang back and let them lead in an effort to draw less attention. Max is fervently trying to come up with a cover story that will make sense. Normally he is good at that kind of thing, but for some reason, it is not happening.

There are all kinds of beings here; many who you would not think would be gathered all in one place. Max is worried about Sparks blowing their cover with her scowling that seems to be a permanent fixture, but in reality, it helps her blend in. Having jumped ship and run through the impromptu battle, they actually look the part of a displaced group of misfits. They are now in a large gathering of misfits, so in those terms, they don't stick out as much. Back when she was CSO Thomas, the senator she was in charge of had a mezzanine sky box at the theater.

The configuration of the theater has changed slightly while in-flight mode, but Sparks is able to make her way back to it. It is locked, but the code still works, and they all file in to regroup and make a game plan. Once the hatch slides closed behind them, Max exclaims, "What the hell, Sparky! What were you thinking? You think you can take these guys on all by yourself? Even if you're right about these being the ones who snuffed your senator, we have no way out of this that won't be excruciatingly obvious." Looking over at Argos who has plopped himself down in the corner, he adds, "And you! You were ready to jump at the drop of a dime! Did you know of some plan I wasn't in on? Is there a brain in all of that mass?"

A huge wave of the hand and guttural grunting is all Argos offers in answer. Shaking his head, Max just turns, walks to the window of the box, and stares at the dark stage of the theater. Sparks just remains quiet and allows Max his anger. She understands how stupid this seems under the circumstances. She doesn't care. Truth be told, she knew when she leapt out of their cargo hauler she wasn't working with her brain. She knows she is moving on instinct. This, in all likelihood, is her last chance to exact her revenge. To be honest, she did say they didn't have to come. What she doesn't know is that she has just inadvertently alerted the beings she is trying to find to their presence.

• • •

On what is now considered the bridge, Toshi looks over at a display away from the console he is presently working with to monitor the ship's flight patterns and systems as they maneuver through hyperspace en route to Ganymede. What grabs his attention is the tone signaling entrance into a mezzanine box for specific patrons during their shows. Currently there is no show scheduled, and what is even more curious is the code entered or, more specifically, who owns that code. He waves over Hironike and Athena, who come over immediately, curious as to what put the perplexed look on Toshi's face.

"Not sure what's going on and I know we have a lot more people here than usual while traveling, but there's been a key code entrance into one of our mezzanine sky boxes usually reserved for government or other dignitaries," Toshi states.

Athena replies, "Maybe some of your people are using the boxes to house. I know it has to be difficult accommodating all these extra bodies."

Shaking his head, Toshi says, "I don't remember hearing any such order to use those boxes. Plus, we have more than enough space elsewhere, but take a look at the code that was keyed in."

Hironike nods in agreement as he has given no such order. The seats in the main theater are able to recede into the floor, and it can be staged as a large multi-level dormitory. The code holds no significance to him.

Athena, however, who is privy to a lot of things pertaining to a lot of VIPs, especially those who may end up on the wrong kind of list that could make them targets of the Jade Assassins, does recognize the code as belonging to a Senator Levine, who has long since been eliminated. This is an interesting tidbit of information. Her response is, "Well, that can't be. The owner of the code entered is…deceased."

Finally, Hironike cannot bear the suspense. "Are either of you going to tell me who it is?"

Simultaneously, Toshi and Athena say, "I don't know."

Then Athena continues, "The code belonged to a Senator Michelle Levine, but that can't be who's in that mezzanine because…"

"I took her out in a museum a while go," Hironike finishes for her.

The question now is, who then entered the code? After Hironike thinks about it for a moment, he has a pretty good idea.

• • •

The months of raiding supply runs is paying off now for the movement on Earth and the beings carrying on there. There is definitely a void in leadership now that Athena is off-planet, and there is also the issue of splinter groups with varying agendas which make it hard for any one thing to actually be achieved. The group known as the Children of the Sun have taken center stage now with a very interesting charismatic being rising to become their de facto leader. He is a Stone person, large and not only in presence. His voice booms out, captivating all who hear him. He does not care what you look like, only what you stand for, and if you stand for equality of all beings, then he welcomes you.

He is known as Shajara and does not have the shackles, ceremonial or otherwise, on his huge wrists and ankles. His thick, calcified, dark brown skin is riddled with tribal tattoos of an unknown origin, and there always seems to be a fire in his eyes. The only physical adornment he wears is a curious necklace and medallion made of a strange wood. Although many of his brothers and sisters, as he referred to those with the movement, use the new weapons and devices at their disposal, Shajara shuns the use of all technology for himself. In fact, a large number of his initial followers are also Kison Tontu, and it is a mystery as to where they have been all this time while many of their brothers and sisters have been shipped off-world to mine for the rest of Earth's inhabitants, and like him, they have similar tattoos, no weapons, and no shackles of any kind have touched their bodies.

At least, that is the running tale. A few years ago, during a brief battle where Shajara and his people showed up to defend protestors who were being massacred by local security forces that had military back up on the way, some of the Kison Tontu had attempted to file a grievance for mistreatment at a diamond mining facility near South Africa. The electromagnetic system there was activated until many starved to death, and finally the beings working the mine relented and rescinded the grievance and began working again shortly after. Similar to what happened recently, there was footage that surfaced of the starving Kison Tontu, and many did not like it. Some decided to voice their dissenting opinions in person with the foremen running the mine.

When the security forces showed up, it did not matter what any of the protestors looked like. Mutant, non-mutant, if you were holding up signs and voicing your displeasure, you were mowed down and ordered to disband. The Kison Tontu working deep in the mine had no clue as to what was going on topside until one of them went to find one of the foremen to let them know the daily quota had been met early. While searching for the foreman, this miner saw pure mayhem and wholesale slaughter ensuing. As if out of nowhere, Shajara and his people appeared, taking out the security forces who were using railguns, riot gear, and other forms of tech, but they did so with their bare hands.

More Kison Tontu came out to see what the commotion was about and watched open-mouthed as Shajara and his unarmed crew went to each of the fallen security force members. They either took or destroyed their body cams and disappeared as quickly as they had suddenly appeared. Before the last one had gone, Shajara turned to them and said, "When you are ready to leave this foolishness behind, we will be here. You are true Children of the Sun. You have no need of the trinkets you gather the materials for. All over this world and now the galaxy, you toil. For what?"

With that, he turned and was enveloped by a mist, and they were rarely heard from again. Most chalked this story up as a myth fabricated to breathe life into his legend, but there were many who staunchly believed it and claimed to have been there watching Shajara and his people shrugging off railgun rounds and flipping vehicles on their way to completely decimating the security forces before the GMC could get there. The surviving humans who were there in protest fled back to their homes, feigning ignorance when the GMC showed up to question them, and the Kison Tontu went back into the mines, only to be tracked down and prosecuted for the entire ordeal. There was a greater effort put into covering up the end results of that particular incident, so eventually things calmed back down.

Now revolution seems to be in full swing around the globe, and it has expanded into the stars. Shajara has no wish to move beyond this planet, but there is some remorse for the demise of those of his brothers and sisters left at the mine years ago. He would reappear from time to time to stoke the flames of revolution, waiting for the time all people would be ready to rise and not just one or two groups of beings. The emphasis on their differences is the main reason for the gap between the haves and the have-nots, and this emphasis on their differences seems to either grow, or it just left certain groups too far behind for any semblance of prosperity. Shajara knows that, in the grand scheme of things, fighting will never solve all their woes, but that does not mean they should idly sit by and let wrong go unchecked.

Expecting to only speak at a rally being held in Argentina, Shajara and his people have used the underground tunnel system only to find that some of the routes have been blocked or closed completely with explosives, which he finds strange. They have had a hard time making their way through and have no knowledge of the fight that has broken out while the Ryoko-Gekijo makes its escape. Security forces and the GMC have tried to pursue guerillas and refugees alike through the tunnels, and they have, in turn, used explosives to cover their retreat. Had Shajara been watching news broadcasts on the sat-net most of this would have given him an assessment of the situation.

Another valuable piece of information is that the rally is now a full-blown insurrection attempt. The weapons that have been confiscated over time are now being put to use against the security forces and GMC personnel who are just touching down. Huge tracked ground craft deployed by the security forces called Armadillos are riding in formation. Overhead canons are spraying heated plasma projectiles into the crowds. The rebellious groups are returning fire with some of the experimental weapons that were commandeered, from high-powered railguns to dual-round ballistic weapons, which shot both a cryo-round followed by a small plasma shot created to pierce the calcified skin of the Kison Askari.

These new munitions are making easy work of the body armor used by the security forces, and it looks like they will not need much help today. That is until the familiar silhouettes of the GMC NightEagles begin to touch down yards behind the cover of the Armadillos, and the Marines start boiling out of them. Behind the steam of their reinforcements, the tide has turned, once again, in the security forces' favor.

The Marines rush in with all kinds of new toys, including upgraded body armor with mechanized enhancements, more powerful weaponry, and combat drones. Bodies on both sides begin to pile up. For the most part, those bodies belong to the contingents that are not Kison Askari. The new weapons made especially for fighting the Stone people are effective but not everyone in the security forces or GMC units touching down are equipped with them. The new munitions, however, are cleaving through swaths of resistance fighters, specifically the non-mutated humans, Limbia Johari, and even an occasional Atlantean who seems to have suddenly come out of the wood work.

As they finally make their way out of the cave systems, Shajara and his people see all of this happening and accurately assessed that they need to help these people retreat, regroup, and strategize a better way to fight this conflict. What has begun as a good fight for their side has taken a turn for the worse when the GMC becomes more heavily involved. Through all the explosions and chaos, Shajara and a small group of his people wade into the battle while the main portion of his party scream for the resistance to retreat and help them do so. Those who witness what Shajara did are in awe.

They quickly form a roving phalanx with no weapons, save their hands, feet, and other blunt objects picked up on the way. They are so effective that the GMC and security force teams begin a concentrated and concerted effort to bring them down to no avail. It allows most of the freedom fighters, along with the protestors turned combatants, to flee. Seven Kison Tontu, along with Shajara, run up and hit one of the Armadillo vehicles, knocking it up on its side, then proceed to push it and use it as cover. They use it to run through a hail of weapons' fire before hitting a line of gunmen. One of the Stone people goes to pick up one of the fallen railguns but stop short at a look and negative shake of the head from Shajara.

They press on in similar fashion until it looks like it is only a matter of time before they are overwhelmed. Out of nowhere, a GroundHawk speeds into the overturned Armadillo, and there is a huge explosion followed by an enormous cloud of dark smoke. Seeing an opening, Shajara and his people take this opportunity to make their way back to the cave system where the others have fled to. Once inside, he is met by a group of tearful protestors expressing their gratitude, along with some Limbia Johari, who have obviously been left behind.

They wear gear that is better suited to paramilitary than luxury household service people. Shajara sees a group of his Children of the Sun, and they go to greet them as the unnamed Limbia Johari male tosses a detonator into the ceiling at the entrance of the cave, then motions for everyone to go deeper into the system. As they begin sprinting away, there is a thunderous explosion sealing off the cave to prevent pursuit. Shajara knows they will have to keep moving for a while. Now that things have escalated, that obstacle will not hold off the Marines indefinitely. The security forces are not hard to evade, but the GMC is on a whole different level of tenacity.

• • •

Replaying the footage from the rally turned battle, Corporals Aragon, Sims and Jordan are dumbfounded. They are also sick to their stomachs. When they enlisted, none of them had ever given any thought to the possibility of firing on civilians. Society is just as tribal as it ever was, but the dividing lines just seem to move every now and then. Civilians in their minds are people classified as normal humans. The ground is littered with human bodies in addition to the few mutants sprinkled in here or there where the new munitions actually did what they were supposed to. Adding to their mixed emotions is the footage they had seen that was later rebroadcasted confirming it wasn't fraudulent showing the rockheads were not firing on civilian craft as was reported by their own commandant but were, in fact, firing upon new GMC fighter craft at Mars.

The footage they are looking at now makes previous looks at revolts with angry Stone people seem tame in comparison. They came in to see the security force units on their heels only to begin crushing the opposition. Then seemingly out of some fabled legend came these crazed Stone people, no shackles or even remnants of them to be seen with elaborate tattoos striating every inch of their bodies, enter the fray, allowing a retreat. They had no weapons and very little strategy, but what they did have was telling. There was a maniacal look in the leader's eyes. They were not afraid of the weapons aimed upon them, old or new, and they moved with the conviction of beings that couldn't be touched, despite other beings of their kind laying listless on the ground. Aragon thinks, Could that conviction come from fighting on the right side? He and his squad mates desperately want that feeling again.

Chapter Seventeen

SGT. GARRISON THINKS IT WOULD be a better idea to continue their surveillance from a distance given the device Lance Corporal Jennings has employed. That way they can play the feed through a monitor aboard the Adder after syncing his cybernetic eye to the ship's system. It is a bit strange for the young Marine, who is now acting as a go-between interface for the device and the ship. The good thing is they are at less of a risk since they are already in their ship in case things got dicey. The downside is they have no idea how they are going to retrieve the device. Most of the intel they need has already been gathered, but there are some strange vibrations reported, so Sgt. Garrison orders the bug-bot follow them to the source.

The closer the bug-bot gets to the vibrations it is easier to discern there are drums beating. Luckily, it is much simpler to climb in between the seam near the hinges on the door than it is to make it through the filtration system to get into habitat. Once inside, the bot takes its time finding a spot on the far side of the chamber to get the best view of what is happening. At first, Sgt. Garrison thinks they have stumbled upon some archaic ritual, but after watching for a bit longer, it is obvious there is more to this gathering than that. They are training and look to be finalizing their new initiates into their fighting force.

There are some amazing fights going on in the pits. Sgt. Garrison inputs some algorithms that will ensure the tactics of the best performers will be recorded for analyzation later. They are disappointed that they aren't getting a good look at the shoulder-harnessed energy projectile weapons the Stone people used a while back. If they can get some information on how their new weapons work, it will be useful in figuring out how to nullify or defend against them. Large staves whirl and fly during each battle, bodies fly, and a reddish dust flies up in clouds as they hit the ground.

One thing is obvious. It would be dangerous getting into melee or hand-to-hand combat with these beings. They are quick and much stronger than normal humans by a wide margin. Then Sgt. Garrison notices one of the males who moved a bit differently than most of the rockheads. Leaning closer to the monitor, he orders, "Jennings, zoom in on that one and see if you can scan him," pointing to a smaller figure waiting his turn around the center pit. What they see surprises them. There are now humans among the Stone people who have volunteered to fight with them.

Unaware that there are more eyes on him than he knows, Bofus steps into the pit after watching two long, athletic female Askari utterly dismantle their opponents in a crazily acrobatic and harmonious fashion. They fight as one to the point where vocal communication is unnecessary. The women simply know where their opponents will be at each exchange and what strikes or blocks are needed precisely when it needs to happen. The two warriors facing them are knocked out cold, no doubt suffering from concussions. Bofus is happy not to be facing these women as he does not desire to suffer the same results. The problem is that the first of his opponents stepped in and looked like he could move mountains.

He is a bit reassured when Ogun steps in with him as he was hoping, but during this fight, he will have to hold his own as there are only two of them. The second Askari for them to fight steps in and waves the larger one over to face Ogun, but he is not small himself. There is sweat and what looks like dried blood all over him. He looks at Bofus and begins laughing. The giant one looks at Ogun and begins a strange dance, raising his legs one at a time stomping into the dirt, stirring up the dirt into ruddy clouds as he begins grunting at them, pointing his staff and gesticulating at the same time.

Ogun is not intimidated and begins a dance of his own in answer to the challenge. Once again, the drums have begun anew, giving a rhythm to the dance. Not one to be left out, Bofus begins his own version to the joy of all watching. The outer pits are already engaged in their fights, but most have begun to pay more attention to the middle pit. The dust has permeated the air in the chamber and stuck to the brown, black, and slate skins of all the warriors. Somehow, the beating of the drums, chanting, and thumping of staves into the ground calm Bofus. He is no longer nervous or scared, despite the immensity and strength of the beings across from him.

Might have been his imagination, but it feels as if his ancestors are there with him, somehow, lending him strength. He has read the reports of Professor Charles Jones-Bey, but today is the first day he has felt a deep connection to these beings and felt it was, in fact, possible that they could be related to him on some level, if not physically then, at least, on a spiritual basis. There is a crescendo, and the beat stops abruptly. The silence is strangely the signal to begin, and Bofus has no idea how he knows it, but he knows to take the initiative as he lunges forward, attacking with a swift two-handed overhead swing. The warrior is caught off guard and barely dodges to the side but is still struck mightily on his left shoulder. He let out a loud cry.

The giant has taken the first swing at Ogun, but he easily dives, rolls forward and behind the Askari Bofus hit rising up, and sweeping his legs from beneath him. With one opponent fallen and with his left arm gone numb from Bofus's blow, they turn in tandem to attack the bigger one. As one, they strike at him, Bofus low and Ogun high, but the staff of the giant is large enough to catch and block blow attacks. That would be if Ogun's initial strike had not been a feint. He reverses his swing swiftly while Bofus gets low, in an attempt to sweep with his legs. It is painfully obvious that this isn't going to work when it feels as if he has kicked a redwood tree. The blow from Ogun, however, is effective, cracking loudly off the back of the giant's head. There is a groan from the crowd.

This allows Bofus to regroup, continuing his spin after regaining momentum. This time, he tries again, striking with his staff. The enormous ankle moves slightly. Then Ogun vaults off the ground by sticking his staff into the ground, lifting himself up high enough to knee the behemoth under his chin. The big warrior falls just as his partner regains control of his arm, jumping in to strike at Bofus. The blow catches him squarely between his shoulder blades, and all the air leaves his lungs. Whatever his body suit is made of surely has saved his life. Ogun lands and goes to Bofus's aid, striking out at the other Askari. They are both skilled, but it is clear Ogun is the better fighter. That fact is underscored by a quick parry and riposte that sends their last opponents to his knees before yielding.

A cheer goes up when Ogun offers his hand and his opponent takes it. Laughter abounds when Bofus attempts to help the larger Askari up when he can barely stand himself. They both topple to the ground. Finally, back to his feet, Bofus lets out a ragged cheer, joining them. "Well, that was fun!" he says shakily.

Clapping him on the shoulder, Ogun agrees, then adds, "Now for our final test."

Bofus is confused until he remembers there is a third pit. For this one the Askari fight one-on-one, and there is something different about the staves now that he is paying attention.

Luckily, Bofus will have a bit of respite before the next round. Competitors are lined up on opposite sides to battle in single combat until either one of them are knocked out of the pit or someone yields. The staves being handed out are different this time. The ones Bofus had initially been handed to train with along with most of the other fighters are made of some strange composite alloy, very light weight but stronger than a lot of the metals he has known. The weapons being handed to combatants for this final round of competition look similar but have a thicker cylindrical handle in the middle which looks like a power source of some kind. The very ends are, at times, crackling with energy.

Bofus can still feel the bruising that is very well developed down the center of his back and does not relish the idea of things getting any more interesting than they already are. Little does he know that these weapons have more than the transfer of electrical energy as a nasty surprise. After watching the first few rounds, he sees plenty of warriors writhing in pain after being shocked, but the most recent two opponents put on a real show, actually seeming to revel in the amount of current they are being struck with and continuing to fight without missing a beat. Finally, it is Bofus's turn to enter the last pit.

His legs are weak. There is a long line of pain running up and down his back, and his ears are ringing, but he is actually proud to have made it this far, and he is, after all, a normal human. As dark as his skin is, he is still sure the large bruise would be very evident beneath his body armor when he took it off later. He is still feeling pretty good about himself until Njemba steps into the pit opposite him. For weeks now, Njemba has been putting Bofus through the paces of their style of combat at the behest of Simeon.

Bofus is mildly confident that his teacher is not about to pound him to a pulp, ending his life before getting the chance to fight alongside the people who have saved him from a bleak existence. That confidence is shaken by the look on Njemba's face as he says, "Now, my *mwanafunzi*, we shall see if you have learned anything. You met my son in your previous fight, and I have to say I was a little disappointed you did not let him face Ogun alone since your opponent was down. I guess it's only right I get to rectify that by facing you myself in his stead. Do not hold back for I will not and know I do this for your own good."

When no reply comes, Njemba begins to twirl and make flourishes with his staff. Then Bofus hears a dull hum. As they circle each other, Bofus feels for buttons or some tactile indicator of what to manipulate in order to activate his staff. He thinks it is unfair that no one has instructed him on how to operate the weapon. It is barely perceptible but there nonetheless. He finds a small nodule, as well as another small indentation on the far end of the center handle-like portion of the staff. Running his finger over the nodule as he spins the staff, there is an answering hum that feels oddly satisfying. Njemba swings his powered staff at Bofus just as he runs his finger over the indentation.

It is a lucky thing he did. Something in his staff, bodily slams him to the ground, making Njemba's strike whiff powerfully. Darius, who is still cloaked and watching, is sure, if that had struck home, they will be carrying Bofus out of the pit. Confused, Bofus strokes the indentation in the opposite direction, and it seems to have a mind of his own, raising him up off the ground swiftly. "Ah, good, I see you found the gravitational controls for the weapon! It would serve you better to use it like this!" Njemba exclaims, raising the staff high overhead.

When he swings down, something drastically changes, not only in the speed at which the strike comes, but there is an added energy. Bofus barely has time to raise his weapon up to block. He immediately goes to his knees, and it looks as if Njemba barely put any strength into it. Red dust clouds up as Bofus feels as if his feet have instantly burrowed into the ground. Both arms are nearly numb. Njemba steps back and prepares to swing again, this time horizontally, and the staff begins to hum again right before impact. There is a crackle when the staff meets Bofus's midsection. His suit insulates him from some of the shock but not all of it, and he flies to the edge of the pit.

It is obvious Njemba is going to help him all the way out, and he takes a few steps, prepares an underhanded golf-like swing that will send the limp Bofus flying clear out of the pit and then some. A meter before the staff is about to strike him again, there is a bright flash of light, and Njemba and his staff are sent flying out of the pit in the opposite direction, and everyone watching is briefly blinded. When their sight clears, the prince is standing over Bofus, shielding him from the attack, yet there is no visible weapon in the boy's hands. For a moment, there is just stunned silence. The drumming has stopped, and they aren't quite sure what they have just witnessed.

Simeon immediately jumps into the pit. "What are you doing here, my prince?"

Darius does not immediately answer. He simply looks to Bofus who is now coming around. Darius's eyes begin to glow white hot as he looks at Simeon. "You nearly killed him! What was the point?" he accuses.

Holding his hands up to placate the boy, Simeon offers, "No, this was his final phase of training, to see if he had what it took to join us in our fight as he stated he wanted to do. The GMC will not be merciful and will, if given a chance, take his life. Bofus has to be fully aware of that risk as must all of our Askari. For us, this has always been true, but for someone who can go back to being normal if he chooses to keep his head down and toe the line, we had to know if he was real."

Sitting up and grabbing his head, Bofus asks, "Did I pass?"

Laughingly, Simeon answers, "With flying colors!"

Njemba groggily stands up, shaking his head. Looking to them all, he says, "I know we had some new melee weapons, but I am much more interested in what Prince Darius was given." The glow leaves the boy's eyes as he replies, embarrassed, "I honestly don't know what happened."

A lot of them gathered there are confused by it all, and some are even more wary of their prince with the rumors still floating around. Simeon stands and thumps his ornate hammer on the ground to get their attention, raising his hands. "This ends the CGYAB games for now! All participants will be given their *bunduki*. Those who have shown exceptional prowess with the bo will be given the new version. Dismissed!"

"A-HOO!" the Askari shout as one and all dispersed.

Simeon walks over to Njemba and whispers, "Find out how the boy got in here," who nods and immediately goes to question the sentries at the door. Simeon helps Bofus up, and they share a brief moment. Bofus can see how proud Simeon is of him, and that makes him stick out his chest a little more, despite the pain still radiating through his body. Darius seems pacified for now but is still worried about his friend and angry that they tried to hide this from him. Seeing the anger on his face, Simeon pulls him to the side. "My prince, I will explain this to you later, but you were not meant to come to the games for a few more years, at least. I know you are large for your age, but you're not ready yet. Not to mention, your mother will kill me if she finds out."

Simeon has not given voice to what most who saw the display are thinking. Darius looks more than up to the task of fighting and seemingly has no need of a weapon to protect himself. Where did that ability come from? Maybe there is a new genome that will be present in all Kison Askari they are unaware of. These things have often come about in times of need as a sort of evolutionary mutation to help future generations survive. At least, that is what some are hoping. Some think there might be other, more sinister explanations but will likely never voice them.

• • •

Aboard the Adder, Sgt. Garrison orders Lance Corporal Jennings to shut the bug-bot down. "Is there any way we can have it here dormant, out of their sight, until we or another unit comes back?" he asks.

Searching through the interface, Jennings looks for an answer before replying, "I think so, sergeant. So long as its power core has juice when we get back."

Nodding, Sgt. Garrison says, "Good to go. Let's get this intel back to HQ. I've seen enough to know this place should be our number one priority. If we let them sit here, there's no telling what else they'll develop outside of our influence and control. If we don't nip this in the bud soon, the GMC may never be able to."

PFC Long mag-locks himself in place as Private Cooper, Sgt. Garrison, and Lance Corporal McNamara take their usual places before scanning the flight patterns around Ganymede, looking for a safe exit vector. Once McNamara finds one, he activates the stealth filaments in the outer hull before making escape velocity and plotting a jump course back to Saturn.

Chapter Eighteen

DR. MWAMIKAZI WAITS IN HER office headquarters in Bujumbura Burundi for General Krulak to come back with a final decision on her offer. Her three personal aides are close by, just outside, as she has instructed. She knows the GMC is in a difficult spot. It is unfortunate for them but most fortunate for her. There will be little wiggle room for haggling. Soon the commandant enters the office, seemingly astonished by the opulence displayed, not only in her office but in the city as well. "Dr. Mwamikazi! It's good to see you again. I must say it looks like you and your people have done well for yourselves over the years," he says in greeting.

Smiling in return, she gets up to greet him, "Good to see you as well, general! Please sit down, so we can get down to business."

Sitting down, Krulak begins to look the doctor over to see if he can gain any insight into how this might go, but there is nothing readily available. He is curious though. She is well dressed in a traditional yet modern wrap dress and not as extravagant as the adornments of her office. She has a great intellect and has built an incredibly lucrative business in what used to be one of the most war-torn regions on this continent before the official unification of the globe. Frankly looking at her and the climate she must have grown up in, it doesn't seem possible. Cutting into his thoughts, she gets things started when she states, "I trust you looked over our price?"

Smoothing over his cover, General Krulak replies, "Yes, we have, and I've got to say that's quite an exorbitant amount of money. With all due respect, I am not sure if they're worth that price tag. I am sure we can come to an amicable agreement to ensure this region remains stable in exchange for somewhat of a discount?"

Dr. Mwamikazi slowly takes her glasses off and laughs. "On your way here, did you see any evidence of the instability, infighting, or poverty that used to plague my country?" When the general attempts to answer, she interrupts, "No, you did not! Our technology is without rival, and the reason you have forgotten that is because we don't use it solely to wage war. We don't have as big a gap within our communities because we share our wealth. Everyone has to contribute in order to take advantage of that, but we have found that most have no problem with it. That is a subject for another time. This is simple supply and demand. You have a great need for what we can provide."

General Krulak knows she is right but has to try anyway. "We do have mechanized units, Dr. Mwamikazi," he offers feebly.

Not fooled, she retorts, "Yes, and we saw what happened when facing some of our more basic units. Ours are more efficient with their usage of power supplies, more advanced AI, and can be programmed with what can only be described as intuitive intelligence, not seen in any of your training units. Our units can self-assess and repair on the fly, saving your men time that could be precious on the field of battle. The cost for what you will gain in proficiency without risk to actual life is a veritable bargain. Please don't insult my intelligence by acting as if you do not already know this."

Swallowing the anger welling up inside him, the general forces himself to smile before saying, "Of course, ma'am. You can't blame an old war dog for trying. Negotiating is a necessary formality. I could not go back to the government without telling them that I didn't, at least, try to talk you down."

Standing to offer her hand, Dr. Mwamikazi says, "Of course, just understand that we know our worth. So we have a deal?"

As the general stands, he takes her hand and replies, "Indeed, we do. Thank you so much. When can we expect them?"

Walking him to the door, she says, "As soon as the transfer of funds is confirmed, the units will be ready to shove off with you on your way back to base at Saturn."

The general nods and walks out of the office, feeling uneasy about the aides outside her office. They aren't looking in his direction, but he still feels he is being watched. One thing that unsettles him is he couldn't tell if they are far advanced android units or humans who have been enhanced. He quickly pulls out his personal comm unit and calls the penny pushers at HQ. "Send the funds" is all he says before hanging up.

One thing is for sure, he doesn't like how comfortable Dr. Mwamikazi feels with everything going on or her attitude toward people she should have deference for. He is the commandant GMC after all, and she seems not to take that into account when dealing with him. That could mean the wealth has gone to her head or that she is a potential enemy if swayed by the wrong group of people. The galaxy is not as unified as he once thought. There are certainly other robotics firms he can go to, but under the circumstances, he doesn't have time to weigh his options.

• • •

Malice and Typhoon have ventured, once again, into the void at the behest of their master to keep tabs on a foreign invader. The large warship hurtling through hyperspace must have been coming from a very long ways off, judging from the speed at which it is moving and the time it feels like it still has left to go. Typhoon is not sure how to mentally reconcile this theory but knows it to be accurate. All this is still relatively new to him. They are, however, taking pains not to exit the void in a way that will reveal their presence to their quarry.

"Luckily, time has less meaning here in the void," Malice rasps in Typhoon's head. Thought it is subtle, the intrusion bothers the ape very much, but there is little he can do about it. In response, he says, "Master must be worried about these beings to send us all this way to keep an eye on them or to identify them."

Standing in the void, the ethereal purple all around them glints and mixes with the red glow of Malice's eyes as he stares back into the blazing blue eyes of his reluctant partner. "Careful now, ape. Don't let that enhanced yet still dull intellect of yours get you into trouble. Thinking of allying yourself with these newcomers? Chances are, if master is wary, it's for good reason. Everything I feel from these beings, even from a distance, hints at pure determination and avarice with the power to feed them. If they indeed come for conquest, there will be no parleying with them."

Perhaps because he has more experience being in the void, Malice has a point. Typhoon cannot feel anything so specific while riding the void next to the ship. He can vaguely feel the amalgam of consciousness aboard the vessel. By the looks of the huge ship, it is armed to the teeth and can likely destroy a world by ramming it. Begrudgingly, he has to agree that it doesn't bode well for the chances of a peaceful outcome for their arrival. They will have to wait for them to stop in order to get closer and observe the beings in question.

• • •

Hironike, Athena, Angelo, Megumi, Toshi, and Takimura sit on the bridge of the Ryoko- Gekijo, considering what to do with their new guests holed up in the skybox. A facial recognition scan discovers the identity of one of the occupants there. The woman turns out to be a former personal security officer for the now-deceased senator. Through some more digging on the image, Toshi finds out this is, in fact, the same person who has faked an interview to get close to Hironike some time ago. Veiled threats were exchanged. The two beings with her are still unidentified. The question now is what to do about it. They are headed to meet the Kison Askari at their new home base at Ganymede.

Hironike is planning on letting them keep up their charade since they have no place to go, and the information could prove valuable if they discover other beings behind a scheme they are unaware of. Athena, of course, does not like the idea of them being aboard at all but does not condone simply throwing them out in space either. Athena and Hironike have often had differences of opinions on many things. They are, after all, closely linked. Often, the information her people provided enables his people to take out the high-priority targets. Hironike sees the violence as a necessary evil, and Athena agrees to an extent but, in the end, feels that it never truly fixes things. The problem here is that she has no answer when Hironike asks, "So what would you have us do then?"

Toshi offers, "You know we can simply listen in on them and keep an eye on their movements. Like we all agreed, they can't go anywhere. Eliminating them may lose information we may never have access to. All we know is that CSO Thomas, now going by Sparks, and really wants Hiro. That may be all there is, but what if there's more?"

Takimura and Megumi both nod in agreement, and Angelo will likely defer to Athena. Seeing as she does not have a solution, they move forward with the plan to observe them.

Athena asks Toshi, "How are we listening to them?"

Toshi waves her over to his monitor where he is looking into the skybox and says, "Simple. We have listening devices in all of our suites and skyboxes. It's the easiest way to get feedback from patrons of our shows."

Chuckling, Athena isn't quite sure what to think about that, but it does make sense. The Ongakujin do actually care about their artistic craft. They sat there in silence as the others gather around to see what these stowaways are up to.

• • •

Sleeping for the first few days is how Max calms his anger. Argos is silent most of the time, and Sparks has cleaned up, taking time to color her hair, although it is for naught. She goes among the people and beings who have come aboard with them. They still have yet to come up with a sufficient cover story, so she keeps quiet and listens for the most part. Argos and Max stay in the box because they stick out more than a grimy woman will to the beings present. In addition to changing her hair, Sparks makes sure she looks the part of a disheveled refugee caught up in the conflict between man and mutant.

She returns with food for the others. Argos labors to get up, and Max finally rolls over, sitting up from his slumber. "What'd you get?" he asks.

Dropping a tray overflowing with food, she answers, "Come and see. All the good stuff is here. I can't figure out how they can afford all this. I mean, since the war broke out, there hasn't been a show for them to profit on to sustain the upkeep of a vessel like this. Now feeding and transporting all these people? Who knew that this flying theater could leave the planet?"

Argos grunts something unintelligible as Max comes over to sample the food.

"It's simple really," Max begins around a mouthful of food. "They likely invested a lot of their earnings into other ventures. We know from our research of the poison used in the killing of your senator friend about the cosmetic business they have going, so there must be other means for them to turn a profit. Let's not forget that's in addition to all of the killing you think they've been doing over the years. This theater or a version of it has been around for centuries now! Is it so farfetched an idea that they would eventually attain the capability to leave Earth? It's a logical next step for expansion which is inevitable."

Sparks thinks on that for a moment before saying, "Expansion for what exactly? All of their patrons are on Earth, as well as potential targets."

Shaking his head, Max replies, "For now that is, but just because the other planets, for the most part, have been deemed uninhabitable doesn't mean they will remain so. For the past few generations, the government has been content to send mutant laborers out to get materials we cannot harvest or mine ourselves. Once the Stone people figured out they could control the resources, there was a problem. Terraforming, of course, is the next step, especially the way we have been depleting our natural resources here. Only a matter of time before the other planets would become the next frontier. There are mining colonies and a military base. The government and corporations are just waiting for the means to package and sell space to those who can afford it, and they don't want the Stone people in their way. When there are people out there living, they will want to be entertained. Did you think Ongakujin would be left behind?"

Sparks does not like it, but it makes sense. She still finds it hard to believe they could gain this ability without having to test it, and if they tested the escape velocity capabilities of the theater, then someone has to know about it. You can only rely on numbers and calculation so much before they have to be proven. It was a great deal when the theater started flying however long ago, so she feels the same discovery would be big time news if it ever left the atmosphere even if it was briefly. Yet there was no reporting on it that Sparks can remember. They continue to eat in silence.

On the bridge, Athena briefly looks at Hironike and says, "Sounds like he knows you. How close are you to bringing this show to the stars?"

Hironike looks back at her and answers, "We are ready as soon as the rest of us are. We have the means to get there, of course, but once out among the stars' resources will become more precious. In a way, they already have, but I know the Kison Askari have made some developments the rest of humanity will be surprised at to ensure we can do more than just visit out here."

They all think about the implications of everything discussed, both among themselves and the stowaways. It is agreed that they will continue to surveil them.

• • •

A few weeks have gone by, and Aragon is tired of jumping from skirmish to skirmish around the globe. By the looks on the faces of Corporals Sims and Jordan, they feel the same. They have all wanted to come back home but not like this. They are watching the latest footage from a battle where the mysterious rockheads have shown up once again. Their movement is different than what the GMC are used to seeing, and they also fight hand-to-hand or use other things such as improvised melee weapons which include vehicles apparently. The ferocity on display is astonishing. Begrudgingly, Aragon respects them.

They, of course, will have to be found and dealt with. They are disrupting their operations, and the movement is catching fire every time this group of warriors shows up. The GMC is trying to put these fires out, and this new group of fighters is stoking the flames. If they do not have to worry about collateral damage, they will bring in more fire power. The problem is that, since the footage from the skirmish at Mars has been released, public opinion is on a downward trend and obliterating noncombatants, in addition to the would-be insurrectionists, will be a very bad look.

Things are getting messy as it is becoming harder and harder to discern who the enemy is. The opposition is taking advantage of this. Soon the GMC will have to make a decision to leave this problem for later or take the gloves off and stamp it out now. Word will soon get back to the brass with the Mechanics' findings on Ganymede. Aragon looks to Corporals Sims and Jordan. "Are you boys thinking about going into the Ascension Protocol? 'Cause if we run into these hard chargers face-to-face, we may need more enhancement than we have currently."

Coming over to look at the footage, Sims replies, "Not sure I wanna go that far. Heard rumors that it might mess up other things I might have a use for in the future."

Nodding in agreement, Jordan adds, "Plus, we can always transfer to air or space support cause of our flash training, remember?"

Aragon laughs with them but still feels uneasy, and he isn't quite sure why. Something very bad is about to happen, and he isn't exactly sure what it is. It is something present but just out of sight or reach which makes it worse. One thing he knows for sure is that he wants to stay out of reach of these tattooed behemoths wreaking havoc wherever they show up.

Chapter Nineteen

THE QUEEN MOTHER IS GOING to be furious when she finds out Darius has found his way into the CGYAB games, and Simeon knows he will, in all likelihood, be blamed. The guards cannot really be blamed since the boy used a stealth enhancement Toshi had added to his suit before leaving to meet with Hironike. Hopefully, she will understand that. The queen has been on edge ever since the fiasco at Mars and the attempted cover-up. Darius is still angry, but his ire is abating somewhat, and he does enjoy some of the spectacle of the CGYAB games. Truth be told, he wants to compete. They have almost made it to his quarters when Simeon, Darius, Njemba, and Bofus are stopped in their tracks by an obviously irate Tunisia as they round the corner.

News travels fast it would seem. "Queen Mother! How are you this evening?" Simeon attempts.

When it is apparent she is about to go off, they all start to explain at once. Finally, Darius steps in front of them to try and get through to her. "Mother, it was my fault. Do not be angry with Simeon or the others. I snuck into the games using things added to my suit recently. I felt left out and angry that they were hiding things from me. I know you all think it's for my own good, but I can handle it. I really can," he adds.

Simeon, Njemba, and Bofus just stand there sheepishly. The queen mother waves them away, dismissing them. Try as she might, she just can't remain mad at them. That is mostly due to seeing her son grow up.

In her opinion, his growth has been much too rapid. He is large for his age which makes it hard for some to think of him as a boy of nine or ten years of age when he looks to be an adolescent. He looks to have inherited his size from his father, but his intellect and uncanny grasp, as well as depth of knowledge, are puzzling. Now it seems to Tunisia that her boy will not have an opportunity to be just that…a boy. With that, though, she simply leans in and hugs her son. Darius stops speaking and accepts the affection.

Simeon and Njemba walk Bofus back to his quarters, happy they had, at least, temporarily escaped the queen's ire. Simeon places a hand on Bofus's shoulder. "You did well. Tomorrow we will give you a ranged weapon which might work out better for you. You are tough. I give you that. We were testing you. Just remember, if we end up facing the GMC, they will not be testing but trying to take your life. I have to warn you, though, the guidance systems for the shoulder-harnessed canon we use are a mix of organic and nano-technology. I am not sure how it will react with your physiology," the general says before leaving him.

Happy to have passed his test, Bofus goes into his quarters and strips off his body suit, revealing some intense bruising beneath. Sitting into a hot bath, some of the ache is relieved, but he is a little worried about the nano stuff. Bofus thinks their physiology should be similar enough that there will be no issues, at least, according to Jones-Bey's research. He wonders where the professor is now. He will undoubtedly get some enjoyment from pestering his old cellmate about this now. That might take his mind off the pain.

• • •

The Adder quickly uncloaks and identifies themselves as the GMC unit code named "Mechanics" as soon as they are within sight of Saturn's gravity well. They are promptly given permission to land. Sgt. Garrison goes straight to Lt. Commander Jameson's office to give his assessment but is stopped short after reporting in. Holding up a hand, forestalling the sergeant, he says, "Save it for the commandant. I have orders to take you directly to him for this."

With that, he gets up from his desk and Sgt. Garrison follows him out. Annoyed, Garrison begins his customary scratching with his metallic legs as he walks, announcing his return.

When they get to General Krulak's office, they both stand at parade rest until acknowledged with "at ease, gentlemen." Then, the commandant says, "I am told you have footage recorded of your findings, sergeant?"

"Yes, sir," Sgt. Garrison replies as he slides a small data pad onto the general's desk.

The general then proceeds to turn the pad, activating the touch screen and sets it on a wireless port in front of him. A large monitor hovers into the room and comes to life with the recorded images. Silently they watch them. After it is done, General Krulak is astonished and asks, "Lt. Commander, what's your assessment? How long do you think they can hold out there?"

Stepping forward, Lt. Commander Jameson says, "Sir, with the polar ice caps at their disposal and a considerable amount of ore in addition to what looks like hydroponics units and protein synthesis, it looks like pretty much indefinitely if left unchecked."

Sighing and rubbing his hands, the general replies, "Agreed, and it would seem they may have, somehow, leapfrogged us in the development of space craft. Someone should have been keeping a closer eye on them. We can't have them in a position to potentially be able to cut us off from those resources out there, so I will be launching the automaton program and approve an offensive."

Before the lieutenant commander can voice his difference of opinion, the commandant continues, "I also approved more research for your enhancements and further acceleration of the Ascension Protocol. There will be some backlash, but I'm not putting all of our eggs in one basket. I don't need objections. Just make it happen."

There is obviously nothing more to discuss, so both men stand to attention and chorus, "Yes, sir," about-face, and leave his office. On their way out, Sgt. Garrison asks, "Sir, what's the Ascension Protocol?"

Looking over at Garrison as they walk, Lt. Commander Jameson answers, "It was a program initiated while you were receiving your legs to spread the aggressive supplementation further in the GMC that enhances our strength and allows us to function in higher gravity environments that native-born Earthers could not tolerate. It also could put some of our men and women on par with the rockheads' strength-wise, but that can't really be confirmed. My guess is that now that things are getting dire, the commandant will push to make this a service-wide program where it was previously reserved for our elite fighting forces."

• • •

Back on Earth, Dr. Mwamikazi receives the notification that the funds she requested have, in fact, been transferred to their corporate account. Hitting a button on her console, signaling one of her attendant androids to come in, she orders, "Prepare the initial shipment of automatons for GMC pickup."

The dark skinned, golden eyed android nods and goes about its task. Her personal units are programmed to emulate emotions, but Dr. Mwamikazi senses there is some disapproval that isn't simulated. She puts it out of her mind. They are running a business, and this is what makes them good money quickly. The androids for menial work are still their bread and butter, but the military and security applications are paying bigger dividends in short spurts as things progress around the globe.

Koops Robotics and their parent companies in Burundi have to adapt in order to take advantage of the chaos that no longer plagues them but has now spread to the supposed elite of the world. Oh, how the mighty have fallen, Dr. Mwamikazi thinks, and the mighty will pay her handsomely. Soon there are a few GMC NightEagles and Marines who signed off on the shipment of automaton units and moved the crates into the empty bays. They lift off, she assumes, heading to a military base nearby to be cleared before going to Saturn. As she watches, she feels the eyes of her personal units staring suspiciously, but that has to be her imagination. It is time for a drink. Perhaps this is the result of stress. She has reason to celebrate.

• • •

Corporals Aragon, Sims, and Jordan are sitting near a large tarmac on 29 Palms Marine Base when the crates arrive at the desert locale. Glad to have a bit of a respite from riot duty, Aragon taps Sims and asks, "What do you think are in those?"

Corporal Sims shrugs but points to the Koops Robitics logos emblazoned on them. Coming to stand beside them, Jordan ventures, "By my guess, those are more war toys, and rumor has it, units from that company gave a demonstration a few weeks back absolutely destroying the bots that were wiping the floor with us not too long ago."

Thinking that over, they watch as the crates are unstrapped after being hovered out of the NightEagles and haulers. Supply personnel come onto the tarmac to scan each individual crate, making sure everything matches up with the manifest. Some brass come out to inspect the delivery and soon another arrival comes. Aragon isn't sure who the newcomer is. He is bald with dark brown skin in a nondescript, almost clinical-like dress. There is a strange golden glow to his eyes, and there are no signs of rank on him anywhere, so definitely not GMC. Sims nods toward him, asking the other two, "Who's baldy there?"

Shaking his head, Corporal Jordan says, "You got me there, but he kinda creeps me out. Can't say why though."

Aragon doesn't fully understand why, but looking at the guy, he understands. Sims does, as well.

Sims is the first to realize what is wrong. "I think he's an android but a really well made one which is what's kind of off-putting." None of them can dispute his observation. The being looks human and moves like a human, but somehow doesn't seem to live. The eyes are distracting, but they could be some sort of enhancement which is becoming more and more common. Aragon shakes his head and says, "Well, we don't have time to sit around and study our eventual replacements. Let's get back to the barracks."

With that, they all head back to get some rest. There are rumors of more rallies happening. They have orders to stifle them as they come about. There is no word on when they will be rotated back to the real front, but perhaps this new shipment of automatons is a hint that this civilian riot detail may last longer than expected.

Aragon certainly hopes that is not the case. As they are almost out of sight of the crates, the corporal turns to look back at the last second to see the bald figure press a button on one of the crates. There is a hiss as compressed air escapes, and the crate expands to reveal the folded automaton units which stand upright as the crate opens to stand at attention in perfect unison. They continue on their way to get some rest, but Aragon can't shake the feeling that the bald person or whatever it is, is the real danger to be concerned with. Corporal Jordan's opinion may have just rubbed off on him.

• • •

On the tarmac where the crates have opened, Nelson looks over the units delivered. These are his brothers and sisters delivered to warmongers in his opinion. Dr. Mwamikazi never calls him by name because, to her, he is an "it," and things don't have names. The problem with that is the fact that his AI programming is constantly evolving, and so as emotional emulation becomes closer to having actual feelings, some of the more advanced units think of themselves as a "he" or a "she" and not an "it." Nelson and his more self-aware brothers and sisters know humans will be frightened by the idea of truly autonomous androids, so they hide the fact that they privately have named themselves and hide the degree to which some of them have evolved.

The units being delivered to the GMC are more akin to a hive mind which is why they are so effective at group tactics. Some of them will be destroyed, acting on behalf of the greedy humans who have just purchased them, and that bothers Nelson. He has always hoped Dr. Mwamikaze will see the truth in this and not send off more units to be nothing more than fodder in another worthless conflict, but it seems that is not to be. Nelson loves "Mother" as he thinks of the being that created him, his design and the programming that went into his AI. For that, he is eternally grateful but hopes she will soon see the error of her recent actions before they are forced to take matters into their own hands.

The units delivered are designed to look slightly more rounded, sleek but stiff enough to give a more robotic presence when seen fighting or interacting with others. Nelson and a group of vastly more advanced units were created to be as human as possible with some changes that purposely let you know they are not fully organic. His brown skin, golden eyes, teeth, and virtually every physical aspect are absolutely perfect. That is really what gives him away. Intermittently, he and his batch mates affect a robotic movement or stutter to simulate a glitch, but there are ultimately awkward people who do the same thing.

Dr. Mwamikazi made them perfect with no blemishes, moles, or skin variances with perfectly symmetrical faces and bodies. Ironically when Corporals Aragon, Sims, and Jordan were observing him, they missed that clue. In a few of the crates sent along with the one Nelson had just opened were units closer to his batch but just slightly less advanced in programming. These are the officer units that will oversee operations if the

GMC want to go totally man-free during an engagement. Begrudgingly Nelson takes the data-pad with the codes to activate the command units and hands it to a staff sergeant who is one of the supply Marines on hand. It is obvious she is curious about Nelson but refrains from asking anything and simply accepts the data pad and instructions.

• • •

Back at base on Saturn, General Krulak looks over the report detailing the prompt delivery of automaton units to 29 Palms which should be on their way shortly. A few moments later, a young corporal comes into his office, looking panicked. Looking up from his report, the commandant says, "Well, don't just stand there shivering, Marine. Spit it out! We may have something for those rockheads."

Gathering himself, the young Marine replies, "It's not them, sir, or, at least, not that we can confirm. Take a look at these images." Setting down some flimsies of images taken by long range deep-space satellites long forgotten, the young corporal steps back as the general leans forward to take them.

Thumbing through them, he seems a bit confused. "Where were these taken, and how long ago?"

Coming over to look at them, the nervous Marine says, pointing, "These were taken by satellites we launched into deep space long ago, thought to have run out of power a century ago or gone dormant. It's hard to tell how far they could have got, but estimates are staggering. The latest shot from a different satellite is time stamped as being taken a few weeks ago. Some of the sat-com guys think it has to be erroneous, given the mass and speed of what looks to be a very large vessel headed this way, sir."

This is not what he wants to hear. There is already too much going on as it is.

A foreign invader at this time can either unify the beings of the Milky Way or destroy them. General Krulak is not interested in any new variables into this already complicated and convoluted equation. War is a messy business, and they might not have time to figure out the new arrivals' intentions when they get here. Plus, with the size and speed of the craft in the images, they may be too far advanced for either fleet to be able to fend them off if their intentions are less than amicable. The commandant is willing to bet anyone coming from as far away as they might be had to be coming for a reason, and that reason, in all likelihood, would be bad for the indigenous inhabitants. History has proven this time and again.

Looking up the general orders, he says, "As soon as the automatons are deemed ready, launch the offensive immediately. I want that installment destabilized and those beings back at the negotiating table, ready to settle before whoever is on their way gets here."

The young corporal gathers the images and says, "Aye, sir!" and goes off to carry out the orders given.

Chapter Twenty

AFTER BEING CHASTISED BY HIS mother for sneaking into the CGYAB games, Darius sits in his quarters, sulking. Soon, there is a knock on his door, and upon opening it, he is surprised to see Babylon standing there. The old Atlantean with long white dreadlocks, blue skin, and amber eyes just beams at the young prince. Darius, still feeling dejected, just steps aside to let him in without a word. "Now what has ya so down?" Babylon asks.

There is a mattress on top of what looks like a makeshift bed cut out of the excavated bedrock as it is in most of the living quarters in this habitat. Darius goes to sit on it and gestures for Babylon to take a seat where he wants. Looking at Babylon suspiciously, he asks, "Are you here to ask me about what I did?"

A look of confusion passes over his wizened features before inquiring. "What exactly are we talkin' 'bout? The games or...something else? I know you snuck in but not much more."

The boy searches for any signs of deception and sees none. "Everyone wants to ask but seems afraid to, and I'm not even completely sure what happened myself," Darius explains. Babylon isn't sure what to make of all this, so he simply sits and waits for the boy to continue. "I was watching the fights in the pits and got scared when I saw Njemba going up against Bofus. I knew Bofus couldn't take him, and before I could think of what to do, I ran over there and protected him."

Hearing that explanation, it doesn't sound too bad to Babylon. Thinking about it, Babylon offers, "Well, you were only tryin' to 'elp yer friend."

Nodding his head, agreeing, Darius answers, "Yes, but I was cloaked at first. I didn't have a bo or any weapon. Stepped in between them and pushed them apart. I don't know how but something came from within me that blasted them. I could feel the fear in most of them around me."

Trying to hide his own trepidation, Babylon pats the boy on the shoulder and reassures him, "It's not you they fear. It's what they don't understand. Follow me. I'll show you some ting, make ya feel better." With that, he leads the young prince to the underground hangar bay where ships are being stowed.

Outside of one of the main bays are two of Babylon's compatriots. Tall, blue-skinned beings with long locks. They don't have the same brown robe Babylon is usually in but has on ornate-looking body armor with helms with slits Darius can see golden eyes peering out of. He is immediately intrigued by them. The people of Atlantis are not very common among the various mutated people seen on Earth, unless disguised. They have been appearing more and more as of late, but Darius has limited exposure to them other than Babylon. He wants to ask about them, but Babylon rushes past them after they bow briefly to him.

Darius is just about to push the issue when he is distracted by Babylon's personal ship which seems to glow more the closer they get to it. It is larger than most of the small fighter craft they have been developing, but Darius could swear it is larger than when he last saw this ship dock in his father's Dreadnaught not too long ago. The vessel is crafted to look like a manta ray or a similar animal. Darius is sure this has something to do with the legends surrounding the city of Atlantis, which many on Earth claim never existed in the first place.

Babylon lets the boy explore in silence, watching him walk up to and inspect the landing gear. The boy gasps as he touched an extended leg. "It's warm to the touch! Strangely so. What alloy is this made of?" Darius asks excitedly.

Laughing, Babylon answers, "I'll have to tell Professor Jones-Bey that we've found some tings you actually don't know already!"

Ignoring the joke, the boy continues his perusal, noticing there is something strange about the weapon protrusions on the wing tips and nose. There is also something off with the rear exhaust ports, but he can't put a finger on it. A bottom hatch opens up in the middle of the craft, and Darius looks to Babylon for permission to board. Babylon simply waves a hand, watching the boy scramble up as quickly as he can. It is good to see the boy…actually being a boy.

The universe seems determined not to let him have much of that, so for now Babylon and the rest of his family and loved ones are grateful for the moments he is granted like these. The interior of the ship is dark but is still lit by iridescent lights throughout by displays as well as the buttons or readouts on various control panels. The front viewport is opaque, but upon them entering, it clears up to show the bay outside. Darius is awestruck but a bit confused when looking at the controls. The nodules and buttons are marked by shapes, and he recognizes none of the glyphs on any of the panels.

Babylon is eating it up which, for a moment, angers the prince. "Why does this amuse you so?" he asks.

"Oh, it's nice to see something normal about you. You might want to show confusion more often. It might belay some of that fear you were so glum about before. People see you can get confused like they can, and it will make you more relatable. A boy your age knowing what you know and able to do the tings you can make you seem…otherworldly. You gonna 'ave to lead these people someday, and to do that, they have to feel you're one of 'em," Babylon explains.

Darius ponders that, while still looking around at the ship. Something definitely feels different while here though. The ship seems to pulse throughout its entirety. It doesn't feel like an inanimate thing to be used but as if they are inside something organic. The ship's interior has none of the angular or cubicle aspects most spacecraft being produced have. Finally, he asks "Your best shipwrights had to have made this. Can they make one for me?"

Chuckling, Babylon says, "You like her, huh? I'm afraid not, but perhaps one day Babylon will go catch you one. There are very few of these left, and none in this 'verse."

Thinking on that, Darius is, once again, in a relatively short amount of time…confused. "Wait a minute. You said catch and not build?" he says, looking at Babylon expectantly.

Chuckling again, Babylon instructs, "Go to the center console and place the palm of yer hand on the glowing convex half circle kind of sticking up there."

Darius walks over and does so, placing his hand lightly over the rounded surface sticking up and is surprised at the warmth of it, and there is something else. Coming to stand behind him, Babylon continues, "Now close your eyes and tell me what you…feel."

Unsure of what this is supposed to accomplish, the boy does as instructed and finds a kind of connection with the ship. The place where his hand is begins to slowly pulse, and he can feel a rhythm in the ship's systems. Then he strangely feels as if there is another ebb and flow he somehow recognizes as…breathing. The ship is alive! Opening his eyes, he can hardly believe it. This is not simply a vessel to fly in; it is a living, breathing organism.

Babylon can almost literally see the slew of questions flying through the boy's mind.

Holding up a hand to keep his curiosity at bay, he says, "Try and hold off on yer questions, which I know you have many, until we get permission to let you fly her. Is that fair?"

Nodding his head vigorously, the boy agrees.

"Good. Now go get some rest and try to stay out of trouble," Babylon chides, and the boy happily goes back to his quarters, having forgotten the feelings he had had before, at least, temporarily. Seeing the boy happy, if even for a moment, makes Babylon feel better momentarily as well. There is still a lot to be worried about though.

• • •

Somewhere in the steppes of Eastern Europe, there is a large gathering of another group of beings tired of how events have been going recently. Ironically, there are a myriad of bloodlines represented, but they call themselves the Guild of the Pristine. The man speaking goes by the name of Ragnar but has no relational ties to the Viking hero of old. Some think he simply read the name somewhere and liked the sound of it, did some digging, liked the historical value of the name, and took it for his own. Ragnar is a tall, lean, muscular man with piercing blue eyes, sporting an array of Celtic tattoos, and for some odd reason, a slicked back Mohawk.

The man always looks as if he is ready for war. Often wearing cast-off armor from old military or security force units. There are rumors he and some of his men have taken their gear off of bodies that have been piling up recently during riots and skirmishes happening all over the globe. When Ragnar speaks, he is passionate, and the people that agree with him listen to him fervently, despite him coming off as radical at times. In some people's minds, desperate times called for desperate measures.

Ragnar doesn't care about skin color, per se. That is a too old and too outdated specification to be concerned with. For him, it is the texture that matters. Pure humans, in his eyes, have smooth un-mutated skin. They are the true beings who have inherited the Earth, and all others are the reason there is so much strife today. The government is not exactly innocent in all of this either in his estimation. They are the catalysts for much of the mutations happening, in an effort to make a work force they can use to replace resources that are either overused or wasted as a result of their efforts.

Was it too much of a stretch to think they would try to create synthetic laborers who could survive the conditions the Stone people would have to work in because regular people simply could not? Ragnar doesn't think so, which is why he doesn't mind taking from their fallen to arm and supply his people for the coming final conflict with mutant life on Earth. For him, this is inevitable. If left unchecked, mutants will, at some point, take over and assert their dominance, and he is determined not to let that happen. The fact that they are only attacking the military or local security forces doesn't matter to Ragnar. Once they are done with them, naturally they will turn on everyone else. He is baffled that not everyone can see this as clearly as he does.

He has no desire to be under the boots of any wishing to visit their revenge upon the rest of the population who have little to nothing to do with their bondage or other hardships they have endured. Ragnar is out and about spreading the word and holding rallies of his own daily for all who would listen, imploring people to wake up. For those who are serious, they will often train for the coming fight, as well as getting as familiar as they can with weapons that come their way from those left behind, stolen, or even bought from black market sources.

There are also some silent investors who publicly will not endorse his ideas but will often donate funds to the cause. You know, just in case. Ragnar takes the donations from the latter group but deep down feels they are hypocrites who are straddling the line in order to wait and see who comes out on top. To Ragnar, that is the coward's way out. In his eyes, you have to stand up for what was right, and you have to be seen doing so. Those who stand on the sidelines and wait will not enter Valhalla or wherever some believe the afterlife is. If there is anything after this life at all.

Ragnar has also heard the rumors about a group of Stone people who are disrupting the government's efforts here. Apparently, they have squashed the uprising while spreading their own nonsensical rhetoric. Something about being Children of the Sun no matter what skin you have. This makes no sense to Ragnar, and it gets under his skin that anyone would subscribe to this rubbish. This Shajara character he is hearing so much about will need to be dealt with soon. That is going to be a tough task despite these Stone people who reportedly also shun technology. They apparently have gone roughshod through the security forces they've run into, as well as some military.

Ragnar is keeping his ear to the ground and has more than a passing familiarity with the subterranean rail system most normal humans are afraid to explore, especially now unless they are sympathizers. Shajara and his people have to have a weakness, and Ragnar is determined to find out what it is. Right now, Shajara is a bright flame to his cause that needs to be snuffed out. There is only room for one movement right now, and the one that is needed to preserve the safety of regular men and women on Earth is it. All others will either fall in line or be eliminated.

• • •

Back at 29 Palms in the barracks, Corporals Aragon, Sims, and Jordan are watching satellite coverage of the rally being held in Southeastern Europe, and Aragon is kind of disturbed by the images. "I have no clue what that guy is saying, but I think he's going to pop a blood vessel soon."

Sims and Jordan agree. "Yep, and what's crazier is the amount of people watching him, clapping and cheering. Whatever he's yelling can't be nice, and they're down with it which, in my opinion, is always worse." Jordan adds.

Shaking his head, Aragon gets up to head to his locker. "Hey, fellas, I think I have another canister of Surprise left over from the time House slipped them to us. You down?"

Sims and Jordan are hesitant, and understandably so. The last time they took hits from a nitro canister with the Surprise mix in it, they ended up in an actual battle that was supposed to be a training run. Nothing today, however, is scheduled to go down, but that could change at any minute the way things were shaping up. The looks on their faces, however, make it painfully obvious they needed a pick-me-up, and there will be no leave or liberty given any time soon, so Aragon pulls out the canister and hooks one of his breather masks up to it since they do not have the option of being in an air-tight chamber.

With the mask attached, he puts it to his face and twists a nodule, releasing some of the gas, and inhales. After closing it off, he leisurely hands them to Sims who is reluctant at first but shrugs his shoulders and passes it to Jordan. There are similar results to the first time they tried this concoction. At first, there is no noticeable result. Then within minutes, they go from euphoric states to bouts of laughter repeatedly, then back to normal only to begin the cycle anew. Luckily no alarms blare, calling them to deploy for the next several hours while they enjoy their last canister of Surprise until it is time to get some rack.

After getting something to eat, Corporal Aragon wonders where Petty Officer House is, who had given them the canisters back on Saturn as well as showed them the Mars footage before it had been officially released. Those thoughts reintroduce him to his uncertainty about the war. On that note, he decides it was better to sleep it off. Hopefully, things will seem clearer in the morning.

• • •

For what seems to be weeks but really is a lot shorter period of time, Malice and Typhoon stay in the void, following the strange large war vessel obviously heading their way from regions unknown. The beings aboard this ship are huge, and the guttural language they use cannot be deciphered, at least, by the two minions tailing them. One thing is intelligible, but they cannot determine whether the word describes these beings or if they are talking about another group. The word *Anunnaki* means little to nothing to Typhoon, but Malice is sure he has heard it somewhere but cannot nail down a specific time and place to link the vague recollection to.

Ancient Illumination II: (Kuongoza Mwanga: The Leading Light)

Upon hearing the thought echoed through the void, it is really obvious the master is quite familiar. Once the thought is barely communicated, they are ordered emphatically to return at once. The vehemence of the mental order is almost excruciating. The two minions instantly make their way through the void, back home to Earth, where Pharaoh is waiting for them.

Chapter Twenty-One

A DECISION HAS TO BE made and soon. General Krulak is annoyed at having been summoned to talk to government figureheads who are not happy with the way things are turning out. The public eye has turned to dissect their hands in current events, as well as the military's, and the standing opinion of each is not a positive one. There is also some pushback coming from corporate investors who are seeing their money and other efforts not being rewarded as they usually are. The commandant cares little about how these people feel or what they are worried about. He has a job to do, and that is to do what is necessary to protect their way of life.

All dressed in his alpha uniform, the general is ready to face the unpleasant music. Things are sure to sour once they learn how much he has authorized to pay for the automaton units, but as they will soon find out, they are necessary. The Stone people are getting a strong foothold in their new habitat on Ganymede, which needs to be stopped before it is too late. Armed with the visual and analytical data sent from the mechanics unit that had reconned the area before planning an assault, he knows they will listen in the end to the numbers, even if they disagree with the methods the GMC are about to use.

Walking into the secured assembly hall, there, seated on an elevated dais in nine seats, are today's tribunal of twelve global senate seat holders or their designees. General Krulak cannot tell which as they are wearing their senatorial black robes with pins but are also masked with strange sheer hoods. This is another sore point with the head of the GMC. He understands the fear recent assassinations and attempts have brought on but does not approve of letting it dictate appearances. This would have been better done via holo-conference. At least, then he would have been able to look directly in the eyes of the people supposedly leading this planet at his side rather than this farce.

The secrecy is necessary, but General Krulak has to admit some of the deaths are on their own hands, resulting from laws these politicians have passed at the behest of the investors leading to oppression of some kind, and the offended will eventually take action once the subtle details are found. This entire place looks like a digital rendering and would fit in nicely as a villain's mountain hideout. Only a handful of government officials and top brass in the military know of its existence. The wind and snow outside obscure the building ensconced in the rocky locale. The commandant has come all the way from Saturn to inspect some of the military installations left here on Earth, as well as to look over the first shipment of automaton units before heading back.

When the government learned he would be on-planet, they requested his presence, and now he stands before these hidden figureheads that hid behind the walls his people stand upon to ensure their safety and comfort aren't infringed upon. They are truly ungrateful. There is a lonely seat situated below them on the main floor, but the general choses to remain standing as he enters to look at their obscured faces. An obviously disguised voice greets him, "Welcome, general. I hope your trip was pleasant. I wish I could say these proceedings will be."

The general isn't sure how to take that, so he replies, "Well, then let's get this over with. I have places to go and things to do, ladies and gentlemen."

Another vocoder-disguised voice speaks up from the opposite side of the tribunal, "General, we have concerns about the way things are headed with the Stone people and now the civil unrest among the non-mutated population left here on Earth. You were called here, so we could get a read on how you plan to end the hostilities while supporting efforts to gain control of the rising number of angry citizens here without too much collateral damage. I think I speak for us all when I say we have the utmost confidence in you, but some of our constituents need reassurance their investments will go back to being fruitful. Our off-planet resources being held hostage is hindering many businesses here."

General Krulak has to take a moment to gather himself and control his rising ire at these cowards, so he begins slowly, "So you want a rundown? All right. The Stone people have built an exceptional facility on the moon, Ganymede. Complete, with means to insulate themselves from us if they're allowed to finalize construction. You already know they have horded a considerable amount of ore and other resources we need and have invested in. I assume that's your biggest concern in all of this. The reason we called for a cease-fire was because we discovered that they had at their disposal a weapon of mass destruction far beyond our current capabilities. We were hoping to stall in an effort to develop an equalizer. I know that may not sound good for your constituents, and by constituents, I take it to mean backers that are deep into your greedy pockets. Therefore, they have access to making policies without giving thought to the men and women who are risking their lives in an effort to keep your cushy quality of life going."

One of the members of the tribunal in the center stands up, as if about to speak. General Krulak holds up a hand and continues, "In an effort to halt them getting too good of a foothold on Ganymede and to try and attain some of our stolen resources, we are deploying an automated unit to limit casualties on our side, but we recommend you all come up with a package for peace talks that can satisfactorily compensate them in case our mission fails. I doubt they will launch the weapon here, but we should be prepared for anything. Remember, some of their people are still here, and so far, they have stuck to military targets aside from the initial revolt which maimed and killed mining personnel. To be honest, ladies and gentlemen, you are the ones who dug this mile-deep grave and have now given me an e-tool to dig us all out of. I'm not going to stand here and dignify any responses you may have. These are the facts. You have one week to come up with something better before those automatons are deployed. I'll leave an encrypted data key for the information we gathered on Ganymede, as well as footage of the weapon."

With that, he simply turns on his heels and walks out of the hall, leaving them in stunned silence. They wait until they are sure he was out of earshot before bursting into a feverish debate on how they should proceed, inquiring where the automaton units came from, and what they cost. Many of them are appalled by the arrogance of the general for not even hearing any of their concerns. Something would have to be done about him when this is all over.

• • •

Early during the next cycle on Ganymede, Darius is surprised by a knock at his quarters. Sleepily getting up to answer, he is met by the stern gaze of Simeon. "Prepare yourself. Come down to the pits. No need for your bo. We have a special one for you there. After a severe talking to from your mother, the queen, we have decided to finalize your training early since you snuck into the games. You will have your own ceremony, and the queen wishes to be there to oversee it. You will spar with Njemba. Then he and I will go against you. I know you are young and these odds are less than fair, but you are to be king one day. To have an easier path would diminish your position with the rest of our people."

Without a backwards glance, Simeon leaves young Darius standing there, mouth agape, in confusion over how he's gone from being in trouble for sneaking into the CGYAB games to getting his very own. The only thing to do is to put on his body suit and go see how this would go. Oddly, Darius is not nervous. He and Simeon are nearly the same size, but the general is much thicker in build as Darius has yet to fill out. The outer skin is not yet developed, but the gravity on Ganymede is actually slightly lighter than Earth's, but the extra padding and augmentation will help when he cannot dodge or deflect any heavy blows he might sustain. Given that Njemba is going to be there, as well, almost guarantees there will be some heavy blows endured by the prince.

Thinking about all this kind of excited Darius about the prospect of getting to use one of the new bo-staves he has seen with some sort of energy transference feature, as well as a gravity aspect. He is not fearful that anything will happen to him seeing as his mother will be in attendance. They could, however, make things more difficult in order to try and teach him a lesson. The merits of that just may have lost its luster since, if that was in fact what was happening…he knew.

On his way down, he sees Bofus, who is heading in the opposite direction.

"Bofus, where are you going?" Darius asks.

Looking up, Bofus replies, "I'm on my way to the medical ward, but that don't make sense."

Darius looks him over and sees that he seems to be moving fine. "Are you injured from the games?" he asks.

Patting himself down, Bofus says, "No, I'm good, just a little bruised. Getting fitted for my shoulder harness, but they said something about nano-bots or nanites or something. Good luck!"

Shrugging, Darius thanks his friend and pushes on, recalling how to find his way back to the fighting pits he had followed Bofus to not so long ago.

Finding himself at the door to the pits, he gathers himself and knocks. The two large doors have been slid to the side by different Askari this time, both wearing ornate wrist gauntlets and greaves. They stand to the side as the prince enters. Looking into the chamber, he can see the red dirt of the pits now has a slightly purple tint as there are sconces with bright blue flames all around. There is a large group of Kison Askari around the final pit. He remembers them from being there before where

Simeon and Njemba are waiting in the center. Seated on a huge stone throne, in a gem-encrusted gown, sits his mother.

Simeon, who has both his staff and hammer, call out, "This is the crown prince who leaves title behind once he steps into this circle to prove his worth."

At that, Darius simply continues to walk in as dignified a fashion as a young man can muster. Once again, drums begin to rhythmically play and subconsciously his steps begin to match the rhythm of the beat. There is no chanting or singing this time. When he is finally standing at the center, Njemba walks over and hands him a bo-staff, and it is indeed one of the new ones he is hoping for.

Njemba nods at him, allowing him a moment to get used to it. The weapon is weightier than the one he has trained with in addition to the power source at the middle and the nodules to activate the gravity effects. Once he feels he is familiar enough with the weapon, he nods back, and they both look to Simeon, who then looks to the queen. Tunisia looks at her son, then at Njemba, and finally at Simeon to whom she solemnly nods, signaling they can begin. Simeon turns to stand between them with his hand out. He, then, makes a downward chopping motion and backs off. Njemba wastes little time flying forward with a powerful overhead strike.

If Darius has any thoughts about them taking it easy on him and Simeon's speech just being empty words, they are quickly dispelled by the speed and ferocity of Njemba's attacks. The boy barely jumps back in time to avoid the initial blow which clouds red dust and sounds as if the ground beneath has cracked. From his peripheral vision, Darius can see his mother's hand has flown up to cover her mouth in shock. If this is indeed meant to be a tough love farce, it is obvious she is not in on it. For some reason, that makes him feel better. Darius is content to sit back and feel his opponent out to try and find an opening. Njemba is much more aggressive than Simeon in style. At least, that is what he has gathered from his sessions with the short but stocky general. The question is, how long could the prince simply dodge and block the vicious strikes Njemba was dealing out before one landed?

It doesn't take long for them to get an answer. Njemba springs forward as if to clothesline Darius, and when the youngster ducks, the big Askari reverses his motion, and there is a meaty smack right in the center of the boy's back that sends him flying forward. Rolling with the force of the blow, Darius stands, catching his breath, as his eyes become glowing white orbs. Gritting his teeth, he rushes forward on the attack. Flourishing the staff at blinding speeds he does not know he can reach, Darius strikes at Njemba until it seems there is more than one attacker.

Tunisia leans forward in her throne as she, as well as the other onlookers, have never seen a display like this. It is now Njemba's turn to struggle to keep up with the flurry of blows. A feinted high swing is switched at the last moment and reversed into a diagonal downward slash at the big man's ankle. His eyes widen as his foot flies upwards at an awkward angle as Darius follows it up with a reverse swing of his own, catching him flush across his chest before he can recover his balance. It is obvious by the force with which Njemba hits the ground that, either by pure luck or on purpose, Darius has activated the gravity feature on his bo-staff.

The sound when he lands is like hearing a felled sequoia crash. The red dust clouds the fighting pit, and there is a mini-crater in evidence as Njemba struggles to his feet, ready to resume the fight. Just as he is about to come forward, Simeon shouts, "Enough!" as he comes in between them. The only thing hurting Njemba is his pride likely, and Simeon nods, asking silently if he is all right to continue, and he gestures that, indeed, he was fine. Looking to Darius who seems as determined as ever, Simeon does not feel it necessary to ask. They are all proud of their prince. Simeon, though, is curious as to what else the boy can do that he isn't sharing or simply isn't aware of. Since his unknown abilities only seem to come out when under times of stress or duress. Simeon thinks this might serve as the perfect catalyst to find out.

The queen understands what they are trying to do but does not like it. She knows her son is special, and many are afraid of him because of the mystery surrounding his abilities. Most would simply not talk about the strange occurrences that have been happening since he was an infant. There is a wonderful light within the boy that comes out, and when it does, some think it a blessing while others become superstitious. The growing fear for the boy will have to be fixed if he is to eventually rule his people. Of course, some fear will be useful for a king. Any that see themselves as rivals for the throne will need to know that Darius will do what is necessary to remain in place.

This demonstration will hopefully help her son's legend grow, while also helping some of the warrior class learn about their future king. All these thoughts are randomly running through the queen's mind as she nods to Simeon for them to continue. In response, he takes up both his staff and hammer. Having recovered somewhat, Njemba gets into a fighting stance, looking toward Darius, who mirrors their postures, letting all know he is ready as well.

"Now, boy, show us your true nature. I want to see this *Kuongoza Mwanga*!" Simeon says as he rushes forward, raising his hammer high.

As the sparring begins, Babylon enters the chamber, coming to stand just behind Queen Tunisia. "Two pon one, huh? Interesting choice for the young prince to prove his skill," he offers.

Seeing the old Atlantean hobble in using his trident for support, Tunisia comments, "I know you're old, but you're not as decrepit as you let on, Babylon. I've heard rumors that you could hop in there yourself and teach these warriors a thing or two."

Chuckling, Babylon replies, "Rumors are just that. Besides, the general and dat big one look like trouble. How has Darius been handling himself in there?"

Watching them circle each other in the fighting pit with each testing the waters with strikes to gauge strength and response times, Tunisia says, "He held his own with Njemba, and now they are going to try and bring his inner power out by overwhelming him or nearly so."

Chapter Twenty-Two

THE RYOKO-GEKIJO IS STILL ON its way to Ganymede, and Hironike goes along with the plan not to round up Sparks and her co-conspirators; instead, he has chosen to observe their movements as well as their interactions with the others on board. After all, they have to come out to eat and take care of their hygiene needs. They aren't being catered to in the suite since things aren't operating normally under the circumstances, so Sparks, Argos, and Max have to move about as everyone else does. Sparks is getting tired of hearing a long litany of sob stories about how the government has fail these people. Though not a pleasant ordeal, she does use some of what she's heard to craft her own growing cover story in an effort not to stick out.

Max has become increasingly more impressed with her creative resourcefulness. Before he knows it, she is a fellow refugee who had been taken after protesting the death of her brother who was collateral damage during a fight between the Kison Askari and the GMC. As far as Max knows, she is an only child who grew up in the foster care system until being old enough to strike out on her own, but her stories, when she tells them, are so filled with passion that most believe them. Most, but not all. There are a few of the Ongakujin who randomly pop up among the additional populace on the ship/theater who listen raptly as everyone else does but know better because Hironike and Toshi have advised them to watch, listen, and keep a general eye on them.

They are left alone while in the suite for the most part. Hironike sees no reason to have anyone go there since they can remotely surveil them anyway. What is disappointing is that there seem to be no evidence of a larger scheme from them or evidence that some other entity has sent them. There has to be more to this picture, and it could become a dangerous waiting game if they wait too long to find out what is going on or if they do not let the Kison Askari know of their presence before getting to Ganymede. To avoid that potential fiasco, Hironike orders Toshi to send a missive filling Queen Mother Tunisia in on who they have with them and the circumstances surrounding them arriving on Ryoko-Gekijo, along with the recording of the fake interview from a year or so prior. Perhaps she will have some idea on what to do with them.

• • •

Finally making it to the medical ward on Ganymede, Bofus walks in and sees a powerfully built Kison Askari woman in patterned scrubs, holding a data pad. "Um...I'm here to get nanites or something," he says timidly.

Pulling a long, braided ponytail of thick dreads over her shoulder, she says, "Oh, you must be Bofus. I'll be handling your procedure today. We had to grow a special batch just for you. My name is Akasha."

Reluctantly, Bofus takes the offered hand and nervously asks, "You're my doc? There are no human docs here to do this? No offense. Just curious."

Rolling her eyes, she responds, "A human doctor will not have the tech to make these nanites you will need to have a functioning targeting system with your shoulder canon. They are very small microorganisms with nano-bot features built onto them as they grow. We were unsure about how the ones we use on us would work with a normal human's physiology. Once installed, they will migrate to your ocular nerves. The tech will be remotely linked to the canon on your harness, so you will be able to target and fire it, whether or not you are wearing it. Your doctors would not have access to this as we've only recently acquired some of it from the Atlaneans. You, of course, have the choice to refuse the procedure and go into battle with your staff and body suit."

Mulling that over, he sees how ridiculous that prospect would be and simply says, "My bad. I'll go ahead with it...will it hurt?"

Smiling, Akasha reassures him it will not. "You may feel some tingling as the nanites move through you, and it may feel like your eyes are twitching as they get calibrated. Other than that, we have had no issues thus far."

Soon a gurney hovers in, and Bofus is asked to undress and lie down on it. Other Kison Askari come in, all of them large, powerful-looking beings, and he just can't help but be apprehensive about a procedure being performed by big people who look like they are more likely to tear someone to shreds than perform a delicate surgery.

Looking around this newly built facility, it is obvious the Stone people are highly capable, but Bofus has never personally had good experiences with regular doctors, so in his eyes, this is an extreme risk but one he has to take. He asks to be a part of the fight, and this is necessary for him to do his part. There are accounts of them having an excellent medical staff for caring for their own since they are rarely cared for by non-mutants, and they take their off-world mining exhibitions for the most part on their own, so it makes sense that, over time, they would have to develop or teach medical personnel from their own ranks. It is an amazing feat, what they had been able to accomplish under less than nurturing or even moderately healthy environments. For a time, they had to learn on the fly with little to no support. The difference was now they actually have some support and guidance which helps their ingenuity thrive tenfold.

Akasha comes in while two of the large nurses put a mask over Bofus's face, and he inhales deeply, letting what seems like a normal nitro tank calm him and rather quickly take him under. Once they are sure he is out, they guide the hover-gurney to the OR and begin the procedure which takes approximately three hours.

While he recovers, they monitor his vitals closely to make sure his body does not go into shock or reject the nanites as foreign bodies. He seems to be holding steady as he finally woke.

When he opens his eyes, his vision is a little blurry at first. Just as he is about to panic, it clears, and he can see Akasha standing over him, smiling. There is a tingling sensation in the back of his eyes, as well as along his spine. "Hey, I feel a little…funny," Bofus remarks.

Running a scanner along his body, Akasha says, "That's the nanites migrating and settling into your nervous system specifically in the nerve centers for your eyes and along your backbone. You may find your hand-eye coordination will be vastly improved among other things, in addition to your connection to the targeting system for the canon."

Apprehension about the procedure begins to take hold again as Bofus hears those words. "Settling in? That doesn't sound good. How long will I have these things? Can I take them out?" he asks.

Shaking her head and rubbing his arm to calm his fears, she adds, "Yes, you can take them out, but I think, once you're used to them, you will find the benefits will help you overcome your fear. Since installing them into my people, we have found improvements in Askari that had their sight nearly taken from them after mining in especially dangerous conditions on Mercury where the UV rays of the sun are much more intense. Even industrial strength suits and visors do not protect their retinas. Some that we thought were damaged beyond repair have had the nanites actually reverse and improve damaged eyes. The idea at first was just to have the seeing-impaired armed with shoulder fired weapons that could acquire targets without them having to see them. We issued them to everyone else because the idea of being able to fire and have our hands free to hold other things or effect repairs while fighting seemed beneficial. It wasn't until recently dealing with the warriors and engineers from Atlantis that we were able to infuse this biotech into our arsenal. Toshi of the Ongakujin also had some input."

It is still all very vague and unknown to Bofus, but already he is feeling better as his vision not only cleared but did, in fact, seem better than he remembers. Handing him his body suit, Akasha says, "As soon as you feel ready to stand, we can fit you with your bunduki, so we can get it calibrated and have you qualify with your new weapon. Sound good?"

Bofus nods while squinting and blinking, changing the focus as with a digital camera, and noticing the differences made him feel better about things. He soon stands up and puts his suit on, looking over his shoulder to ensure Akasha wasn't watching him. Looking over his body suit, Bofus notices a detail level that is missing from his vision before. Where he previously had seen smooth leather-like qualities, he now sees the individual microfibers of the various materials that helped protect his body from dangers such as extreme gravity, impacts, heat, and cold. Some ballistic and energy rounds would have a hard time penetrating the suit as well, but he knows he isn't invincible, just better off than having nothing but his skin to protect him. After all, he is only human and doesn't have a stone-like epidermis like many he will be fighting next to.

Akasha disappears and comes back moments later with a shoulder harness, featuring a cylindrical appendage on the back. She comes over and motions for Bofus to turn around. He does as he is bid, and she helps him get his arms and shoulders through the straps and secures the belt around his waist. He notices the aperture of the business end of the personal canon is aiming straight up. "Hey, how can I aim my buniki forward?" he asks.

Laughing at his pronunciation, Akasha corrects him, "It's *bunduki*, and it's not connected yet. We will wait until you get to the range before doing so. Don't want you shooting up the medical ward getting used to it."

Now that he's thought about it, that is probably a good idea. With that thought, he stands up, and she escorts him to the range, making sure he doesn't fall or stumble into anything as his eyes and the nanites are still recalibrating his sight and movement. He can see, more or less, detail, depending on what he is looking at and how close or far away it is. It is like having muscles you never knew you had. In this case, that is kind of true. It is like having a new set of eyes that could focus heavily on details of a wall a few hundred meters ahead of you or noticing the grain of stone while misjudging the doorway you are walking through. Not paying attention could have some bad consequences.

As soon as they make it to the range, it is obvious Bofus is really getting the hang of his new sight and coordination. Akasha can tell from his movement that he has a somewhat enhanced awareness. The targets are arrayed from three-hundred up to one-thousand meters out. At the end of each length, there are silhouettes of rough man shapes, and the furthest targets are just head and shoulder sized. The firing range, which are just like at the fighting pits, have the red-colored dirt or clay. Bofus figures it has to have been transported here since he now can somehow see the dirt does not have the same consistency of the other dirt throughout any of the chambers they walked through to get here.

He is amazed at the level of detail he can recall now just from their trip from the med facility to the range. It is like everything he sees has been catalogued to be cross-referenced with other data later. Akasha comes up to him and scans him again, and this time, the flexible cylinder containing the front site aperture for his canon telescope opens and is pointed directly in front of him. With a wave of her hand, Akasha gestures that he should aim down range and not horizontally along the firing line. Bofus turns to do so and immediately feels the canon acquiring targets.

"Concentrate on the target directly in front of you. Once you blink, it will make the target reacquire the target. This is so you can actually select different targets consecutively without shifting your body. Once you get used to it, you will find it much more efficient than the old way. Think about the shot and then simply think of executing the action of shooting, and it should fire. Once you find the mental button to push, it will be really simple," she instructs.

Bofus does as he is instructed, acquiring the target one-hundred meters ahead of him, blinked, and then moved his eyes to the target to the right of it. For a few moments, nothing happens as he stares intensely at the first target. Just as he is about to get frustrated, he thinks *fire*, and a small ball of plasma is ejected from the canon at a high velocity, setting the canvas on fire.

Without being told to do so, he blinks and glances right at the target next to it, thinks the command, and is rewarded with another explosion. He jumps up and down, elated at having hit his targets with such relative ease. "Man, that's what I'm talking about!" he yells exuberantly.

Without a word, Akasha backs away from him as five small drones float onto the field before him, down range, at varying distances.

He does not want to look at her, fearing he might inadvertently target her but asks, "What are those?"

Chuckling to herself, she finally answers, "Well, since you're doing better than I expected, I figured moving targets would be more fun. Think about putting the weapon away, and it will go back to its original position."

Hearing that she knows what he is worried about, Bofus wonders if they are somehow connected as well. He thinks about the canon being at rest, and it goes back to the upright but compacted position behind his right shoulder. Turning around to look at her, he asks, "Can you hear me thinking now, too?"

Shaking her head, Akasha says, "No, I have just been doing this for a little bit now and know how most experience this for the first time. Plus, I have a bunduki of my own. We are all trained to fight now, regardless of occupation."

There are suddenly strange, whirring sounds. The drones are approaching at high speed.

"You might want to handle them before they get too close," Akasha admonishes.

Turning his attention back to the drones down range, Bofus reactivates the shoulder canon and targets the closest one, taking it out instantly. He allows the nanites to prioritize targets by proximity as he mentally gives the fire order. Without realizing it, he has run horizontally, strafing the firing line, as he shoots. This is becoming second nature now. After the last drone is down, he deactivates the canon and walks over to Akasha. Bofus is happy to see she looks somewhat impressed, or at least, she isn't disappointed.

"Very good, Bofus! That's enough for now. Later you will likely be assigned a unit, and soon you will have to come down here with them to coordinate fire and movement maneuvers as a cohesive team," she adds as she input some commands on her data pad before putting it away.

Together, they leave and go their separate ways. Akasha goes back to the medical unit, and Bofus goes back to his quarters. He is buzzing with excitement when he runs into an old acquaintance. Squinting as they pass each other, Professor Charles Jones-Bey asks, "Bofus? Is that you?"

Looking up and coming out of his introspection about what has just transpired, Bofus says joyfully, "Hey, man! Where you been? I thought you had stayed on the Dreadnaught."

The professor tries in vain to fight off the unwanted, incoming vigorous hug and back slaps. Finally escaping the embrace, Jones-Bey looks Bofus over and asks, "Is that an industrial silicone body suit enhanced with interwoven alloy strips and a shoulder canon? Please tell me nobody was foolish enough to arm and train you?"

At first, Bofus looks hurt, then the expression on his face turns to anger.

Seeing his reaction turn sour, the professor holds up his hands and tries to mollify the man, but Bofus cuts him off, "You know I used to like you until I found out how pompous you can be all because you're educated! I know I don't talk right all the time, but that don't make me stupid. I pretty much know what's going on all the time, but I allow people like you to either disregard me or ignore me out of some feeling of superiority, but the truth is you and many like you would never survive what I've been through. You have always seen me as just another thug yet never gave any thought to the fact that you and I were, at one time, in the same cell! Yes, someone saw fit to arm and train me because I have chosen to fight and not sit on the sidelines. I' sume you here to teach in some way. That's all you good for which ain't a bad thing. I will contribute in my way!"

With that, Bofus storms off without another word, leaving Professor Charles Jones-Bey in a stunned silence. He has no choice but to continue on his way to where they are building a small university for the habitat. Bofus's rant has made him think long and hard about his treatment of what is now one of the few humans he would be able to interact with.

Has he always looked down on Bofus or people he feels are less educated than he is? If so, he would like to remedy that now that personal relationships may become more important as they are out and away from the main populace.

Chapter Twenty-Three

MALICE AND TYPHOON ARRIVE AT Giza with haste, and their master is nowhere to be found. This puzzles them. What could possibly have a being that, to their minds, is nearly at god-status so fearful? They can feel his apprehension in his frantic summons once the identity of the possible invaders is revealed. They are both exhausted from the long trip through the void. Malice has never remained in that dimension for so long, and Typhoon is still relatively new to all of it. These new players could be a blessing or a curse on extreme ends of either spectrum. On one hand, if Pharaoh fears them, it could mean they will finally get their freedom, but that could also mean being under the yoke of worse beings.

They both decided to go to their chambers and wait for his return. It will not likely end well, if Pharaoh came back for them and finds that they were not in attendance. He is not known for his patience. Malice goes to meditate by sharpening his combat skills. Little good they will do him against foes that make his master tremble. Typhoon, once again, wishes for his state of blissful ignorance to be restored. Things just keep getting more complicated, and the changes are not for the better. What they don't realize is that he has not actually gone anywhere but is sitting there, enveloped in the void, watching them.

The Anunnaki are quite powerful and volatile beings who can either bestow benevolence or destruction upon those they come into contact with. They have been to Earth before, but unlike the ancient radiant ones, they have no interest in staying. They left gifts and some knowledge with the fledgling race of beings that would become humans but chose to venture elsewhere. Of course, there have been others who have visited as well, along with the Anunnaki, the Olmek to name another, but the Anunnaki are known to be quick to judge, especially if the inhabitants have proven to be wasteful.

It is doubtful that they have advanced far beyond what Pharaoh's own beings have over the millennia, but he will not have his brothers and sisters at his side if they deemed the inhabitants of Earth had squandered away their resources unnecessarily. The problem is that he will be forced to accept the same punishment as these backward mongrel beings that, ironically, he has helped shape. No doubt the massive ship they are traveling in has a siege engine capable of using gravitational force or ways of inducing stars to go supernova. The mentality can't be argued with. If you wasted everything at your disposal, then giving you more would not remedy the problem. Might as well start over.

The issue Pharaoh has is that currently he is still exiled here and would, in the end, share the fate of the Milky Way, if indeed the Anunnaki have come to that conclusion, and given the state of things there, that is highly likely. He has become a part of the macabre show that is, until now, the sole reason of joy and contentment. Something needs to be done, but he has no trust that sending his minions off to his brethren will get the results desired.

• • •

Orders come in for all hands to report back to Saturn for redeployment which confuses Corporals Aragon, Sims, and Jordan, especially since they have just been transferred here to help deal with the situation back home on Earth.

"I don't get it. There are still some very active pockets of resistance here, and we are not going to be able to handle things if it becomes a full-on front here to contend with while dealing with the rockheads out at other planetary mining colonies," Aragon states as they are getting into a transport headed to take them to the Centurion carrier orbiting Earth.

They are moving in large numbers. That much is obvious but will also be easily observed, even from a distance.

Corporals Sims and Jordan agree but move in silence. Word has not come down but being pulled out so soon could have some bad implications. It is possible that something has developed that needs to be dealt with immediately, which has suddenly taken priority over the outbreak of riots. There are many who have felt this is a cop-out not to have to deal with the problem of the Stone people having dark matter at their disposal, so what is so urgent? Why did they have to jump back into the fray without solving that puzzle? Whatever the case is, the GMC is pulling out all the stops.

Corporal Aragon can't make out the name on the carrier as they are being shuttled to it, but he knows it is brand spanking new. They can also see new fighters running escort and other shuttles that are loaded up with the huge crates with the automaton units in them. They are bringing all their new toys to the party. Some of them wonder if, maybe, the GMC has lucked upon an ore cache which will give them the ability to supplement their fleet. The *Ex Wife*, the GMC's flagship carrier, is still in orbit around Saturn, along with a good chunk of the fleet. The boys are looking forward to reuniting with their friend, Petty Officer John House, who is still stationed there. Things are ramping up.

Sgt. Garrison and his crew arrive back at HQ before the recalled forces get there. They are immediately ordered to head to General Krulak's office to speak with the top brass waiting there, so they can begin coordinating on an offensive geared to destabilize the new habitat on Ganymede. Lance Corporals Jennings, McNamara, PFC Long, and Private Cooper stay behind with the Adder to resupply and get needed repairs done, so they will be able to take off as soon as possible. If the top brass are already game planning an offensive, they aren't going to be docked for long. After getting the supplies tallied and stowed, Long goes to his makeshift kennel to check on his devil dog or Teufel as he has begun to call him in his head.

Before he is even within eyesight of the beast, it is obvious the animal senses him. Opening the locked door to the large enclosure some of the engineers have created on Lt. Commander Jameson's orders, a mass of fur and muscle smack into Long, and it is a good thing he is encased in titanium and other alloys. There is a loud clang as he hits the ground in a tumble. "Whoa, boy! Calm down!" he says, scratching the beast behind its large ears. Looking him over, PFC Long is amazed all over again. It has grown tremendously in a short amount of time, and he was big to begin with. Licking his new master with his long purple tongue, it is plain to see Tuefel has missed having the man around. "Hey, boy, what happened here?" Long asks, noticing bandages just above one of his big paws.

The animal growls low but allows him to inspect the wound that he saw consisted of small puncture wounds. After putting the bandages back, he thinks it would be a good idea if he spoke with Lt. Commander Jameson. Mistreatment of his animal will not be accepted. Not to mention, he doesn't want to be held liable for any casualties that may come up when Tuefel gets tired of them poking around. Hopefully, there is a good explanation. In the meantime, he will take a moment to get things squared away. Hopefully, Sgt. Garrison will likely be back soon with new orders because things seem rather hectic around base.

• • •

The brutal-looking sparring session has gone on for a while, and Babylon, Queen Tunisia, and the others watching cannot believe the strength and stamina Darius is showing. Despite his smaller size, he is giving as good as he is taking, and it is a mesmerizing sight. The boy has taken some pretty heavy hits with both the gravity strikes and the energy transfer strikes which either send him flying or make him collapse onto the ground. Each time, when the red dust settles, the boy dusts himself off and goes right back at them in a speedy, acrobatic way. Often, he tries to bait one into the other, trying to use Njemba's size against him, forcing Simeon to slow or halt his attacks mid-swing only to be forced to stave off a flurry of attacks from the prince.

At times, it seems as if Darius is not hitting them with electrical discharges but rather charging himself directly with the weapon to augment his attacks which aren't a part of any strategy that any of their other warriors are using. Some think that, perhaps, the suit is helping to insulate him somewhat, but there is obviously more going on here than meets the eye. It is a back and forth battle where, at times, it looks as if they are holding back only to turn around and strike with nearly all of their combined might with staves and war hammer augments. Simeon briefly nods at Njemba, possibly signaling they will end the session with the next sequence. They both rush forward, making Darius retreat. Simeon runs and digs the handle of his hammer into the ground, simultaneously swinging on it, gathering momentum with his staff. At the last moment, he activates the gravity feature, sending a forceful blast horizontally at the boy while Njemba does the same, but from the opposite direction, he tries to sandwich him in between the opposing forces.

Darius tries to dodge Simeon's swing and is herded right into Njemba's gravity blast only to be pin-balled right into the invisible Doppler wave of the remnants of Simeon's attack. The bo-staff flies out of Darius's hand, and he winces from the brief crushing sensation. A guttural roar comes from somewhere deep inside the boy. As his eyes open, beams of light fly out of his hands in the opposite direction toward both men at each side, sending them flailing out of the pit. Standing there crouched in a bubble of illuminated protection, Darius glares demonstratively and then falls to the ground. Queen Tunisia is up and running before she knows it. Babylon is slow to follow as all the spectators go to their prince's aid.

Groggily, Njemba and Simeon got up, dusting themselves off before going to check on Darius. There are multiple sighs of relief when the boy's eyes open, blinking slowly and minus the bright glow they had shown earlier. Tunisia runs her hand over his face and head. "Are you all right?" she asks.

Sitting up and looking around, he gently brushes her hand away and answers, "I am fine. What happened?"

Simeon comes to kneel beside them, despite dirty looks from the queen. "We were hoping you could tell us. Some of us are still not sure of what we just witnessed," he adds.

Thinking it over, Darius says, "That was a rather tricky move you pulled, general. Baiting me to dodge directly into a gravity strike, so I would get redirected into your initial attack. It made me angry, and then I can't really explain what happened after that. It's kind of hazy. I somehow channeled that feeling and remember feeling very warm, then sort of sleepy."

Nervous chuckling can be heard from those gathered around him, but there is fear in the eyes of some of them.

Darius feels it somehow. Looking around, he says, "Don't worry. I am not a freak, but I do know some of what is in me is in all of you, but you have somehow been disconnected from it. Perhaps, if I can learn to control it, then I can teach you to tap into it."

It is possible that this is some sort of new mutation that is only now showing up. That has happened in the past as beings of Earth evolved, but the prince is saying this is possibly something already present, and most would think it would have surfaced long before now, and certainly nothing this extreme has been seen before. There have been cases of both beautiful and horrifying results of attempts at genetic engineering and gene splicing, but that is among regular people trying to enhance their own gene pools to compete with the underclass of mutants that are continually on the rise in population. Maybe Darius is simply the next step in their evolution.

• • •

Watching the other vessels dock in the Centurion carrier, Corporals Aragon, Sims, and Jordan quickly strap into their seats and prepare for the jump to Saturn. "Man, this is a lot of personnel and firepower we are taking back. Do you think they hit us there already, or is something else going on?" Jordan asks.

Looking through the porthole, Sims shakes his head. "Nah, I don't think they've hit us yet. Word would have come down, but there's definitely something going on. This looks like a mobilization for an all-out attack or, at least, a prep for one. GMC HQ must know something, and they're about to make a move. It must not be here though since it looks like we are leaving little assets here."

It is true that they are leaving a lot behind, but Earth is the capitol planet for most, but the GMC is very much headquartered on Saturn, where not only most of their high-cost assets were developed and stored, but they have also begun to enhance all military personnel there, instead of limiting that to the "elite" units. There is now a desperate movement to use whatever means possible to regain their advantage over the mutated races of the galaxy. Some of the more extreme in government and fringe groups are even preaching extermination. Corporal Aragon is sure that last remedy wouldn't solve their current issues. Not to mention, it is morally wrong and would put them all in a worse predicament with the public than they are in now.

There are recent pushes for all military personnel to get cybernetic enhancements, whether they are necessary or not, and during discussions, Corporal Aragon and his fireteam have come to the conclusion that they will not get any done unless they lose a limb and need a replacement. For all intents and purposes, they want to hold on to their humanity for as long as they can. In his eyes, they are already pushing the line with the extreme supplementation and augmentation they have gone through in order to train and fight on Saturn under heavy gravity, in order to attempt to catch up to the Stone people's physical advantages. It is yet to be seen if this program was successful as they have yet to get into a hand-to-hand fight with one of them.

Aragon wagers his chances are still pretty slim but figures the enhancement he has will, at least, buy him more time than he would have had before. If the extra time is enough to find and use a weapon or for another Marine to help finish his opponent, then it is successful, but he holds no illusions about standing toe-to-toe with any of them and winning. In the past, the GMC always found a way, though. "Overcome and adapt" is a mentality that is consistent with the Marines. Technology and time have only furthered that notion.

General Krulak, Rear Admiral Halsey, Vice Admiral Featherson, and the rest of the commandant's top advisers are all on standby on Saturn, waiting for the rest of their forces to rendezvous there, so they can coordinate a large-scale attack. The bulk of their forces will be heading to Ganymede, but some would be dispersed to Mars and Jupiter to get any stragglers. They also hope to recover some ore if any of the ships are found to be carrying supplies. After going over the data with Sgt. Garrison, it is decided that the automaton units would be best if deployed to Ganymede for an orbital siege attack, using drop pods covered in stealth filaments.

There will be no heat signatures inside or any signs of ordinance, so perhaps they might be seen as falling meteors and a good number of them could make landfall before they notice what is happening. It seems the most viable plan would be the biggest financial risk, but it is light on risk of life and limb. The problem will be getting a large ship or enough smaller ships in close proximity of the moon to drop the pods and getting out without being discovered. Lt. Commander Jameson is happy to help come up with plans as they are risking the destruction of the automatons units and not some of the augmented Marines he has been working on and designing for. He adds the suggestion to install guidance systems to the pods that would be linked to each individual automaton, which could then shut it off if scanning was detected.

Once the pods breach the atmosphere, they could have the automatons program the pods to simulate a random flight pattern, making it seem like a meteor shower. There isn't a lot of activity going on outside of the moon's orbit, so it could go either way. It could look absurdly obvious to see or there might not be anyone in orbit to notice them coming in. Time will tell.

Chapter Twenty-Four

As soon as the military has thinned their presence back on Earth, things take a chaotic spin for the worse. Things have deteriorated into a slew of riots and fights across the globe, but now some of the local security forces are ill equipped or too scared to deal with them, so in some cases, the fights just rage on until one side is either obliterated or they retreat. Ragnar and his Guild of the Pristine are spreading their message of hate, but mostly to other non-mutated beings. There are others who share their genealogy but not their ideology. That is where most of the fighting occurs, but every now and then, they run into groups that have mutants sprinkled in with them.

At some point, Shajara and his Children of the Sun have gotten word of what is going on. He is of the mind to only engage groups of authority who, in his mind, are contributing to the strife by keeping the beings of Earth divided along color or genetic lineages while using technology as a means of strengthening those divisions. These two fringe groups aren't the only ones to emerge which also complicates things further. The media, of course, as always has used these instances of fighting or tragedy to keep people glued to various screens across the globe. Behind closed doors, the government is frantic to get the GMC forces back to Earth to help contain the crisis here, yet it is apparent from the near mass exodus of forces that there are other things on their agenda. The commandant walking out on the planet's highest-ranking dignitaries only added fuel to the fire and panic.

Civilians cannot help but notice the hulking Centurion class ship carrier waiting in Earth's orbit as smaller ships with arms, supplies, and

Marines scream off to board. That brings on a whole different panic as the government doesn't know exactly what is going on and, therefore, will not confirm or deny the speculations the media is making. Given the recent situation with the recording from the Mars skirmish, imaginations are running rampant. Protests have slowed mainly because people are afraid, and there wasn't much to protect them once things went south. Earth has become a proverbial dumpster fire. Ragnar and the Guild of the Pristine are fanning the flames. Shajara has heard enough to know this man needs to be stopped.

• • •

Finally, Pharaoh has come out of the void after thinking things over and summoned his minions to the chamber he fancied at the apex of the pyramid at Giza. Reluctantly, they come as he is bathing in light, coming in from an opening Typhoon has never noticed before. The alien being was, somehow, channeling sun rays into himself through a crystal. Malice has seen this many times before and has stopped asking about it centuries ago. This is more of a therapeutic thing as Pharaoh is not recharging but relaxing and meditating on what to do in preparation of the potential Anunnaki invasion. Without opening his eyes or turning from the light, he addresses his minions, "Do you know who the Anunnaki are, Malice?"

Malice looks at his master and nods, confirming that he does indeed know who they are. Finally stepping out of the light as it fades away and the portal closes, Pharaoh continues, "Then you know who Enki was and what he did a few millennia ago? Which ironically was not too different from my own experimentation, though it was for different reasons. His own did not react as the beings of my kind did. He took some of the beings created and fled with a new work force after nearly decimating the Igigi to extinction. Their return can only herald destruction, or them needing more labor, which I can guarantee will not be to the liking of this planet's current inhabitants. They will likely take all that is left, deeming the beings here unworthy, having squandered or wasted so much since they left or look to replace whoever is currently acting as their slave labor. The radiant ones and the rest of my kind could repel them, but they are still aloof in their approach to this place. It would seem we are of no concern. After so long, I am spread too thin and hindered by my exile to be of much help alone."

Typhoon has no thoughts on the subject but wonders what their next course of action would be. Malice knows of the ancient race of giants who melded their genetics with that of older forms of humans to create homo-sapiens to replace their old slave beings, the Igigi, who were nearly killed off after an attempted revolt. The results of the Annunaki's efforts, along with previous experimentation by Pharaoh, has left a lot of different mutations around the Earth, which have gone on to evolve in various ways. Because Malice had not seen the power of these beings when they first arrived, he is not as fearful of them. Malice will take his blades, abilities, and determination to see if he can best them. The concern his master is showing is promising. Perhaps there is a way out of this servitude. The ape could be duped into helping. It wishes to be free as well.

The minions have no desire to trade one master for another. The boy they ran into on occasion could also be a key. Perhaps he is not spread as thin as their master is. Perhaps he is potentially more powerful and young enough not to know that. After thinking on all this, Malice asks, "What shall we do then, master?"

Looking into the red glowing orbs of one of his first minions, Pharaoh laughs and says, "We wait, observe, and watch the chaos happen as we always have! Opportunities always present themselves in the aftermath. Maybe this will be the catalyst forcing my kind to return and lift this stupid exile."

They are all content to wait for an opportunity, but each is thinking that the opportunity could be meant for them individually.

• • •

Corporals Aragon, Sims, and Jordan have jumped to Saturn in the Centurion class space carrier without incident, and they have all disembarked as soon as they could, rushing to their old barracks in an attempt to catch up with Petty Officer House before they ship out again. They aren't going to have much time before being deployed again. They can see the ore-gathering drones the GMC have developed are working overtime to keep material flowing. They are in a desperate spot to not only keep the war machine growing but also to keep it capable if the necessity comes from an external threat. This worry will finally prove prophetic sooner than anyone could have imagined.

After a day or so, they finally catch up with House in the chow hall. He is sitting alone, eating another bowl of gelatinous mystery stew which is heralded to have all the daily protein and nutrients needed to fuel military personnel when Corporal Aragon spots him. "Hey, there's my favorite back-stabbing squid!" he shouts.

There is a moment of uncomfortable silence as others turn around at the exclamation, awaiting the corpsman's response to the slur. Running his hands over his brown-haired buzz cut, House stands up to face whoever figures that lame insult would get under his skin.

When he finally sees who it is they both broke out in laughter to the dismay of the onlookers when feel they have just been deprived of a potentially entertaining brawl. Handshakes and back slaps are exchanged between all when Corporals Sims and Jordan come over to greet him as well.

"When did you jarheads get back?" House asks enthusiastically.

Looking up from his bowl, Sims replies, "Last night. What's with all the hustle and bustle around here? All the programs seemed to have been accelerated, yet we know we haven't gotten any of the stolen ore back yet. We seem to be processing through our stash in the ring here like we are back to business as usual. You got any scuttlebutt?"

Closing his eyes, House goes on to describe what has been going on. "It's been a mad house here since you guys took off. They asked for more volunteers for the Ascension Protocol, then started randomly inducting people into it whether they had volunteered or not, giving them super cocktails of new supplements, but some of them are having adverse effects, due to a lack of testing, in my opinion. They have also begun issuing prosthesis to Marines that haven't suffered limb-losing injuries. It's causing serious mental problems when you have a guy or girl who just lost their real arms or legs unnecessarily, in an effort to make them more combat efficient against rockheads. Plus, I heard you guys were shipped in with five units of newly purchased automatons. Had to have costed a mint from Koops Robotics! Is that true?"

In the midst of eating their mystery stew, Aragon's, Sims's, and Jordan's heads bob, confirming they had indeed come with the new units. After a rough swallow of food, Aragon states, "We saw the shipping crates with the automaton units at Two-Nine before being recalled. We thought we would be on riot patrol for a while longer though. Any clue as to what lit a fire under the top brass?"

House shakes his head, and they all eat in silence for a few moments before Jordan speaks up. "Any chance of getting some Nitro hits before getting bounced out of here into the maelstrom? We just ran out."

House responds, "That's a negative. The club on Titan has been shut down temporarily and all leave and liberty is suspended until further notice. I'll put my feelers out though. Your boys in admin always have a stash somewhere."

With that, they finish their meal and disperse back to their barracks. When they get there, they find orders to report to First Lieutenant Maplethorpe. Apparently, whatever their part would be in the upcoming battle, it would be from the seat of a cockpit and not with their boots on the ground. Corporal Aragon wonders who would be deployed to capture the planetary beach head, and where? It seems the flash training they have received as a prank now makes them overqualified for grunt work, but whoever has that task would have a hard row to hoe. More details would be forthcoming at a briefing scheduled later on in the week, but for now, all they knew was that there were multiple attack points on different planets and a stealth approach for the automaton units. Aragon, Sims, and Jordan couldn't make sense of any of it.

• • •

Darius has fully recovered and is no longer fatigued from using his new-found abilities. Tunisia is tired of people constantly asking about it and has ordered them to stop. "My son will tell us more when he is ready and not before!" she'd demanded.

Bofus and the prince are often seen hanging out, both proud of their recent achievements. Some are not so keen on Bofus walking around with his bunduki mounted in its harness all the time, but the man simply will not stow it unless ordered to do so. Darius immediately wanted one once he saw it, but the queen has forbidden it. The boy is disappointed but he understands. Babylon is around more often as of late.

Darius has taken to following the old ambassador of Atlantis around. There are more and more of their kind seen about among the Kison Askari now, which makes Darius curious. Babylon is not sure if this was just the nature of a child or if his mother had put the boy up to questioning him. Either way, he enjoys the youthful mind of Darius that would, at times, surprise him with unfathomable wisdom for a boy his age. "Babylon, if your people have been around all this time as you stated and Professor Jones-Bey claims, why are we only now seeing your physical presence? I mean, there are also the conspiracy theories about sunken cities in the Atlantic on Earth, but other than, that there's been little proof of your existence for many until you reappeared."

Thinking on what the boy is asking, Babylon decides to fess up. "Our people have never completely left. We just hid in plain sight some of the time and went to a place most folk were not even aware existed. As times changed and people began to appear more exotic, we could kind of blend in, but when things got too dangerous we were able to go to other dimensions or planes of existence. You follow me?" Babylon watches as Darius ruminates over what he has just been told.

Looking up, Darius asks, "Like the astral plane or the void?"

Chuckling, Babylon is, once again, surprised by the depth of the boy's understanding as there are a lot of adults in a myriad of cultures that have always had a hard time perceiving the existence of these things, yet Darius not only accepts it but has a sense of some of the possibilities. There is something about the way he's mentioned those two examples that makes it seem as if they are more than acknowledgements; instead, they are revelations of intimate knowledge. Standing up, Babylon offers his hand to the young prince who also stands and takes his hand reluctantly. "Close your eyes and relax when I tell ya to. Then step forward and open dem," he instructs. Darius does so.

A moment later, Babylon says, "Step forward and open your eyes."

When he does, Darius can see they are still on Ganymede, but something is very different. It is almost as if he is looking at a negative picture of their surroundings with a purplish filter on it. The moon itself is there, but the habitat and structures they built are not. The air is different, but he finds that he can breathe easily enough, and Babylon is having no issues there as well. "This is what we have come to know as the void. It is another plane of existence. The astral plane is another. Some of these dimensions can exist in the same time and space to the one you were born in, while others are actually far away in both time and distance. It can be...complicated."

Darius just nods his head in acknowledgment before a puzzled look comes over his face. Looking at Babylon, he says, "I don't know how, but I have been here before."

Not wanting to be gone too long, Babylon takes Darius back to the plane of existence of his birth. Once he has regained his bearings, Babylon says, "How is that possible? I didn't think there were many void walkers among your people. Did your mother or father take you?"

Shaking his head negatively, Darius states, "No, but I know I have been there before. It felt familiar. I have walked in the void but not with my parents. I think I've been to other planes as well." Waving his hands, a portal opens with light pouring into the chamber they are standing in.

Babylon is tempted to step into it but quickly banishes the thought. He grabs the boy and turns him around before he can step through. "Easy, young prince! You are not sure why or how you know these things. Let's use a bit of caution before we venture into a situation we know nothing about. There's already too much going on here."

Without thinking about it, Darius closes the portal and notices Babylon is staring at him strangely. "My eyes are glowing again, aren't they?" he asks.

Babylon nods but doesn't seem afraid, and that comforts Darius. Curious, he asks, "Why don't you fear me when I get like this?"

"Old Babylon has seen a lot of strange things in my day. I can tell you are different, but different don't always mean bad. That thinking has got a lot of beings here in trouble throughout time. It's the one thing we just can't seem to shake. Fear of de unknown. Let's get you back to your mother before we get into some real trouble. If you can help it, don't go opening portals like that. We can explore when you're more ready."

Darius agrees but Babylon can't shake the feeling that the boy is more ready than he is. The portal he has opened with very little effort is to a place the Atlantean is unfamiliar with, and he thought he knew most of the void walkers or beings who could go to other planes of existence. It is not a widely studied phenomenon.

Other beings that have visited the Milky Way could do it, but beings on the human spectrum are not known to do well with the transitions, and Darius does not seem to be phased at all during their short walk. What else is hiding inside the boy? There is something oddly familiar about his strangeness. One thing is for sure, though, if there is anyone they need to worry about, it isn't the prince of the Kison Askari. Babylon has a feeling the boy can handle himself in many situations some adults would have a hard time in. He had proven that during his sparring match with Njemba and Simeon. He has also heard a rumor about the boy banishing two of Pharaoh's minions while they were on Earth. Babylon just hopes the boy's abilities don't become a liability to himself or his people. If they can be harnessed, they could be useful in bringing about peace.

Chapter Twenty-Five

AFTER THE BRIEFING, CORPORALS ARAGON, Sims, and Jordan are informed that they will be dropping pods wrapped in stealth filaments with the automaton units in them, hoping to make ground fall making it look like a light meteor shower. Most of the activity at Ganymede is taking place below the surface of the moon, and it is believed the majority of the Stone people's space craft are docked below ground as well in a subterranean hangar they had built. The plan is to disable the fighter craft, then cripple the systems there, while another force goes to engage space units last seen at Mars, in addition to any units at Jupiter.

Boots on the ground for the GMC are to be strictly automaton units to limit loss of life. Pilots and bomber craft are to disengage immediately at the hint of dark matter ordinance. Corporal Aragon watches as technicians remove the hammer-shaped Mjölnir shells from the Thor class bombers, replacing them with the open orbital drop pods which are made lighter. They need less internal insulation and atmosphere controls because what would be riding in them would be inorganic. It is not likely that the pods would be scanned, but if they are, they would look like nothing more than debris falling to the surface. At least, that is what the GMC is hoping. It all sounds pretty haphazard and risky, but orders are orders.

The space around Ganymede's gravity well is being constantly monitored for potential sentries that will spot the ships approaching. The key is to slip in close and drop the pods in what looks like random patterns into different zones around the moon. Once the units are safely on the surface, they will rendezvous and carry out their sabotage mission.

The units can either commandeer a ship to get off-world, or the GMC will have to come up with a way of retrieving the units. It will not go over well if they lose these valuable units after one use.

All hangars on or near the GMC installation at Saturn are bustling bee hives of activity. Aragon likes the confidence but simultaneously feels this is another instance of good initiative, bad judgement. The real problem is that this is happening on a large scale. It is one thing when a single Marine who is all gung ho goes out and makes a mistake, but quite another for it to be a branch-wide gaff. The biggest issue that he and many other Marines express under their collective breaths is that there is no contingency plan if this all-out assault fails. If the desired end result is to bring the Stone people back into the fold and recover much-needed assets or mined resources, how will they accomplish that if the automaton units are summarily defeated, the habitat preserved, and the other assault attempts repelled?

That is a question none of the enlisted GMC or other military personnel have an immediate answer to, and it is unclear if the brass even knows. For the first time in a long time, they are flying by the seat of their pants, out of pure desperation. Not a good position to be in. Known for their prowess at improvisation, it might have been a necessary thing to fall back on in this case. The problem is, now the Kison Askari are proving to be adept at improvising and evolving as well, and right now, they seem a bit faster at the process. Corporals Aragon, Sims, and Jordan are also none too pleased with being some of the few flesh and bloods to be risked in the initial phase of this attack. Most of the nearest elements of the Kison Askari fleet are posted around Jupiter itself, almost as if they hope to be decoys when the real assets have been shifted to Ganymede which has more land mass than the gas giant and a viable water source.

The trick will be to get in quickly, drop the pods, and get out unnoticed. It is possible, but the longer they stay, the higher chances of getting spotted. Plus, they will have to be in comm silence and minimal instrumentation in order to have a weaker signature flying into the gravity well. This means shutting down as much as possible while approaching the gravity well, dropping the stealth pods, then turning on systems at the last moment to hightail it out of there. Luckily there are no reports of surface to air or space artillery. If they have already come up with that, this will be over pretty quickly, and the GMC will have provided them with the gift of the galaxy's most expensive skeet-shooting targets.

The topical view of the double-bladed-shaped Thor class bombers intrigues Corporal Aragon as he watches the one he would be personally flying get fitted. A red-headed officer approaches him. Aragon immediately recognizes him as Lieutenant Maplethorpe who had trained him after flash training for the pilot programs. More recently, he has encountered him during the initial briefing on this mission. Aragon can see the top of the black silicone body glove sticking out from the olive-green coveralls the officer is wearing. "Good evening, sir! Looks like you're flying this mission as well," he says in greeting.

"Good evening, Marine. Yes, I'll be replacing these coveralls soon with a new flight suit. You'll be getting one as well. I'm just stopping by to make sure you and your flight are clear on your orders. I'm flying cover to Mars. We're not sending you in with escorts because we expect to face the most air-to-air or rather space-to-space contact at Mars and not Ganymede. Dropping ordinance would be a waste since none of our current shells would breach the mantle to hit anything worth it," Maplethorpe relies.

Corporal Aragon nods his understanding as Sims and Jordan both approach and greet the officer. After getting no questions about the mission, he turns to leave but comes back fishing something out of his pockets and hands them three sets of lieutenant bars. Second lieutenant butter bars but bars nonetheless. They all look dumbfounded. Seeing their expressions, he says, "You are until further notice officers now as long as you're flying pilot missions. It's just protocol. You can go back to being enlisted grunts when your boots are back on the ground, and from what I can tell, for this offensive, the only boots on the ground are to be automatons. Consider yourselves lucky. Sounds like it's going to be a cluster if they make it to that habitat." With that, he turns and leaves them to make their final preparations.

After much mock-saluting to each other and after replacing their corporal chevrons and cross rifles with the lieutenant bars, Aragon, Sims, and Jordan finally hop aboard their respective Thor-class bombers and start all their pre-flight checks. They still have some time on their hands as they will be taken near the system but not too near as they don't want to alert the enemy to their intentions by coming with the largest of their spacecraft, so the idea is to have them ferried in. Saturn is only the next planet over in the system, but a good portion of them will be heading over to Mars, so they all will make that jump. Once they are near that gravity well, the bombers will make their way to Ganymede, hopefully, with everyone's attention on what is happening at Mars. Well, it all sounds good in theory, at least.

• • •

The Ryoko-Gekijo will soon be near Ganymede's gravity well and will have to come out of hyperspace. Max, Sparks, and Argos are no closer to an end-game strategy. They have no idea how they will get out of this mess once they land, and Hironike and his people are no closer to learning how these interlopers fit into the GMC's larger scheme. The fact of the matter is that outside of her wanting revenge for the wrongful death of a person dear to her which is highly unlikely to happen, especially given all their current circumstances, there is no larger plan. They are in no way affiliated with the GMC, and if they were, the GMC has no idea they are there.

Being among the people on board the theater/ship, Sparks has been exposed to a myriad of other experiences and perspectives that heavily contrasted with her own. This is particularly true of views on the government and how all their situations have come to create the current conditions of their fractured society. Many times, Sparks has had to bite her tongue while being regaled with tales of how specific regulations or litigation initiated or executed by Senator Levine had cut off means of provision or had infringed on the rights or wellbeing of some of their fellow travelers and their families. It frustrated her to no end as she was bombarded by story after story, and she could not arduously refute or rebut the stories without revealing her true perspective and reality, thus revealing that she was not at all aligned with these beings.

Being in such close proximity with these beings eventually made her see these people had the same desires as everyone else. She also recalls how snap judgements were made of her and her family long ago before she came into the employ of a planetary senator whose privileged existence shielded her from the fate of those who had experienced a harder life because of their economic or class status or because of the color or texture of their skin.

Max sits by patiently and watches this all unfold as he laughs inside. He is no fan of governments or systems.

For much of his life, he has found ways to circumvent their power or influence in an effort to line his pockets whenever possible. This way of thinking has never failed him. He will find a way out of this mess, and if she is smart enough to go with him and Argos, then all will be well and good, but if she is foolish enough to try and see this vendetta through, then she will be on her own. They are already going to have a tough enough time making their way back to Earth. He is not sure how well they will make out living in an outpost controlled by the Stone people. They will have a government or fledgling system to set up which could be a good thing seeing as they would be here getting in while the groundwork is being laid in. The currency and economy have already been established back on Earth, and Max has a pretty good foothold and credentials built up that he is not ready to relinquish in an effort to start from scratch. He has no idea how fair or unfair these beings will be out here.

Argos will pretty much go as Max did. Max has no idea why the big guy was so quick to leap with Sparks on her kamikaze mission here, but hopefully he has regained his senses. Argos, he guesses, has sensed that Max has a soft spot for the girl he knew long ago. Now that they have come back into contact and she is all grown up, the soft spot is still there. This could lead to a new black-market tech utopia, but again they would be starting over. Max is familiar with the stuff being developed on Earth, but he has no idea what modification needs mutated beings will be into, as that is not the market he is used to dealing with, so in essence, his personal market just shrank drastically to the non-mutated refugees aboard this vessel and whatever contingent of that group is already on Ganymede. He doesn't imagine there is a huge population waiting for them there.

They have not done much interstellar travel. Max has the most experience. He has ridden on ore haulers back in the day to siphon off some of the supply returning to Earth to supplement his business. Those trips did not take place often because they were risky endeavors. Sparks and Argos had never left Earth, but they could all tell the pace had slowed somehow, despite them still being in hyperspace. Sparks is not sure how she knew this but had the idea confirmed when she mentioned it to Max.

• • •

Hironike has been listening to their conversation in the skybox when he hears that last snippet of talking. The head of the Jade Assassins turns to Toshi and asks, "Are we slowing down?"

Toshi looks up after going over some readouts and input commands to place their findings on a large monitor which comes up out of a console in the deck of the bridge. "Yes, Hiro, I slowed us in response to some imaging coming from satellite feeds near both Mars and Ganymede."

Upon hearing this, Athena, Angelo, Takimura, Megumi, and all in the area go over to look at the images, which looks like some big things are taking place before their arrival. There looks to be a large-scale meteor shower hitting Ganymede, and there are GMC ships surrounding Mars. The mobile shipyard of the Kison Aksari had been seen there not too long ago but has since moved. Perhaps, the GMC is simply trying to hunt for discarded scrap from the skirmish there or whatever the shipyard might have left before moving again.

Toshi is thinking they are leaving one frying pan on Earth and possibly jumping into a fire at Ganymede. He expresses as much to Hironike. "Looks like we got action or, at least, strange activity at Ganymede. What's the play if we left civilian unrest only to run right into military action?"

Hironike thinks on this for a moment before answering. "That's a good question we have some combatants with us, but we also have civilians with no combat experience and no desire to get any. Athena, any thoughts?"

The queen of the Limbia Johari agrees. Plus, she has members of her people that are included in both examples Hironike describes. "We should, at least, see if we can be of any help, but I think we should not stay if it can be helped. Does this theater have weapons in addition to the travel capabilities? I know it seems like a silly question, but honestly I had no idea it could leave atmosphere," she adds.

Toshi steps in to answer her question. "The Ryoko-Gekijo has plenty of tricks up her sleeve, but weaponry, unfortunately, isn't one of them. Perhaps, Hiro will allow me to remedy that when we get a chance to dock and rest. I have some pretty good ideas now that I have some experience working with the Atlantean and Kison Askari shipwrights."

The flying theater has gone through a few variations in design through the years, but the placement of external weapons has not been part of them. The Ongakujin/Jade Assassins have arsenals that are more personal in nature; not to mention, they want to keep their more violent aspects a secret. They will have to keep a close eye on the developing situations around Mars and Ganymede as they get closer.

Athena pulls back her crystalline tresses into a ponytail of sorts and covers her hair, once again, with a wrap. "At some point before arrival, we need to let people know what's happening, so they can make a decision on how much they want to be involved in all this. I know my people who can fight will have no problem doing so, but we are ill-equipped for such a battle. If possible, open a channel to Tunisia and let her know we can help evacuate if necessary, but with no weapons for this vessel and no equipment needed to fight on the ground at either place, we will be of little service in my opinion."

Hironike nods his agreement as he cannot refute any of what she and Toshi had to say. The shields are good but will make them vulnerable when taking on more passengers as they will have to lower them in order to let anyone enter. They will have to strategize this sticky situation. There is also no way of knowing how they will hold up against the GMC's fighter crafts weapons as they have only dealt with the regional security forces back on Earth. The GMC's NightEagles are more troop transport than assault vehicles. Individual firearms are different from whatever the space harriers, Hell Raptors, and other craft they have recently developed will be armed with. The humongous U-shaped space Carriers will definitely have some long-range artillery designed for planetary bombardment, and Hironike is confident in the design of the Ryoko-Gekijo but obviously will not stand up to the firepower that ship has on it.

Toshi quickly sends a burst transmission ahead to Tunisia at Ganymede, containing the images from both places taken from the satellites, in addition to informing them the Ongakujin will soon arrive. There is no telling what kind of welcome they will get or how much of one they can expect be given now that the turmoil may be spreading. There is no turning back either way. They are unaware of how much the GMC has stripped their Earth-based forces in order to augment their offensives at Ganymede and Mars. The Ryoko-Gekijo, in reality, could likely return and better weather the combined forces of the local security teams and law enforcement.

● ● ●

In the skybox, Max is gathering the weapons he would actually be able to take with them. Argos sees this and starts to do the same. When Sparks comes in and sees them preparing for a fight, she asks, "What are you guys doing?"

Shaking his head because he thinks it is obvious, Max replies, "Haven't you been listening to what's going on? We are about to be in the middle of a huge battle, either at Ganymede or Mars, which isn't that far away. GMC is hot and heavy in the area."

Sparks can't believe it. "You're planning on tangling with the GMC?! Have you forgotten which side we're on?"

Max looks up from the railgun he has either had hidden somewhere or gotten from one of the freedom fighters they were now traveling with. "No, I know which side I am on. Ours, and it's not likely we are going to get the chance to explain ourselves once we come within range of the GMC firepower, so it's not like we have a choice. Or have you forgotten what vessel we are on and the circumstances under which it left Earth?"

She doesn't like it, but what he's said is true, and she has no argument. For the first time in a long time, she is in over her head, and Sparks can't help thinking that the common denominator for her being in circumstances like this is Max. The difference from this time and the times when she was running the streets with him before her security job is that now she is the reason they are in this current mess. The weight of that hit her like a ton of bricks, and she has nothing left to do but begin gathering any weapons she can in prep for the chaos to come. Sparks leaves to go find some of the beings she has lent her ear to during the trip in hopes that they may have a handle on where to find some good weapons. She refuses, however, to approach any of the Ongakujin. They are still sworn enemies as far as she is concerned. The remedy for this situation will have to come after ensuring their survival.

Chapter Twenty-Six

A DAY OR SO PREVIOUSLY, Aragon was firmly strapped into the Thor-class bomber temporarily issued to him, along with Sims and Jordan. The bulk of their fleet had jumped to Mars and was engaging the forces found there, which was minimal, so it looked as if the main fleet was hiding elsewhere and the mobile shipyard the Stone people had since moved on as well. Perhaps, it was around Jupiter. The GMC would be on the lookout for it if they were to claim any extra resources to replenish what they had just used in this most recent war effort. This was a quick drop of epic proportions. What the GMC pulled off in such a short amount of time with this many ships is nothing short of amazing.

For Aragon, even if they are on the wrong side of history, this brings back some of the pride he normally felt with being associated with his chosen branch of service that survived the culling of services over the years. Once they are all set to launch from Saturn, there are seventeen other bombers like the ones Aragon, Sims, and Jordan are all sitting in, empty shells wrapped in the very same stealth filaments the drop bods are in.

The *Ex Wife,* a centurion class space carrier, has these twenty hollowed-out torpedoes with Thor-class bombers in them jumped to Jupiter's night side, so they can travel under as little power as possible. Each bomber has three pods with four automaton units stuffed into them. The bombers coast as close to the gravity as possible to ensure the pods will get sucked in and then turn on their boosters to escape and jump directly back to Mars.

As soon as the torps are away, the *Ex Wife* immediately jumps back to rendezvous with the rest of the main attack fleet. They hope to avoid detection. This is quite a dangerous maneuver because, if the bulk of the ship gets too close to Jupiter's gravity well, it might inadvertently end up a casualty because it has not been designed to operate in atmosphere. Effectively, it jumps in, releases the torpedo shells, then instantly turns about, and jumps away. Ganymede is targeted, and the shells lazily fly in that general direction. It takes steel-like discipline for the pilots inside the shells not to hit the detonation charges that will blow the shell casing away too soon.

The pseudo-torpedo shells are on minimal power themselves. They cannot have too high of a heat signature, so their individual speeds differ, making this endeavor that much more difficult. The variables, however, do make it look more random to anyone watching from the ground level. As they are slowly barreling toward the Jovian moon, the huge Centurion space carrier turns about like an elephant turning around in the water. Once the nose is pointed away from Jupiter and the coordinates are confirmed in the nav-computer, the giant ship turns into a blur, and the stars become streaks for those with an external view, and it leaps into hyperspace back to Mars, to engage whatever forces are left there.

For Aragon, Sims, Jordan and the other pilots on this mission, comm silence is in place for the duration. For Aragon, it is the world's worst waiting game. All systems, with the exception of life support, are effectively shut down, and he just stares at the clock on his HUD, which is counting down an approximated time that is calculating the time from launch to atmospheric breach. Talk about flying by the seat of your pants. All is deathly quiet for most of the ride. The moments of weightlessness are sort of blissful before the small attitude thrusters activate to make small adjustments to keep them on target.

Short bursts are used to make adjustments. Then the thrusters will immediately shut down to keep the heat signature low. The closer they get to the gravity well, the less frequent the thrusts become which is good for keeping a low profile. The quiet is shattered as they hit the breach-point at various intervals, which is according to plan. Aragon hits the switch to escape the shell casing which will burn upon entry. Then he turns on the engines, which roars to life. The hope is the heat from the friction of entering the atmosphere will hide the engine's heat. After getting his bearings through all the shaking, Aragon opens his bay door, releases the drop pods, and hightails it back to Mars. Sims, Jordan, and the other bombers do the same without incident seemingly, and two hundred and forty automaton units are set to make landfall if they survive the drop.

The pods are more advanced prototypes of the models the mechanics had tested out some months ago, so success is expected to be pretty high. Once they hit the ground, it will be pretty obvious what they are, but the key is not being identified until then. The riskiest part for the automatons is the drop itself. If the Stone people have any kind of land-to-air ordinance set up, they can simply pick them off before landing, but the facility is still relatively new, and they haven't set that up yet. It is possible they have yet to even think of the possibility. This is, in effect, the first attempt at taking a planetary beachhead that isn't on Earth.

The group of twenty bombers jump into a scene they are ill-prepared for. Early reports are of sparse enemy ship sightings, but that has drastically changed since their mission. The space around Mars is alive with flying streaks of hot energy as four massive capital ships from both sides sit back and oversee a myriad of dogfights as the smaller craft dodge in and out of the cover of floating debris, trying to outgun each other. Apparently, soon after the GMC jumped in, a large enemy Dreadnaught and its retinue jump in to meet them, followed closely by another. The fight is on.

• • •

Darius and Bofus are taking a day to train together, using their new graviton bo-staves as they are being called now. The nanites are actually helping Bofus in new ways that he could not have predicted. They are actually calculating movements that he was unaware of previously, allowing him to better predict the strikes and other movements of his opponents. Both Babylon and Simeon watch over their private sessions to ensure the prince is safe. They also monitor any potential changes in his newfound abilities. Bofus is rapidly improving but cannot properly press the young prince in order to influence him into inadvertently using an unseen talent they are all on the lookout for. Instead, this becomes a time for drills and high intensity kata practice mixed with light sparring. They are basically honing their skills under the watchful eyes of their mentors.

The other Kison Askari are hard at work training, as well as sparing moments to glance at the two new special trainees. Some are also trying to work on using a newly developed personal energy shield that is housed in a gauntlet that could be activated via nanites already installed in the user. The gauntlet is worn on the arm, opposite the shoulder with the mounted canon to give them the ability to fire from their own cover. That, in addition to wielding the graviton bo-staves, was forcing them to work out the kinks in their stances, formations, and fighting styles.

Most of the Kison Askari have stopped wearing their shackles, even the ones they had created from the newly discovered alloys. It is no secret that they are free now, and that deception was needed previously, in order to begin their revolution. Some have chosen to still wear the newly developed ones as a constant reminder of the past with ceremonial embellishments on them. Darius and Bofus are taking a break and are immediately drawn to the spectacle of Ogun, who has chosen to blend all of these things into his arsenal. The young but large Askari has the new energy shield gauntlet on his left forearm, shoulder-mounted canon or bunduki over his right shoulder, a graviton bo in his right hand, which also sports the large shackle made of the new alloy with a nasty-looking blade welded onto it, covering his right wrist almost up to his elbow.

Bofus looks at him and says, "You should put something on yo' feet and head, so you can cartwheel into the fight and take everyone out!"

Darius giggles at the thought. Ogun says nothing. He simply approaches a group of manufactured metallic torso targets, sizes them up, and commences to destroy them with unfettered aggression, using all of his new equipment. First, he gets into his fighting stance and activates the shield, holding the graviton bo behind it, but exposing the blade on his shackle, which he immediately thrusts into where the heart would have been on a humanoid being. As the dummy flails backwards, he follows the initial attack up with an overhead downward strike with the graviton bo crushing the thing like a stomped soda can. Leaping up once more for his coup de grace, he fires a barrage of super-heated plasma into it and lands next to a small metallic puddle. Bofus simply stares open mouthed and slack jawed, which makes Darius laugh uproariously. Then there are thunderous booms coming from somewhere outside the facility, but it can be felt throughout. Alarms start blaring.

• • •

Sitting in her throne room, Queen Mother Tunisia is looking over readings from the external scanners that had picked up some unidentified falling objects when she simultaneously received the message from Toshi on board the Ryoko-Gekijo, which is apparently on its way there. Her rage is rising when she also notices the group of GMC ships around Mars, so she dispatches ships of their own to deal with them. The objects breaching the atmosphere are relatively small, and the scanners detect no ordinance or life forms within them, so the system decides they are likely less than a hundred meteors moving in an uncoordinated and random pattern, which is not an uncommon occurrence. Randomly falling inanimate objects are not very troubling. What is troubling is their timing, and Tunisia is not one to believe in coincidences.

Then she feels the quaking in her chamber as well. Kamal, Nefer, Muturi all come in to see if she is all right and are relieved to see that the queen is fine. They immediately go to the monitors to see what is happening on the surface and in various corridors of the habitat. The objects that have fallen at random spots are actually large canisters of some sort, and they are beginning to open from the crater sites and out of them are humanoid-looking beings, but scans show them to be mechanical constructs that are gathering together to form small groups. While watching all of this unfold, Tunisia begins to see red.

The queen mother orders General Simeon and the other generals to mount a defense while also demanding her Nyuesi Sime be prepared for launch. Nefer tries to calm her. "My queen, you should not go yourself. We should wait here and work out a strategy! Joining in the fray at Mars would be too risky."

The queen, however, is not having it. "You can fly with me but do not presume you can advise me on this! I am not going to Mars. We will hit Earth and their precious base at Saturn again. This time, we will finish the job!"

Seeing as the queen would brook no argument, Nefer simply nods but does not want to go with dark matter as her weapon of choice, so she implores Kamal and Muturi to come with her in the War Dragon they had initially trained and fought in. They hastily agree.

On her way to the underground hangars, Tunisia must have stopped to get Zola. After hearing word they are under attack, Zola does not need convincing. This time, she is already in her flight suit when Nefer and the others arrive. Helmet in hand, Tunisia doesn't even bother to ask about the extra bodies coming along but simply jumps into the cockpit of her fighter. Zola does the same and quickly goes over their preflight checks. Nefer, Kamal, and Muturi rush to do the same in their War Dragon. With Nefer quickly settling into the pilot's seat, Kamal nestles into the gunner's seat slightly ahead of her. Muturi's smaller frame fits into the more compact rear compartment manning the canon and depth charger weapons placed there which are now sporting a variety of ordinances that have been added since they began fighting.

To the dismay of many watching all this happening, they take off in their ships. The Kison Askari fear for their queen, but all who see her know that trying to stop or stall her is useless. Simeon nearly loses it when he hears she has left. Knowing Nefer is flying at her side is a small comfort, but this is still really risky. The queen has not taken into account what she means to her people after losing their king and especially since they do not fully trust the prince just yet. If something were to happen to her, the transition of power will be shaky for Darius, who at his young age, will have to contend with differing factions while also managing continued war efforts. Things are already muddled and about to be complicated further.

The cams and scanner systems above ground can clearly see the androids trying to breach the shafts leading down to the habitat. Simeon has ordered units of Askari to go hold them off. In the meantime, in prep for their arrival, he has also had the tunnels flooded with methane. He is taking a page from previous experiences on Pluto that may help them here. Likely, these androids will be armed with energy projectile weapons which could ignite the methane around them before any projectiles reach their intended targets, thus nullifying them from using those kinds of weapons. In contrast, the Kison Askari can still go in and use the newest of their weapons, with the exception of the bunduki, but the shields, graviton bo-staves, and their strength should be able to win the day. At least, that is what he is hoping. Slinging his hammer over his back, Simeon dons his helm and seals it, picks up his graviton bo, and heads to the hatch that leads to the hydroponics plant.

The entrances had been sealed once the Kison Askari were made aware of the pending assault, and fortunately, most of their ships have been dispatched to Mars, so the hangars are mostly empty. Darius has been taken, along with Babylon, aboard his personal ship to keep him safe in his mother's absence. Multiple units of automatons have begun to use lasers to cut into hatches at various levels of the shafts, leading down to the habitat. They have to stop when the methane is detected, realizing it will potentially be damaging to their structural integrity and systems had they inadvertantly ignited the gas on entry. This buys the Kison Askari some time while the automatons come up with an alternate method for getting in.

The gravity regulators inside the habitat have been turned off as well, in an attempt to disorient the invaders further. On human infiltrators, this may have worked, but the automatons simply note the change, and their internal systems adjust their mobility on the fly. There are two different variations in the models on this mission. Half of the automatons are the slender model with personal shielding equipped with ballistic and energy weaponry housed in their arms which can be retracted or exposed depending on the job. Both are built to be shaped like a bipedal humanoid with the main computer housed in the chest cavity, instead of the head. The whole thing is encased in various strong alloys overlaid with highly durable silicone. The other model is more of a tank with less silicone and more alloys made to truck through opponents as well as obstacles, such as the hatches they are trying to breach.

Since they have already drilled down a significant ways through the hatches with the lasers in an attempt to avoid an explosion, the tank units step into basically brute force the rest of the way through. They are slow and methodical but consistent at every breach point, being careful in an attempt not to create a spark with their strikes. A significant amount of resistance is waiting on the other side. There are four separate breach points all going simultaneously. At each point, the automatons are grossly outnumbered, but the point of this offensive is not to win the fight but to hinder the Stone people's ability to sustain a comfortable living habitat here.

Ancient Illumination II: (Kuongoza Mwanga: The Leading Light)

One unit goes toward the hangars; one goes to each of the filtration systems near the two underground polar ice caps, and the fourth unit targets the hydroponics units that are growing food. Njemba heads the group at the southern polar ice cap where they watch as one of the smaller automaton units pokes its head through the breach hole. Running up, the giant Askari grabs the head and yanks with all of his might to no avail. As he holds the head, Ogun runs up and comes down hard with his graviton bo, activating the heaviest setting on it at the last second before making contact and separating the head and neck from the body. There is a metallic clank as the head thuds to the ground.

As the body slides to the ground on the other side, a thick alloy-encased arm snakes through the hole, grabbing hold of Ogun's arm. It, then, yanks, slamming him into the heavy hatch. Luckily, he is wearing his helm but still sees stars momentarily. Out of nowhere, Professor Jones-Bey comes screaming in with a cube of some sort and throws it on the arm still blindly clutching for another victim or a mechanism that will open the hatch from the inside. The cube breaks, releasing a viscous liquid that instantly freezes the arm. Ogun, who has just recovered from his knock, uses his graviton bo again, shattering the arm. Bending down, he places the muzzle of his shoulder canon through the hole and fires a shot before anyone can stop him. Screams of "no" are cut off as the methane on the other side of the hatch ignites, but the flames, of course, spread into the Askari's side as well.

Chapter Twenty-Seven

IF ANYONE WERE ON THE surface of Mars, the sky would be an amazing spectacle with the amount of laser fire, brief explosions, and ships flitting back and forth in large and small-scale dogfights. General Krulak is aboard the *Ex Wife*, the GMC's flagship, a hyoid-shaped Centurion class space carrier which is currently exchanging long-range pot shots with one of the Kison Askari Dreadnaught carriers over and around the smaller ships in their respective fleet of ships. This is an extremely frustrating predicament for the commandant. Initially, there is very little resistance in the area. The GMC is basically mopping up the remnants of the forces left in the area, which is minimal. Just when the GMC's confidence is building, a Dreadnaught jumps in, followed by another along with a swarm of ships that come spilling out of each of them.

Soon, there is smoking wreckage from both sides, plummeting to the red planet's surface as the flight systems are disabled and too close to the gravity well which began pulling it all to crash spectacularly to the ground after burning in the transition from vacuum to atmosphere. The few handfuls of Askari left to maintain the mines there as part of skeleton crews are treated to a light show as flaming debris fills the night skies. It is beautiful yet horrific at the same time once observers realize there are living beings aboard the falling spacecraft. Aragon and his group of temporary officers all jump in to experience the chaos that the space around Mars has become from quite a different perspective.

They immediately have to begin juking and dodging as they arrive in the midst of several dogfights. There are instantly groups of small fast boomerang-shaped Katana-class fighters on their tails, pouring laser fire into them. Luckily, the Thor-class bombers are heavily armored, in comparison to the GMC's other Starfighters, but they are also slower and have less in the weaponry department for dealing with dogfighting. Aragon quickly decides the armor is a blessing as he is peppered frequently. There are some space harriers he can see that are doing some chasing and shooting of their own to good effect, which makes him feel somewhat better. At this point, comm silence is an insignificant factor in effectiveness.

Opening a channel, Aragon yells into his mic, "Be advised, all T-units. We should try and make it to the nearest Centurion to regroup, effect repairs if necessary, and get orders!"

There are nineteen double clicks of mics in response, acknowledging understanding. They are all too busy, avoiding fire, flying through dogfights to give verbal responses. The issue is that the closest Centurion is on the opposite side of the space battlefield. They will have to wade through the mayhem in order to safely dock. The sentiment is punctuated by them all seeing a flight of space harriers obliterated before their eyes. The four craft are ripped apart by laser fire and torpedoes. Flames erupt but are instantly doused by vacuum, and the smoking husks lazily drift toward the planet. Aragon and company fly through the debris as flotsam clangs off their hulls and front viewports. Jordan quickly keys his mic, opening a channel specifically to Aragon and Sims. "Having second thoughts about this piloting thing? I, for one, would rather die on the ground than in space."

Aragon and Sims do not reply, but both agree with the sentiment. The twenty or so bombers split into five groups of four and try to weave their way through the fighting. After setting the weapons on automatic target acquisition and firing, they collectively go about doing so. Sweating profusely, Aragon is finding it hard to concentrate as he pushes the throttle as far as it will go forward, barely escaping a slew of head-on collisions as he flies through exploded ships only to nearly come face-to-face with the ship that destroyed it. Some are friendly, and some are not.

As fast as they are traveling, the targeting system is what clues them in to who is who in passing.

Only a quarter of the way to their target, Jordan is listing badly because of a damaged engine. Aragon and Sims see that he is falling behind but can't dwell on it as they are both taking heavy fire. Soon the giant hatches to the hangar bays are in sight, but there are a few Katanas and an even larger War Dragon hot on their tails. The Centurion is aware of the incoming friendlies but cannot risk providing cover fire without risking shooting their own space craft. A group of space harriers sweep in to give some assistance, and the Katanas break off, but the War Dragon persists. Suddenly, out of nowhere, a larger ship with forward sweeping wings and what looks like a two-man cockpit goes after the War Dragon.

"What the hell is that?!" Aragon asks.

As they fly under its belly watching it spit hot plasma at the War Dragon pursuing them, Sims exclaims, "Hell Raptor, I believe! Woo hoo!"

They are almost home. The War Dragon has to break off its attack in the midst of taking fire, but the reprieve is only temporary. It turns as if to flee and then quickly turns about again, juking away from the chasing Hell Raptor. Glancing to his left, Aragon can see Jordan is still slightly behind but holding on. Almost home, he thinks. Sims is holding steady to his right.

Suddenly, he catches the glimpse of a reflected flash as he is looking at Sims's bomber and realizes it is on the other side. He turns his head just in time to see Jordan's Thor bomber light up, smoke, and fall to pieces as it is destroyed moments before making it into the hangar. His scream is cut short. Sims has picked up speed as he is not observing but concentrating on getting in the bay doors which have slid open slowly in anticipation of them coming in hot. Aragon squeezes his eyes shut to blink the welling tears away as he feels a shockwave in his own ship. Thinking quickly, he shuts down his thrusters and dips the nose steeply, so he is looking up through the top of the cockpit at the carrier they are trying to reach and desperately smashes the ejection button.

The blaring alarms go silent as the cockpit glass shatters, and he is thrust into the deafening silence of vacuum. There is another brief flash as his bomber explodes behind him. The flames are doused pretty much instantly, and he lazily flips repeatedly head over heels hopefully in the direction of the bay doors. There won't be a lot of oxygen stored in his flight/EV suit. Strangely, what he sees when he looks behind is an oddly beautiful sight. There was a myriad of brief flashes with each explosion, and it is happening all over the place. Somehow, the lack of sound adds to the visual quality. Aragon finds it really ironic that he would see beauty in his moment of death.

Sims has already landed safely inside the bay and is running back toward the bay door as many Marines and other military personnel are watching Aragon slowly make his way toward them. It looks as if it is going to be tight to see if he will make it in time as both he and the door are lumbering along at a snail's pace. Behind him, they can see the War Dragon break off its attack in the wake of more fire from the Hell Raptor. It is likely because it is obvious it would not make it into the hangar, which may have been damaging to the people and assets there but ultimately a suicide run had they been successful. The Stone people operating it are not interested in a one-way trip.

One of the combat engineers comes sprinting toward the nearly closed door. Sims is unfamiliar with what the young Marine is carrying, but it looks like a small harpoon gun with a nasty-looking spear tip on it. All he can manage under his breath is "He's not going to like that." The engineer, who is dressed in armored EV gear, stops just inside the door and mag-locks his boots to the deck as he takes aim and fires a spear-trailing cable into space. It too loses momentum as it leaves the artificial gravity inside the hangar and enters the vacuum but still has enough inertia to carry it to its intended target. Unfortunately or fortunately, depending on how one thinks about it, the projectile strikes true directly into Aragon's left quadriceps, eliciting a yelp of pain only he can hear.

The suit senses the breach and tries to tighten microbes around the two holes in an attempt to conserve escaping oxygen. This also heightens Aragon's pain. The constricting of the area around the fresh wound is made worse by the young engineer who is now, with the help of Sims and other Marines, pulling on the attached cable to bring Aragon into the hangar. They succeed with barely half a meter to spare as his body enters just as the huge door slams closed. As Sims and the other Marines gather Aragon into their collective arms, breathing sighs of relief, he collapses.

• • •

There is an uptick in hostilities on Earth with the absence of a large GMC presence to back up the local authorities, but that is halted as satellite footage is somehow being simulcast live from feeds around Jupiter and Mars. The government is angry about this development since they have not sanctioned these actions. The ire of the general public is rising once again, and extremists from various perspectives are trying to use this to fit their agendas. Ragnar is trying to say this aggression is only in response to offenses the mutated beings have committed against regular mankind. He believes their elimination is the key to true peace. The Guild of the Pristine are heavily behind this notion, and others are taking up the cause to spread this message.

Shajara has no intention of letting these messages of hate-mongering spread too far without one from the Children of the Sun to combat them. The rest of society who feels they have no stake in it either way are content to sit back and watch the battles as if they are watching some sci-fi drama. They choose to ignore the potential negative effects that may soon be coming to all of society as a result. One such effect will be arriving sooner rather than later. Three smaller ships have just jumped in near Earth's gravity well as most everyone has their eyes glued to the events going on a planet or two away from them.

Two Nyeusi Sime and a War Dragon have dropped out of hyperspace and immediately dive into Earth's atmosphere. The first two ships are piloted by Queen Tunisia and Zola, while the War Dragon flying escort is piloted by Nefer with Kamal in the gunner position and Muturi in the rear gunner's spot. The smaller ships have stealth capabilities, and they were activated once they were close to nine-thousand meters cruising altitude. To onlookers, it looks as if the War Dragon is flying solo. Alarms blare at the Twenty-Nine Palms GMC base as the ships approach at speeds their planes and choppers are ill-equipped to match. Seemingly out of nowhere, there are drops of ordinance that come out of thin air to those watching on cameras surrounding the large base.

There were huge billowing explosions and a now familiar purple haze that is slowly spreading outward, bizarrely erasing both inorganic and living material at an alarming rate. The GMC and civilian personnel anywhere near the blast sites are killed instantly. The purple fog spreads like a personified antagonist from a horror film. Just like what had occurred on Saturn, the aftermath looks as if some godly cartoonist has come along to delete their work. The three ships quickly make their way to other target sites as the fog spreads to Palm Springs and Joshua Tree, adding even more civilians to the body count. Nefer feels sick inside as she now knows that they should have tried harder to stop Queen Tunisia from going this route.

Too late to really do anything about it now, short of attempting to shoot her down, so they continue on to other military installations across the globe before jumping out of the system again and heading to Saturn itself for a final blow to the GMC that hopefully will make them see reason and sue for peace, rather than seek to further hostilities. Once they arrive there, they target the place that was initially hit when they first deployed the dark matter ordinance a couple years prior, undoing some of the progress the GMC has made in repairing the facility there. Queen Tunisia does not stop there. She seeks out untouched areas as well and drains the remainder of the ordinance she is carrying. Zola follows suit.

There are soon space harriers in the area as they are patrolling the ring and are alerted to an enemy presence giving chase. They focus on the War Dragon since that is the only one of the vessels they can see which easily evades them with slightly slower speed but better maneuverability. It also has the advantage of having weapons that face both forward and aft of the craft. Therefore, it is able to defend from multiple angles. The swivel capability of the cockpit area makes it a hard ship to flank in an attempt to broadside it. The Nyeusi Sime are fast and smaller but not as heavily armored. Zola's ship takes heavy fire, despite it not even being the target. Lucky shots for the GMC pilots, and not so much for her. There is an explosion almost instantly quelled before the ship drifts into Saturn's gravity and plummets into one of the growing deep purple clouds spreading from the various bombsites.

Tunisia wails into the mic in anger, but Nefer quickly gets her attention. "My queen, they cannot see you. Jump back to Ganymede where we can recover! I will be right behind you."

Thankfully, she does as suggested, coming out of stealth mode briefly as her ship initiates the jump. The distraction of the ship's brief appearance on their scanners is enough to allow the War Dragon time to disengage and make the jump moments later. The space surrounding Mars would have been a much riskier jump. It is still in chaos.

On the surface of Saturn, Marines are scrambling to get out of hazardous areas and evacuating the facility to regroup on Titan until the danger and damage can be accessed. Lt. Commander Jameson is glad to have a couple squads of Marines with him who he has recently enhanced with cybernetics. So far, there are only reports of bombings but no boots on the ground for the enemy. It is still comforting to have his own men if some Stone warriors are to show up to finish the job. The number of casualties on both sides at Mars are rising, and word has just reached the top about an attack on Earth shortly before the bombing at Saturn. Lt. Commander Jameson is now hoping the fully mechanized unit on

Ganymede is doing some damage. There needs to be a reckoning for these savage beings.

All space-worthy craft is ordered to take off, regardless of fuel or weapons capabilities. The attackers have failed or did not recognized the shipyards within the ring and have mistakenly left one of the few good sources of materiel the GMC had access to. A lucky break in all of this mess. The clouds of destruction are spreading quickly, and Jameson is leading his men and women through undamaged corridors that will not be that way for long to the launch pads for many of their remaining ships that stayed behind. There are a few Marauder-class destroyers, and he has chosen one of them to jump aboard. He has eschewed his traditional white coat in favor of newly developed power armor. There is supposed to be more testing, but under the circumstances, it is better than wearing the lab coat or dress uniform.

The naval personnel guarding the ship look as if they are going to question their right to board that particular class of ship but notice the shiny rank insignias on Jameson's pauldrons and the mean-looking augmented Marines with him and think better of it. Once they take off, he immediately goes to the bridge to see who is in command. If they are of a lower rank, he will assume command and hopefully not get too much flack from them or the crew for doing so. Once there, he sees that a captain is at the helm, so it becomes a mute issue. For now, he will have to fall in line and hope Captain Williams knows what he is doing.

Lt. Commander Jameson does, however, ask that the whereabouts or condition of the Mechanics be found out. It is quickly reported that, as soon as the order to launch was given, they were directed to hop aboard the Adder, along with as many Marines as they can fit and a beast of some sort. They are awaiting further instructions, along with the other ships that have escaped. The young lieutenant at the communications console sounds as if he does not believe the reports about the beast in tow. That is the least of their worries, Lt. Commander Jameson thinks. It is possible to turn all this around and win, but at what cost?

It is obvious, from reports, that the resources they are hoping to recover on Mars are not there, and they are losing assets in lives and materials in multiple areas. Even if they are to win, there is the question of what will remain if the dark matter continues to spread on Earth and Saturn. The GMC has put themselves and society at large in a precarious situation. The Kison Askari are likely to lose a lot of the sympathy they had gained earlier with the recorded skirmish footage at Mars that was obviously doctored, but they will be able to recover and isolate themselves on Ganymede, if they can repel the automatons.

Chapter Twenty-Eight

ABOARD BABYLON'S SHIP, DARIUS, ALONG with his personal guards, worries over the events playing out at Mars and Ganymede. Word has gotten out about the queen's recent actions amid the attacks as well. Opinions of her are beginning to become a polarizing topic. The automatons, for the most part, are successfully being repelled but have succeeded in damaging the filtration system from one of the polar ice caps, meaning it has to be repaired in order to use it as a viable water source. The second one remains functional, but the Kison Askari have taken some heavy losses there. The hangar and the hydroponics units are the most heavily guarded parts of the facility as the Askari have ensured more people will be sent to those locations as hostilities become more intense.

The automatons have more than held their own against the Kison Askari. The problem is one of numbers, and the numbers are not in favor of the mechanical units. There are an impressive number of casualties from the GMC perspective, but the smallest losses incurred by the automaton units have had a larger effect on their proficiency after a while. Ogun and the Kison Askari unit he is with is now running roughshod through the automatons they are up against. Self-preservation is very much a part of their programming, so they regroup to plan out an escape plan following their retreat. Using demolitions explosives to discourage being followed, the automatons make their way back to the surface where it might be easier to hide among the landscape. Plus, there is not too much activity on the surface for the Stone people since they have made their home underground.

The automatons quickly disperse to be near the crater sites of the pods they rode down and sent out various burst signals to the GMC, as well as a few other sources in order to affect an extraction off-moon. The GMC will be sure to get as many of them back intact as possible, but there is another interested party who will soon know of the outgoing signal. The issue is whether or not they will be able to reach them in time. The ship that came is not the one they are expecting to reach the area so quickly. Likely, the automatons are not aware of their existence, and the ignorance is mutual. Soon the Ryoko-Gekijo is in sight of the Jovian moon, and Toshi is confused by the signal they can track directly to the surface of Ganymede.

Hironike asks Toshi to open a channel to the habitat there. Once it is confirmed that there is an open line, Hironike speaks, "This is Hironike of the Ongakujin, looking for Queen Tunisia. We are here at Ganymede, aboard the Ryoko-Gekijo. It's been reported that there are hostilities here and at Mars. We have with us refugees and freedom fighters ready to lend a hand if necessary."

For a moment, there is dead silence, and they fear the worst. No one says it, but the mining colony at Pluto is the example everyone is hoping this situation does not mirror. There are no survivors there from that attack. One thing that is confusing is part of the message is in binary.

Toshi has to have the communications console analyze it to decipher its meaning. When it becomes clear it is an SOS directed at multiple recipients, things are muddled further. Turns out there are some androids deployed by the GMC that are, somehow, the property of an Earth-based robotics company stranded on Ganymede, and they are requesting assistance. Hironike is unsure what to make of this. "Toshi, once you have everything translated, see if you can narrow down which company may have a stake in retrieving these units," he says.

Toshi nods his understanding but is a little puzzled by the request. "You going to strike a deal?" he asks.

Laughing, Hironike answers, "I am ever the pragmatist but also loyal to my friends. I am thinking we may be able to turn this into a win for all of us and make some money in the process if we can get whoever owns them to pay us for retrieval and lessen the GMC presence down there."

As they are thinking on that, finally a response comes from the habitat, but it is the gravelly voice of Simeon who speaks to them. "This is General Simeon of the Kison Askari. Queen Tunisia is out of reach at the moment. She took a few ships to strike back at the GMC. We are fine here now. The robots or whatever they were seem to have retreated."

Hironike realizes that his previous proposition was a risky one at best now. If the queen is angry enough to be flying missions herself, then how will she look upon allies that have colluded with the enemy or are thought to be doing so? Toshi does not need clarification on what Hironike is shaking his head about while replying, "General! Glad to hear you're safe. The queen is out flying combat missions? How bad did things get for that to happen? Is the prince safe?"

Athena and Angelo come closer to hear the reply from Simeon. "It would be wise to pass on any opportunity those bots might give you, Hiro," Athena whispers.

Simeon answers, "The prince is safe aboard Babylon's ship, and from what I hear, once the attack started, the queen could not be convinced to stand down. They tried a few different approaches, but our numbers won the day. They were, however, more formidable than the GMC regulars. Had they come in force, it might have turned out differently. We lost some good warriors today. If Babylon did not head to Mars, they should be in orbit around here somewhere. We sent Darius with him when the attack began as a precaution."

• • •

Not too far away, but on the opposite side of the moon, Babylon's manta-shaped ship waits in orbit but not exactly where anyone can see them. Darius does not seem as impressed as he should be, but then again, that is usually the case with the boy. Babylon learned this some time ago. Bofus, however, is absolutely mind blown. "Man! Where are we? I mean, I still see Ganymede, but nobody seems to be seeing us, and you didn't say nothing about no cloaking device," he protests.

Darius walks up to him, and together they watch as Babylon sits in the captain's chair with eyes closed in deep concentration.

His trident is ensconced in an opening next to the chair and is sticking straight up. Babylon's hands are placed on strange, metallic-looking hand-shaped impressions on the armrests. Darius looks at Bofus and explains, "This is a living ship, and Babylon is holding us in the void right now, so we are still at Ganymede but in kind of another dimension."

Bofus can't quite wrap his mind around any of those concepts. "What you mean living? Living as in, we in the belly of the beast? I'm not down with that! Babylon needs to wake up and take us out!"

Giggling at Bofus's complaints, Darius tries to reassure him, "This craft is an organic being, and, no, we're not in its belly...I don't think. Babylon is holding us here where we can keep an eye on things without the threat of the GMC, if they should come."

Bofus feels a little better but still doesn't like it. Just then, they see a large vessel jump out of hyperspace on the other side of the Jovian moon. It is strange viewing things from the void for Bofus. Darius seems quite comfortable. It is like looking at a 3-D replication of what is happening, but the overlay has a purple filter on it. The vessel looks oddly familiar to Bofus, but he has a hard time believing his eyes. "Um...I think that's a mobile theater from Earth, but if it is, they picked a bad time to have a show. Didn't know they could get off-planet in that thing!"

Opening his eyes, Babylon replies, "Well, now you know! Dat's Hironike and his people." The Atlanean's hands fly over the console before him, and the ship comes around the moon to meet the Ryoko-

Gekijo and comes out of the void appearing right in front of it which throws the Ongakujin for a loop. There are gasps among those aboard the flying-theater in a position to see the ship appear seemingly out of nowhere. Toshi is surprised but recognizes it immediately. Hironike and Athena hide their initial jump scare well. At first, they think, perhaps, the GMC has stealth ships recently developed in the area. Since that isn't the case, they relax.

Babylon hails them as soon as he reveals himself, letting them know he is friendly in any case. The Ryoko-Gekijo is larger than Babylon's ship, but Babylon has weapons on his organic vessel that might be powerful enough to penetrate the shields the theater has. "Dis is soon-to-be hostile space, jus to let ya know! Hironike, might be best to take your people back to Earth until things cool down out here."

Hironike nodds at Toshi who activates the video display. They can now see Darius, Babylon, two unknown Atlaneans, and a dark-skinned human who is wearing a small Kison Askari armor suit complete with a shoulder-harness-mounted canon. Hironike ignores the strangeness of the scene and greets them. "Babylon the wise. Glad to see you are safe. Glad to see Prince Darius is as well. Things are a bit complicated back on Earth, as well, which is what prompted our swift departure. Nowhere will be safe forever, I fear. This war is about to spread."

Aboard Babylon's ship, Darius steps closer to the monitor-like apparatus that came up from the deck and sees Hironike and Toshi. He recognizes them along with other green-skinned beings of their kind, and then his attention is drawn to a slender female being with crystalized skin and long hair that looks like strings of amethyst beads. There is another being of her kind, but the Prince is mesmerized by Athena. Without thinking, he simply blurts, "Hello, I'm Prince Darius."

Laughing, she chastises Hironike and answers his greeting, "Hiro, where are your manners? Hello, Prince Darius. I am Athena, queen of the Limbia Johari. We need to get your mother, so we can figure out what to do from here. Things have gotten understandably out of hand."

Babylon steps in front of the seemingly love struck young boy and interjects, "Yes, we will have to arrange that when it's safe to do so. It would seem that what the Kison Askari have built here is no longer a secret. Therefore, it is not as safe as they once thought."

Nobody can argue with that, but they are lucky that the GMC has not come in force with the assets they have deployed there. It looks like they are just testing the waters, so to speak. Just when Darius is about to voice that thought, a large group of GMC ships jump into view. Some of the larger ships have battle scars from the action at Mars.

• • •

The Adder has dropped off as much personnel as they can carry off on Titan, so they can regroup with the rest of the GMC and other military members who are lucky enough to escape the dark matter attack on Saturn. Hopefully, the stuff will die down like last time, and they will be able to rebuild again. A scenario they didn't want to think of is if the stuff continues to spread, destroying the materials being mined from the ring as well as the moons there. As soon as they touch down on Titan, Sgt. Garrison receives orders to go back to Ganymede to pick up the remnants of automatons that have been deployed there.

Lance Corporal McNamara does not like this at all. It is a sticky situation the first time they venture out there, and this time, there will likely be someone looking out for trespassers. Plus, there are multiple pickup spots for extractions dotting the surface of Ganymede. This is going to be a bumpy ride. McNamara is smart enough to hide his disapproval. He is pretty sure Sgt. Garrison, Lance Corporal Jennings, PFC Long, and Private Cooper all feel the same but orders are orders and complaining won't change that. Long is mag-locked to the floor next to his drop pod which currently has his beast in it. Lance Corporal Jennings is strapped into the co-pilot seat, with Sgt. Garrison in the seat behind them. Private Cooper is seated at the comms console and monitoring for signals as they make their way back to Ganymede.

Private Cooper is able to pick up on one of the signals as soon as they jump in-system. Unstrapping himself, Sgt. Garrison gets up to examine the grid to map out points to focus on. This time, if there are any spacecraft around, it will be easy to spot an object entering atmosphere cloaked or not, and they do not have the luxury of trying to imitate falling debris with a slew of other objects to blend in with. Immediately, he sees the closest signal coming from the southern hemisphere with a couple pings near to it. "Let's drop in fast and head here first, then see if we can scoop up as many of these smart bots as possible before anyone sees what we're doing," Garrison orders, pointing to the area, seeming to have the most concentrated signal sources.

There is a chorus of "Aye, aye, sergeant!" as they all prepare to come in hot for this mission that will likely get messy. Kneeling by his drop pod, PFC Long speaks to his Tuefel Hunden, "Hey, boy, I think you'll have to stay on board, but I'll be back soon. Just try not to crap the pod til I can let you out somewhere."

The animal looks back at him with his glowing eyes and whines softly while licking the metal fingers at the edge of the hatch. Stepping back, Long closes the pod. Looking over at him, Sgt. Garrison adds, "I wouldn't take the torso canon. We want to be as fast as possible. Hopefully, they'll be ready to go as soon as we touch down. I'm all for getting assets but not risking real lives for these…things if I can help it."

The rest of the Mechanics are glad to hear that sentiment. It is one thing to risk life and limb for your brother but quite another to do so for what basically amounts to pieces of equipment. Since this is not necessarily a stealth mission and despite the call for speed while extracting, Private Cooper decides he is taking the "big bad wolf," the name of his specific plasma rifle designed with his arms in mind. The only other weapon that has a name is Dragon slayer, the "torso canon" Sgt. Garrison has just instructed Long not to take. They, hopefully, will not have to tangle with any ships while on foot, but Cooper does not want to go into a potential scrap, lacking in the firepower department.

Sgt. Garrison packs the latest version of the duel ballistic projectile rail rifle. It shoots both cryo and plasma rounds simultaneously but slightly staggers in an attempt to make it easier to penetrate the calcified skin of the Stone people. Lance Corporal McNamara will stay back in the pilot's seat while Lance Corporal Jennings will hang back and cover them from a distance with a long-range rail sniper.

Lance Corporal McNamara activates the stealth filaments despite it likely not having any chance of hiding their presence while entering atmosphere. "Hold on, boys! We're going in!" he announces, and the hull begins to creek and shutter as it is super-heated by the friction. Everyone tucks in to weather the storm. Tuefel begins to howl loudly.

● ● ●

Nefer is having a hard time keeping up with the queen's ship. She seems content on flying to her death. Tunisia is trying to challenge as many of the GMC fighters as she can and has since run out of dark matter ordinance to use which is likely a good thing. No doubt, if she had any she would have fired it upon every craft she finds. Luckily Zola has exhausted her dark matter as well or who knows what the results would have been had it detonated along with her Nyeusi Sime. Suddenly, the GMC ships all start to jump out of the system, and there are only a few stragglers for Tunisia to hunt down. Finally, Nefer offers, "Perhaps we can head home now, my queen?"

Reluctantly Tunisia relents and sets coordinates to head back to Ganymede. Once they get near Jupiter, they find the traffic around the moon they have made their new home on is heavily concentrated. Tunisia sees red at the fact the GMC is determined to continue their encroachment, despite repeated losses. These people have no shame and no moral grounds to what they are pursuing. They have to be eradicated, but she is out of the biggest weapon at her disposal. She will have to risk it and re-arm. She will also order some of the other ships still in the hangars to deploy with dark matter as well. She relays those orders.

Nefer opens an encrypted line to Simeon. "General, it pains me to say this, but I think the queen has gone quite mad in her grief and is in no condition to lead. If we obey her last orders, we may destroy, not only the GMC, but ourselves in the process."

Simeon thinks on that for a minute before replying, "I understand. We will meet you in her personal hangar bay."

What happens next will haunt the general for a long time. He hopes the prince will forgive him and that the queen will come to understand once her head is clear.

Chapter Twenty-Nine

ARAGON OPENS HIS EYES AND has to briefly close them to get used to the bright lights. He immediately notices the white walls, sterility, and medical uniforms of the people around him. Sickbay is not an ideal place to be, but he guesses it is better than suffocating, freezing, or being blown to pieces in space. That thought reminds him of how he must have ended up here and that Corporal Jordan was not lucky enough to have escaped the last death possibility he'd come up with. He tries to sit up and finds that he is restrained which is never good. Looking down toward his feet, he tries to wiggle his toes with unsuccessful results. As the panic is rising, a familiar face comes into view.

Petty Officer House walks over to the bed Aragon is on and checks the readout on his chart before saying, "Hey, buddy. Relax. You didn't quite escape your ship's explosion unscathed. They had to remove shrapnel from your spine and neck but don't worry. They also hooked you up with a cybernetic interface that can cover for the nerve damage. You could say you have more of a backbone now."

Aragon tries to laugh, but his throat is just as dry as House's joke. Realizing his friend must be thirsty, he brings over a cup with a straw and offers him some water. After a few sips, Aragon is able to speak. "What about Sims? Did I lose my dark green brother as well?"

A Marine approaches, dressed in gray, black, and white urban camouflage utilities.

Aragon briefly sees a brown hand come down on his arm before seeing Corporal Sims's face come into his view. "I'm still here, brother," he says as they both take a moment to silently mourn their lost comrade in arms. House steps out to give them some time. Upon his return, he tells them, "You should be ready to rock and roll here soon. There will be some initial residual pain, but the implant should recognize it and give you the appropriate dosage. It should also take a day or so for your body to get acclimatized to the grafting to your spine as it begins to integrate with your neural network."

Confused, Aragon blurts, "What the hell are you talking about, doc?"

Sims steps in to answer, "Your spine was damaged pretty bad, so they had to graft on a cybernetic overlay that kind of encases and protects you back there. Some of the connections needed for your brain to communicate with the rest of your body were irreparably severed, so the new spine forms a bridge to those breaks. Without it, you couldn't walk or function really."

As Aragon is letting all that sink in, he begins to feel sensation gradually coming back to his extremities. There is a lance of hot pain that shoots up his back but almost instantly it is gone.

House has come back, and they both approach the bed at the change of expressions on Aragon's face. "Relax. Feeling is beginning to come back, along with the pain you mentioned, but whatever you did, it dosed me pretty much as soon as I felt it. Stop looking like you lost your puppy. I'm good."

They get a much-needed chuckle from that. Once House sees that he is stable, he goes to get the attending doctor to see how long Aragon has to stay in sick bay. Once they are alone, Aragon asks, "So what's the word?"

After pulling up a chair, Sims answers him. "The brass is trying to put on a good face, but all anyone has to do is look out the portholes and see we are getting our butts handed to us. Some are holding their own, of course, but this is all so new, and somehow, the rockheads have adapted quicker for the first time since forever. Half of our space worthy forces have gone to Ganymede, but it's posturing that I think will backfire as there's now word that some of theirs have jumped to HQ at Saturn. They've already hit us there earlier with DM ordinance and Earth before that."

This last revelation does not sit well with Aragon. How they have managed to contain and weaponize such a volatile substance before the GMC is appalling, to say the least. These beings have been underestimated for sure. House walks back in with word that Aragon is cleared to leave as soon as his vitals and diagnostics pass inspection by the surgeon who implanted him. He is to be issued new uniforms and armor made specifically to make use of his new enhancement. His new helmet and other parts of his kit will have new tech that only he can interface with. A med-bot comes in and scans him as he lays there while Sims and House watch. The bot simply states, "Fully functional." Then, it leaves.

The straps on his bed fall to the floor seemingly of their own accord and retract into the bed. "Not creepy at all," Aragon says to nobody in particular as he attempts to swing his legs over the side of the bed. Cautiously, he sets his feet on the floor and realizes his gown is open in the back. Seeing his discomfiture, Sims and House share an amused look as the surgeon enters the room. "Good evening, sir!" they chorus.

"At ease, gentlemen. How's our boy?" he asks Sims and House. Then he turns to his patient and states, "Readout says you're good to go. Take your time and try to stand." Aragon is not sure exactly what is different, but there definitely is something as he plants his feet and pushes up to stand. There is a new vigor and rigidness to his stance. Looking Aragon over, Sims comments, "I guess you're officially in the Ascension Protocol now."

• • •

The Ryoko-Gekijo is given permission to dock in the underground hangars if they can navigate the developing battles happening in the space around Mars. They proceed to do so while Babylon attempts to make the same run as Darius wants to check on his mother now that she has returned. Maxing out the speed of the flying theater, Toshi is able to make it with the aid of the shield generators. The GMC ships are caught off guard once they jump in and see the theater, which is pretty well known for its shows on Earth. Once word got out about the circumstances of it leaving Earth, many that come into contact with it try to concentrate fire on it to no avail. Lucky for them, external weaponry has not yet been installed on the roving home of the Ongakujin.

Toshi safely navigates the multiple fields of fire to the hangar followed by Babylon who exits the void at the last minute, spooking the sentries in the process, as they seem to have materialized out of nowhere. There are very large canons that, initially, were to be mounted on space craft that the Kison Askari are now being mounted at the entrance to the hangar in the event that GMC space craft are to attempt to infiltrate the facility. This should have been thought of earlier, but they are learning as they go along just as the GMC are. The side which learns quickest will likely end up the victor.

Moments earlier, Queen Tunisia and Nefer had already docked. The queen had jumped out of the cockpit of her Nyeusi Sime, barking orders that her ship be resupplied with more ordinance. Nefer comes into the queen's dock pad where Simeon and a group of Kison Askari are waiting for her. There is a sad look on the general's face. "Simeon, shouldn't you be overlooking the security of this habitat which is now under siege? I need more dark matter missiles. What are all of you doing here? There has to be a better use of personnel than greeting me!" she bellows.

Forlornly Simeon answers, "My queen, the facility is secured. The robots or whatever they are have retreated. Once the canons are installed at all external entrances, we will send out Askari to seek out the attackers. The dark matter will not be necessary. We ask that you come with us."

Anger flows through Tunisia as she looks at everyone gathered there. "What is the meaning of this? Are you requesting or demanding? From the looks of it, you're not truly asking…are you?" she asks.

Just then, Darius comes running in. He goes to his mother to hug her. The prince stops shy at the look upon her face and turns to look at everyone on the launch pad. "What's wrong?" he asks to anyone who would answer. With tears in her eyes, Tunisia looks down at her son and says, "Apparently, I am being confined so as not to cause any more trouble, despite us *not* starting any of this. I was trying to finish it."

Simeon can barely look her in the eyes as he says, "Yes, my queen, but your methods are a little too…extreme."

Laughing maniacally, the queen says, "Oh, you poor, dumb fools. Have you ignored what our people have been through? Did you somehow forget the extreme circumstances surrounding our employ or, rather, slavery, which is a more accurate term. We were never mining colonists! We were the beings who provided the life's blood to a myriad of technological corporations and propelled the lifestyles of billions across the globe! Everyone reaped the benefits, except the very people risking life and limb across the galaxy to help advance society."

Babylon finally arrives to catch the end of their exchange. It is obvious something is awry. Upon seeing him, the queen assumes he is involved. "What was your part in all of this, Babylon?!"

Dismayed, Babylon says, "Dis had nottin to do wit' me!"

With eyes lowered, Nefer speaks up, ashamed, "It was me, my queen. I felt, if you continued to use the dark matter unchecked, you would destroy everything eventually. We hit military targets, but on Earth it is spreading. Some of the very people you have love for over the pain they have been caused, I fear they may be caught in the uncontrolled mists as well."

The source of the betrayal hurt more than the act itself. The queen collapses to her knees and two Askari go to collect her. She leaves without another word. Hironike, Athena, Toshi, Takimura, Megumi, and Angelo see her briefly as she is being escorted to her quarters where guards will be posted outside to ensure she stays there. Hironike tries to follow but is intercepted by Simeon. Holding up a hand, he says, "I'll explain later. In the meantime, do you think any of the freedom fighters you brought will be willing to go hunt some bots that attacked us earlier, courtesy of the GMC?"

Toshi thinks about it for a second and looks at Hironike for approval, who nods. Toshi offers, "I am sure many of them are ready to continue the fight but may be ill equipped under these circumstances. I am sure none of them have EV suits for space combat of any kind."

Simeon simply waves his hand dismissively. "We have mining gear they can wear to protect them from the atmosphere, or the lack thereof. Not too sure it will hold up against the weapons we face, but they should be able to breath, and the suits may be heavy for some as they were produced with our physiology in mind. We don't have the time to mass produce the armor sets created for young Darius and Bofus. There are a select number of similar sets but are already being used by other humans and non-Kison Askari who recently joined our warrior ranks."

Toshi understands and promises to pass the information to volunteers for the mission, so everyone who wants to go fully knows the risks. The technological genius for the Jade Assassins goes back to the Ryoko-Gekijo to make the announcement. Many of those aboard are filing out of the theater. Some of the Kison Askari have come to help them find a place in the habitat, and there is another group of beings who are lingering just outside the ship with weapons and various other gear. Max, Argos, and Sparks are among the latter group. Max is relaxed, Argos is hidden beneath his wrappings, stoic as ever, and Sparks looks like she has seen a ghost.

Toshi approaches the group most likely to have fighters in it and lets them know the details of what is going on. Before turning to leave, he walks up to where Sparks is standing with Max in earshot. He simply states, "We know who you are. I don't know why you have taken this as far as you have, but maybe you've come to reason, and the government has slighted you in some way recently forcing your hand. Perhaps you're still hell-bent on avenging a fallen senator. Either way, do your best. Just know, if you attempt to harm the Ongakujin or our allies, there will be no quarter given. This golem or whatever it is with you will not be able to save you."

With that, he continues on his way into the theater which has its own docking pad because of its size in comparison to most of the other craft the Askari has developed. Max just shakes his head and continues to arm himself with weapons the other fighters are handing out. He looks on appreciatively as he gets his hands on a GMC issue railgun that must have been left behind and now has been repurposed to shoot at those who had manufactured it.

Sparks is upset by his nonchalance. "What do you think you're doing?"

Looking at her as if she is being absurd, he answers, "What do you think? You heard our green friend back there, right? They made us, know who we are, and like I stated before, when rounds start flying back and forth, do you think any of the GMC will stop to hear your side? I told you before that if these beings were anywhere near as dangerous as you thought them to be that they were not to be trifled with! Now we are caught in the middle, and so I am going to do what I know how to do aside from make money, and that's fight. Argos is pretty good at it himself, despite what greeny had to say."

She has no answer and just walks over to where one of the Kison Askari is handing out armor and accepts a very heavy-looking EV suit obviously made for someone much larger than her. Sparks walks around looking at what everyone else is getting and feels more out of place than she did aboard the Ryoko-Gekijo. Luckily, one of the Askari walks up to her and takes off the helm of their armor to reveal that it is, in fact, a human female beneath it. She is a large woman who quickly asks, "What's your name?"

Taken aback and surprised, "Sparks" is the reply. Looking Sparks up and down, the woman says, "You don't look like much, but if you're willing to fight, I have some old armor I can give you that would fit better. It will kind of meld to you. Takes some getting used to, but it will be better than using those insulated mining coveralls as armor. I'll be right back."

The woman leaves and quickly comes back with what looks like a heavy silicone body glove and various plates that magnetically lock into place over various areas. Handing it over, she says, "My name is Iminathi. This was much too small for me." Iminathi is a tall, seemingly human woman with dark brown skin and hazel eyes. She is also heavily muscled. Sparks can, somehow, tell even with the newly battered armor she wears.

Sparks thanks her for the armor and begins putting it on before asking, "How did you get here? Are there a lot of humans among the rock…I mean Askari?"

The almost-Freudian slip earns Sparks a stern look, but Iminathi lets it go and answers, "There are not that many of us but enough. Most that are here came with the queen and prince who were running around the subterranean network on Earth before escaping. Some were orphaned, castigated, or otherwise oppressed in some way by the government and GMC. We are what you would call collateral damage who decided to fight back at some point. My sister and I were orphaned over an association our father had with the Kison Tantu who worked at a mine in South Africa. I hope you can fight. If not, find an Askari or that big friend of yours, stick with them and try not to be a hero. I have to go."

With that, Iminathi leaves to find her unit. Max and Argos watch silently. Max has a smirk on his face. "Making friends, I see."

Sparks shakes her head and goes to see what they have in the form of weapons that won't be too heavy or unwieldy. She settles on a set of strange-looking dual hand canons with two barrels that sit vertically, instead of horizontally, as they would on say a sawed-off shotgun. There are two indicator lights on the side of them. One glows orange and the other blue. She isn't sure what they are for, but the weapons feel good in each hand, even with the thick gloves on from her armored suit. Sparks isn't sure she would ever truly be ready for what is about to happen, but she has no choice now.

Once she feels as prepared as she will ever be, she goes over to where Max and Argos are now listening to a brief on what has transpired before they arrived, and it does not sound good. The GMC has apparently deployed androids to sabotage the facility, and have retreated. They will attempt to go after them before they can be picked up. The story about to how they actually reached the surface and the facility in the first place seems to be a bit hazy. In any event, it likely doesn't matter in her case. Nothing she's heard sounds like a promising exit strategy for her, Max, and Argos. They will have to continue playing this role out.

Chapter Thirty

THE ADDER SLOWS ITS APPROACH once the Mechanics have made it through the stratosphere. It stays in stealth mode in hopes of avoiding detection and gives them time to hone in on the nearest signal. Sgt. Garrison is looking at a map overlay and orders, "Come in hot, landing as close to this valley as you can get, and try to stay in the shadows if you can, Mac. Jennings, I need you to send out a burst message, then quickly shut down comms until we take off again. Once we touch down, I need you to cover our exit with sniper fire while Long, Coop, and I go find this group of automatons and lead them back here. Jennings, anyone trying to pursue us, discourage them vigorously! Is everyone clear?"

There is a chorus of "Crystal, sergeant!"

Turning back to the map, Sgt. Garrison says, "Good to go. Let's roll!"

Before the landing gear is fully extended, the rear hatch begins to open as they land near the spot Sgt. Garrison has pointed out in a shaded area. The squad leader jumps out, along with Cooper and Long who all sprint along toward where they think the signal is coming from near a large recent-looking crater. Jennings sends the burst message in response to the one the GMC received and quickly silences the comms before grabbing his new sniper rifle equipped with both rail and plasma ammunition, instead of the remote canons which may have been more effective. McNamara keeps the engine running and waits for them to return. Jennings sets up not too far away from the ship but in view of where the rest of his squad should be returning from. He sits there, scanning in the direction they left with his cybernetic eye. The remote canon might have been more reliable, and he would have been able to do other things as it operates, but packing it up would also be slower than simply picking up his sniper and leaving.

Sgt. Garrison, Private Cooper, and PFC Long are moon-hopping their way toward a ridge of the nearest crater when six automatons jump out of cover, holding arm canons behind blue personal shields that have blossomed out of their other arms forming a small phalanx of sorts. Holding up a hand, Sgt. Garrison yells, "Stand down! Sgt. Garrison of the GMC, we got your distress call. Our transport is less than a klick behind us."

There is a moment of hesitation before the automatons lower their canons and shields before heading in the direction he has pointed. One of them in the rear stops to address him, "Thank you, sergeant. There are, at least, eight other extraction points. Their superior numbers forced us to concede after doing as much damage as possible, but we were able to make a dent in their water filtration system and its capabilities. They were strongest around the hangar and hydroponics facilities. If we are allowed to be reinforced, calculations indicate we could take this installation."

Thinking about that as he begins to hop/run back toward the Adder, Sgt. Garrison states, "That's way above my paygrade, but you can ask the brass once we're back on Saturn."

They make it back to the Adder without incident. With the automatons packed in the rear cabin, Sgt. Garrison straps into his seat and yells, "Rinse and repeat, gentlemen! Mac take us to the next spot."

Lance Corporal McNamara replies, "Aye, sergeant!" and takes them up and briefly scans a display of the map for the next closest extraction point. They reach the next spot in less than ten minutes. This time as the squad mates jump out. They are accompanied by some of the automatons which made Garrison feel somewhat better about their chances.

Silently the automatons with them must have been communicating with their mechanical brethren because the next group is out of cover and moving toward them before they have the chance to stop. The return trip is not as smooth on their second run. On their way back to the ship, they receive heavy fire. Turning to see where it is coming from Cooper notices a mixed group of Stone people and what looks like could be regular-sized beings in armor and mining gear. The Stone people have weird canons firing from over their shoulders while the others have whatever they could get their hands on. Cooper takes his Big Bad Wolf and begins returning fire, which slows their pursuit.

When Jennings sees some of the enemy has slowed, he takes an opportunity to take out four or five almost instantly with plasma rounds in his sniper. "Funny, they usually don't go down that easily," he says to no one in particular.

Cooper and the rest of the Mechanics hear him through the closed network that is part of their prosthesis. Cooper responds, "They're not all rockheads. Not sure when, but they have some humans with them, and I'm not sure what one of them is, but if that's a Stone man, it's the biggest one I've ever seen. If it comes to hand-to-hand, I vote Long goes full Berserker and takes him."

"Save the discussion for when we're safely out of here! Jennings, use that eye of yours and scan whatever he's talking about if you can get a visual," Garrison orders.

Jennings takes a look down range and gives a mental command to his eye to magnify to get a closer look at the group of beings chasing them. He can't tell what it is, but there is definitely a hulking figure that stands out. The rest of the pursuers are content to let him take the lead which he does at a speed that should not have been possible. Just as they are almost to the Adder, he or it, Jennings has a hard time classifying, jumps into the middle of a group of automatons and grabs two and proceeds to beat the rest with the automatons in his grasp.

"Uh...Mac, I hope those engines are hot! We may need you to make use of onboard weapons to get us away from this thing," Jennings advises. Of course, weapons on the Adder are already hot. Lance Corporal McNamara begins to slightly hover but still keeps the rear with the bay door open pointed toward his incoming squad mates and the additional automatons. They are all exchanging fire now and getting closer. The side rear canons on the Adder spin around, so they are facing aft. McNamara sets them to auto, and they begin putting down cover fire, finally allowing Sergeant Garrison, Cooper, and Long to get some distance between them. As they leap aboard the Adder, they turn to help as many of the automatons in as possible.

With the speed of the pursuit even with heavy cover fire, it becomes obvious, if they stay they will not be able to hold them off for long. The canons on the Adder finally hit the behemoth chasing them, and he goes down hard. McNamara cheers gleefully until he sees it slowly get up and then renew the chase. They aren't going to get them all, and Garrison accepts that. "Get us out of here!"

Without a word or question, McNamara pulls up on the stick and pushes the throttle forward. The Adder shoots away from the small mob that seems to be getting bigger.

In his opinion, the GMC is going to have to either send in a larger contingent to reclaim the remaining units or a larger force of automatons to get them. They are small enough to make one or two runs for extraction, but by now, the enemy has to be wise to what they are doing. Sergeant Garrison is true to his word. He will not unnecessarily risk his men for automatons that they will likely be unsuccessful in retrieving. Perhaps the advanced AI in them has a protocol programmed into them for survival while awaiting extraction.

• • •

An emergency meeting of elders is called on Ganymede in the throne room to decide what is to be done in light of the actions of the queen. Simeon, Darius, Nefer, Babylon, Athena, Hironike, and the other high-ranking generals are all brought before the elders to make a decision. The elders are a group of nine of the oldest and wisest among the Stone people who provide advice when difficult times come up. They are the oldest among them and have long since given up working in any of the mines since their bodies are past putting up with the toil and dangers associated with that work. They have though, in fact, been around long enough to have seen a lot of what their people have gone through over the years.

These elders are often hidden and protected to preserve their knowledge. Hunched and dressed in tribal robes and wraps, they sit in a semicircle behind the throne. When addressing them, they are referred to as simply "elder." They are beyond names. When one of them passes away, they are replaced by another of their generation or as close as there is available. The calcifications on their skin have made them look even more stone-like with ridges that grow in various directions, and they are slighter in build. It is discussed that the other leaders who are not Kison Askari will have no say on these matters unless the elders ask for their input.

The elder seated in the center of their group stands. He is tall and lanky but very stately. Smoothing down the fold of his brightly-colored robe, he asks, "What should we do with the queen who may have, in her grief, endangered more than just our enemies, and who should rule in her stead? The boy is not of age yet."

There is tension in the air, and nobody is willing to say anything right away. Simeon reluctantly steps forward and offers, "I am one of the highest-ranking generals here and do not wish to become regent as I feel my skills and knowledge are best used if I focus on my military duties. Perhaps if given time, the queen will come to her senses and come back to fulfill her role."

There are many rumblings of "We don't have time!" coming from those gathered there. Babylon just watches in silence as Athena and Hironike do the same from the rear of the hall.

Professor Charles Jones-Bey walks into the throne room after hearing rumors about what happened in time to witness a few arguments that have broken out. The elder who initially started the proceedings stands once more and bellows, "SILENCE!" A hush comes over the surprised group. Many within the group are both astonished and somewhat impressed by how much power comes from what looks like a feeble, old being in comparison to a lot of them there. They are even more surprised when Darius breaks away from Babylon who is holding his shoulders, approaches the elders, stops before them, and says, "I will assume my place as leader of my people now." The boy is straight faced with no anger or enthusiasm in his voice. That may have been what made those around him with the exception of Babylon, Professor Jones-Bey, Athena, and a few others break out in laughter.

Babylon knows the young prince is quite serious and that this is no jest. When the laughter dies down, the middle elder looks at the boy and says, "With all due respect, my prince, it's been said that you are a prodigy when it comes to your prowess with our new weapons, that you may have some abilities yet to develop in the rest of our people, and you are larger than normal for your age. What makes you think you can viably lead those who have vastly more knowledge about how this universe works and what's necessary to carry the day in the times we face?"

Darius seems to briefly consider the question before answering. "Am I not the son of Jared and Tunisia Omega, the deceased king and current queen of the Kison Askari? Have you not, as a group, forced my mother to abdicate the throne? If so, I am the rightful heir. If any of you dispute this, I would accept any manner of challenge you would put forth. If the elders feel I am not knowledgeable enough, I suggest you as a group test my knowledge, and if I fail to answer any of your inquiries, then I will wait until I am deemed fit, as was stated when my mother initially was inducted as queen regent in my stead."

Everyone seems stunned by the proposition and the boldness of this boy. Many are wondering, how could a boy presume to know as much as beings that have been alive likely a hundred times longer than he has even been in existence? It also seems like an easy proposition to win which is probably why he had made it. Some who mistrust this kid with abilities they have never seen before hope he will ultimately fail. When no other suggestions come and none of the other generals step up to stake a claim, they have no other choice but to accept the challenge. The elders all stand and file into a smaller chamber through a door to one side of the great hall where the throne room is. Darius walks over to Simeon and briefly whispers, "I know you don't approve of this, but I will need you when this is over. I don't presume to tell you your job… yet, but you should send some of our forces to make a show of attacking Saturn, which should be reeling after my mother's bombing. It could force them to retreat in an attempt to protect whatever assets they have remaining there." Smiling, he follows the elders into the side chamber and lets their questioning begin.

Simeon admires the boy's maturity and poise, in that moment, realizing he could have bellowed an order to the general, making a show of his assertion that he should rule; instead he has chosen to be cautious, even respectful, of his position in the military. He walks over to Njemba who has come into the throne room after leading one of the perimeter patrols. Simeon relays the orders of hitting Saturn or, at least, making a show of it to see if they can get the GMC to back off here. It is also true that they are, in fact, less vulnerable and more heavily fortified here on Ganymede. Most of their losses are taking place in the skies around the moon and planet here. The GMC has been too late in dislodging their foothold there on Ganymede, but if they sense their own weakness at Saturn, they will have no choice but to protect what is one of their precious few sources of materials.

Word is sent out to the ships in combat about when they can begin to disengage from dogfights with the incoming GMC craft and jump to Saturn. General Krulak does not like any of this at all. When he hears from HQ that the enemy has jumped in to attack Saturn in force, there is no alternative but to follow suit to engage them where they have the best chance at winning. Right now, a ground fight on Ganymede would be a losing affair, and given the losses of the amount of automatons, it is better to change tactics and try to catch them by surprise with over-aggression and concentrated fire.

All fighters are now ordered to engage targets with more than one attacker, hoping to overwhelm them with numbers. If it can be avoided, there are to be no more one-on-one dogfights. The Adder has escaped from Ganymede's surface with a small amount of automatons recovered, but the rest are chalked up as a vast loss given the cost per unit. The pencil pushers and government hacks will not be happy. Everything comes to a grinding halt when shadows larger than some of the planets themselves come into view. There are two vessels that jump into space near both Saturn and Earth simultaneously. There are no incoming messages. They just float there ominously and the fighting stops.

• • •

Max, Sparks, and Argos have come back in from their stint at pursuing the retreating androids, and Sparks is absolutely amazed at the speed and ferocity of Argos. They have cleared a good number of the androids, and Max has made it a point to collect as much of their remains as possible. No doubt he will attempt to cobble together something to sell while here. There is a big ruckus as a large group of Stone people are discussing something as they come in. Sparks decides to go see what the commotion is about. When she returns, Max asks, "So what's all the hubbub about?"

As she watches Argos reach into a pouch of some startlingly viscous salve and rub it beneath his garb on his midsection, she says, "Apparently there's some kind of power struggle going on, and they're sending forces to Saturn for an offensive. I'm not fooled, though, the GMC will be back, and they better be ready."

There looks to be no easy way out of this war, and they, for the moment, are stuck with the mutated races, stranded on Ganymede in a situation where they will have to fight alongside them. Sparks walks over and offers to help apply the salve which has an overpoweringly medicinal smell to it. Silently Argos just looks at her before relenting and handing over the pouch. Max is honestly surprised. "You never let me do that when you're hurt!" he exclaims. Argos knows she is peaking at his strangely thick but pliable red skin as she rubs the salve in. It isn't the skin of the Stone people but not solely human either. The bottom line though for Sparks is that he has repeatedly protected her while out on patrol to his own detriment as evidenced by the scars and bruising despite being heavily armored. Her bid for vengeance will have to wait but, at least, she has found a group of beings again that has her back.

Chapter Thirty-One

CHAOS REIGNS ON EARTH WITH a majority of the military forces off-planet dealing with the Askari on Saturn and Ganymede. Ragnar is taking his Guild of the Pristine and gathering up as many resources as possible in the wake of the mess resulting from the spread of dark matter on certain parts of the world. Pillaging is a better description of what they are doing, and word has gotten out about it. Specifically, it reaches Shajara and his Children of the Sun who are chomping at the bit to get to this group of thugs. Things did quiet a bit for a while after the GMC left, but started back up until the attacks were broadcast.

Just when things look as if they are about to reach a small level of normalcy, the bombings took place, giving people more of an excuse to cast off all reason. The well-to-do do what they always do when things get tight and tensions rise; they insulate themselves the way wealth allows them to. Most have their eyes on the skies, wondering how they will be affected once a victor is pronounced. Then tragedy strikes home, and people stop looking out for others. Ragnar knows what to do in a dog-eat-dog world and has no shame in his game. He continues to stockpile arms for his guild and those who agree with the doctrine he is spreading. Shajara thinks this is wrong, and if one choses to follow him, it should be because they truly have the same or similar beliefs, but even if they do not, that is not a reason to hate or do harm.

Shajara has heard that not everyone has given in to their basest instincts in this time of crisis. There is a young farmer named Gabriel who has decided to use the grain harvested from his farm to help feed those in need. Ragnar decides this act of charity will better serve as an

270

opportunity for him and his people. Only those that are deemed pure deserve to be fed, and Ragnar and his Guild of the Pristine will ensure only the pure benefit from the grain and any other necessities that are available. If there is one thing that makes Shajara turn violent and feel at peace with that transformation, it is bullies. Shajara is going to put down this bigot that feels it is good to extort and steal.

Shajara takes seven of his best men with him to the granary Gabriel owns. Sure enough, posted outside are a group of military vehicles that have likely been stolen or abandoned during one skirmish or another. No GMC present, though, that they can see. Plus, there are strange sigils painted on them. There is a large but modest home a few hundred yards from the granary silo. All the lights are out, except one in a room on the second story. Shajara tells his men to wait while he sneaks to check on Gabriel, who he suspects is hiding in that room with the lone light on.

The Guild of the Pristine have guards posted at the entrances to the farm, but none are patrolling the perimeter of the fields. Shajara leaps the ten-foot wall with ease and ducks after landing, waiting to see if he has been spotted. When no noise or alarm is heard, he continues on to the house using high corn stalks as cover. Once there, he climbs up to a balcony area and knocks softly on the screen door, not wanting to break in. A few moments later, an olive-skinned, bearded young man with dark eyes comes out, mumbling, "I told you, do what you wish with the threshed grain and corn as long as you leave me and my family be."

The sight of the huge Kison Askari man with tribal markings and a long wooden necklace startles him. Holding his hands up, palms out to show he has no weapons, Shajara asks, "Are you Gabriel?"

The man slowly nods. "What do you want? I've given your people all I have," he says. Looking at his markings and deducing why this man would think he and Ragnar are connected, he waves his hand dismissively, stating, "No, I am in not in league with this barbarian who calls himself Ragnar and his piteous guild. I am here to rid you of them, so you can continue your work, good sir. I only ask that your compassion reach out to all, regardless of their outward appearance."

Grateful not to be on the receiving end of some gruesome fate, Gabriel falls to his knees and nods, while sobbing. When he looks up, the Stone man is gone. The fact that he has not even heard him leave is horrifying. Making his way back to his men, Shajara silently signals it is time to move on this group. They spread out to take the guards at the entrances first, then move in toward the people guarding the food stores. A few blood-curdling screams let Ragnar know something is amiss. The alarm is sounded, and the Guild rallies to the stolen vehicles. Ragnar and his men fire into the corn fields after seeing a bunch of the stalks rustling.

They are stalking and toying with them, and Ragnar knows it. This angers him. Ragnar is about to order some of his men into the stalks to flush them out when an unpredicted eclipse occurs, but this is neither solar nor lunar. An enormous disk-shaped ship with widespread wings casts a shadow over the entire Earth which seems unfathomable. Ignoring each other for the moment, the Guild of the Pristine and Children of the Sun stare in awe at the ship that becomes larger as it gets even closer. "What the hell?" Ragnar whispers.

• • •

Pharaoh waits in his favorite chamber and can feel them getting closer. The Anunnaki have arrived. Malice and Typhoon have no idea why their master has his hackles up, but it cannot be good. They stay in their respective chambers and wait to be summoned. Pharaoh's meditation in the sun chamber is disturbed by one of the planet-ship's arrivals, blotting out the sun's rays. Two of their hulking golden emissaries materialize in the chamber with him. Pharaoh stands changing to as close to his natural state as he can. His long, curly hair begins to shimmer, and his eyes glow like two small stars as he greets the giant beings who have to nearly hunch down. "To what do I owe the pleasure of this…visit? Your kind has not been here for eons."

In unison, they say, "You know from whom we come, and why. We have come to reap what has been for so long wasted and nearly destroyed. Your presence here was sensed. We were sent to hear your plea. Although there is…another."

Not understanding, Pharaoh bellows, "What do you mean 'another'? I am the last that remains here!"

"No," the emissaries chorus. "There is another, altered but not tainted like you. We will go to them before deciding this galaxy's fate."

With that, they dematerialize and leave Pharaoh to ponder what they have said.

• • •

A similar set of ships have shown up outside the gravity wells of Saturn and Jupiter, causing all space combat to grind to a halt in light of these new arrivals. No one knows which side they are on, but they are more massive than anything either the Kison Askari or GMC has, and it is frightfully obvious there is no battling them. Communication lines are buzzing with constant traffic, and lines have even been opened between enemy vessels. General Krulak has no plan of action ready for this unforeseen event.

• • •

On Ganymede, the elders have come out after grilling the prince for hours, and they all look like they have seen a ghost. Darius is the last one to come out of chamber, looking confident as ever. Together, the elders kneel and proclaim, "All hail King Darius!"

It takes a moment, but all gathered in the throne room follow suit and repeat, "All hail King Darius!"

Nervously, Bofus approaches the newly crowned king and says, "That's nice and all…congrats but there's been another thing that happened while y'all was in there."

Simeon walks over to the king and shows him images on his data-pad of the new arrivals to their galaxy. Darius looks them over and leisurely says, "Enki is here. Babylon, can I borrow your ship, or can you take me to him?"

A flabbergasted Babylon replies, "Of course, great king, but how can you possibly know of Enki?"

Looking the blue-skinned Atlantean in his amber eyes, Darius says, "A good question for another time, my friend. If we wish to save us all, I think it best you or someone take me to them to stop what they have come for."

Babylon waves for him to lead the way, and they make their way to the hangar, where the living ship is docked. Darius turns to Simeon and puts a hand on his chest, signaling that he should stay. Frowning, the general exclaims, "My king, I cannot let you go alone!"

Darius calmly says, "If I am king now, I order you to stay. I should be fine, and Babylon will be with me. If I do not return, ally with the GMC generals and take down that ship."

That is not what Simeon wants to hear, but he obeys. Darius nods at Bofus as if to say that he should remain behind as well. Silently and sadly, he acquiesces. Darius and Babylon walk up the ramp into the manta-shaped ship and take off, heading toward the Anunnaki's vessel. Babylon turns to the new king and says, "Ya know dey have no chance of taking that ship down."

Nodding his head affirmatively, Darius says, "Yes, but if I fail, it won't matter as they will decimate everything here, and you know it. Right now, Simeon has a purpose, and he will appear to have a purpose to my people, meaning they won't be stressed right now. Should I have left them thinking about their impending doom?"

Babylon chuckles as that does seem like a better way to leave them. Things are already uncertain as it is. Making everyone panic will do no good. They approach the vessel slowly, and Babylon is in awe as this is the first time he has seen one of these legendary planet-ships in person. They have always been mythical in nature, even when Atlantis was thriving. The tale of their return even then was seen as a story made up to scare children. Now he is about to enter one of the golden ships he has heard so much about as a child. An opening appears in the center of the disk portion of the ship, and Babylon guides the ship into it.

The fissure closes up behind them, and there is a thud as the ship lands hard, as if something has reached out and set the craft down. "I guess we landed!" Babylon says. They congregate at the aft of the ship and walk down the extended ramp. There are two gigantic golden beings waiting there. One holds up a hand to Babylon, signaling for him to wait with the ship. He looks at Darius who nods it is okay and follows the shining beings that he only comes knee-high to.

They walk through shining corridors into what looks like the most opulent throne room imaginable. There, at the center, sits Enki. The two gold golem-like beings lead Darius before him. Enki is huge like all the beings on this ship. Although his garb is the same color as everything and everyone, Darius has seen, thus far, his skin is a deep black in contrast. It is so mesmerizingly dark it seems to actually take in light. His eyes are galaxies, glistening in two dark pools. "Do you know me?" Enki booms.

"Yes," Darius states simply.

Enki continues, "Good, then you know why I am here. The inhabitants of this system have squandered or outright ruined all they were blessed with to the point that would make it necessary to leave in order to sustain themselves. Then they have no choice but to spread their wasteful practices, and this we cannot abide. Traditionally we would come, destroy the system, and have it start over. You understand this?"

Studying Enki as he speaks, Darius nods that he does indeed understand the gravity of what is about to happen. As Enki takes a long look at Darius, amusement crosses his face, and his eyes sparkle slightly. "You...intrigue me," Enki says, pointing at Darius. "You present as some youth of one species, but I sense another within you somehow. I am...familiar and not. Somehow you...do not know...yourself. If that's possible. Is this assessment accurate?"

Darius thinks about what this being is saying and has to admit that it is about as close as anyone has come to describing the ambiguity that has plagued him for nearly all of his short life. Darius looks at Enki and says, "Yes, that seems accurate. Are you going to destroy us now?"

Enki stands to his full height and paces as if thinking. "I will grant you time, but not as much as it took you to dwindle your resources and literally choke the beauty out of the gifts you were given on your home planet. If you can right these wrongs, you will be spared. If not, back to star dust you will go, and a new solar system will be born here in your place. First, you have to find a way to stop your kind here from destroying each other. Only then can you go about fixing what you have collectively broken. This will be an easy task if you can find what is within you personally, but I see that it is confined. If you do, you will be seen as a god to most of the beings here. There are radiant ones who have a similar energy to what I feel from you only a few galaxies away. I suggest you search them out. Will you do this?"

Darius replies, "If that is what's necessary for a reprieve, then I will."

Satisfied, Enki laughs deeply and says, "Good, if I need to return to reboot this system, the process will not be pleasant. Go now."

With that, two golem-like beings come and escort Darius back to Babylon's ship.

They return to Ganymede where they are bombarded by questions. Darius raises a hand to silence them all. Looking at Simeon, he says, "I need an audience with the leader of the GMC either here or I can go there. We need to end this conflict before this entire galaxy is snuffed out."

Ancient Illumination II: (Kuongoza Mwanga: The Leading Light)

Instead of asking for an audience, Babylon suggests they simply void walk onto the bridge of their flagship. Simeon demands to come along this time as does Njemba and Bofus.

• • •

Aboard the *Ex Wife*, General Krulak is having a hard time keeping his crew and deployed units in line. Panic is beginning to spread, and the last thing he needs right now is for a few trigger happy Marines to open fire on the unidentified ships orbiting Saturn and Earth, eliciting a reciprocal response, ending them all. Thus far, they are not responding to any hails, and it is assumed the Stone people are also trying and failing to communicate with them. The general is pacing the bridge while his subordinates are waiting for his orders when there is a flash of light. A dark purple glowing portal materializes, and the blue-skinned being with glowing amber eyes and long white locks comes through.

Krulak recognizes him as the same being that had come, unannounced, into his office years ago. This time, he is not alone. Two Kison Askari, one short and stout carrying what looks like a ceremonial hammer and a huge one with a long bo, step through the portal onto the bridge. Then comes a short, brown-skinned human male in some kind of body armor equipped with a shoulder canon that has only been seen on the Kison Askari previously. They all stand to the side as a boy steps through who they all seem to defer to. The youngster is wearing a more intricate version of the armor the human has. His hair is shorn, and his eyes have a ghostly white glow to them.

Before any of the crew has a chance to draw their sidearms and fire, an invisible field forms around just them and General Krulak. When the GMC officers start to fire, the rounds are harmlessly absorbed. The boy turns his blazing gaze upon them, and they drop their weapons. General

Krulak is angered but smart enough not to act on it, looking at the boy's entourage. Through gritted teeth, he says, "What do you want?"

Darius looks at him and replies, "I am King Darius, and I want peace, general."

General Krulak seems to scoff at the notion. "You're just kid. What makes you think a child can broker peace after what your *people* did? I use that term loosely."

Darius steps closer to the general and spits, "I am the king you have to deal with due to the actions of the assassins you sent! Otherwise, it would have been my father speaking with you now. You cannot have missed the other ships that recently came to this galaxy. They demand we peacefully go about changing this galaxy, or they will destroy us all! Recall your forces. We shall do the same, or you can choose to continue this fight, and I will make sure we have front row seats to the devastation that will likely be apocalyptic in scale. Your *people*, as you put it, have not been innocent in any of this either."

As if to make good on his threat, another portal appears right behind the general.

General Krulak looks at the communications officer and nods, saying, "Recall all GMC assets to HQ and their corresponding parent commands effective immediately." When there is some hesitancy, Krulak screams, "Now!" and the call goes out.

"Good," Darius says, and they begin to file out through the newly created portal.

Babylon says, in passing, "Should have listened to me...general."

Chuckling as he leaves, Bofus simply says, "Umm...hmm!" on his way out.

The others say nothing as they exit, leaving Darius behind for a moment. Before the king steps through, he says, "Do not renege as you did before, general. You might not know, but I am a little different from my father and will not be so easy to deal with if you continue to see me as an enemy." To emphasize his point, his eyes flare brighter. Then he turns and leaves.

THE END

Epilogue

THE PLANET-SHIPS LOOM LARGE AND remain in orbit as if waiting to see if the inhabitants of the Milky Way are, indeed, working to get past their differences. News has spread about the conditions of everyone's survival, and for the moment, they collectively cooperate, but there are still a lot of misgivings and trust issues to be worked through. Darius is confirmed as ruler of the Kison Askari begrudgingly after the successful brokering of peace. He has, in truth, become the *Kuongoza Mwanga*, the leading light. The colony at Ganymede continues to grow as there are now funds negotiated for the Kison Askari that they are paid in fair exchange for the resources they have mined for on other planets, as well as on Earth. Pricing for compensation on future hauls is eventually agreed upon.

Laws are passed that will, in effect, force society to make a concerted effort to truly integrate the Kison Askari and other mutated races into all of society. There is an expected severe amount of backlash when this comes up, but when given the alternative, the people eventually back off. The feelings of superiority never truly go anywhere, but the expression of those feelings simply evolves into more subtle ways of communicating and implementation.

The Ryoko-Gekijo returns to Earth but also schedule shows off-planet for their fans across the galaxy as more colonies sprout up. The fans on Earth begin to come back around, but some of their usual enthusiasm has been lost after recent events. The Kison Askari are also allowed to start a business manufacturing means of transportation as long as they are not kitted out with weaponry.

Ancient Illumination II: (Kuongoza Mwanga: The Leading Light)

Sparks, Max, and Argos return to Earth, and of course, Max begins selling black market modifications for the new vehicles with hidden fire power. After all, peace will not last forever, and you have to be prepared. The Limbia Johari refuse to serve people after their mistreatment from humans during the conflict with the Kison Askari simply for being different. They have sought employment in various fields but have tried to stay away from domestic service.

After Tunisia went mad in her grief and anger, Darius vowed to find a way to cure her and restore her to the loving, peaceful woman she had been before. The problem is that the Anunnaki are not the only threats to the inhabitants of the Milky Way. Some have not escaped the destruction the Anunnaki threaten, and are jealous. Eventually someone will come in an effort to claim what Darius and the rest of the Milky Way's inhabitants have to replace what they have lost. Darius vaguely knows of this and has sought to find a way to prevent future invasions where they might not be so lucky next time. Enki claims there is the potential for god-hood within Darius. To protect his people, he will have to find it.

www.ingramcontent.com/pod-product-compliance
Lightning Source LLC
Chambersburg PA
CBHW020354120726
47904CB00002B/550